love in bloom

Books by Jenny Proctor

The Some Kind of Love Romantic Comedy Series

Love Redesigned

Love Unexpected

Love Off-Limits

Love in Bloom

Romantic Comedy

Love at First Note

Wrong for You

Inspirational Romance

The House at Rose Creek

Mountains Between Us

love in bloom

Jenny Proctor

✻ Four Petal Press

Copyright 2021 Four Petal Press
All rights reserved.

No part of this book may be reproduced in any form or by any means without express written permission of the authors, except for quotations used in an official book review.

Cover design by The Red Leaf Book Design www.redleafbookdesign.com

ISBN# 9798418578266

*For Charleston
and all your lovely stories.*

The pineapple is an iconic part of Charleston's identity as a port city, most notably depicted in an elaborate fountain shaped like the fruit in the city's Waterfront Park.

Traditionally, it is a symbol of Southern hospitality and denotes warmth and friendship.

Chapter One

Darcy

Hating Cameron Hunter shouldn't be this easy.

At seven years old, I talked my friends out of being mad at Tabitha Sharkey, the mean girl who wouldn't stop pulling my hair, because "she was probably going through something difficult at home."

At sixteen, I spent every lunch period of my junior year hosting a "friendship booth" where new kids or lonely kids or any kids at all could eat in a judgment-free zone.

I'm basically a golden retriever puppy. I love everyone and want everyone to love me.

Which is why hating *anyone* with my whole entire soul is so bizarre. So . . . unexpected. So *irritating.*

He's leaning against the bookshelf across from me, his ankles crossed, his eyes fixed steadily on his phone.

His pale pink button-down looks freshly ironed, and his sleeves are rolled neatly to his elbows. His khakis are the perfect combination of tailored and casual, like he could really relax and be comfortable in them, but also like they cost him five hundred dollars. They're cuffed just above his pristine Sperrys, worn without socks, of course, and an off-white sweater with a thin navy stripe hangs over his shoulders, the cuffs linked at his chest.

He looks like he belongs in a freaking catalog.

Or on the cover of *Yacht Club Weekly*.

Not that I have any idea if *Yacht Club Weekly* even exists. The Charleston Yacht Club is far from my scene. But if it does exist, Cameron Hunter could be their poster child.

"Staring isn't nice, Darcy," Cameron says without glancing up.

I cross the room and pull a copy of Pat Conroy's *Prince of Tides* off the shelf behind him, leafing casually through the pages. "Don't flatter yourself," I say coolly. "There are so many things in this shop I would rather look at than you."

He finally lifts his gaze, the startling blue of his eyes catching my attention regardless of how much I don't want to notice anything special about Cameron Hunter. "And yet, here you are," he says, not even trying to hide the disdain in his voice.

I roll my eyes. "Because this is where my tour group is supposed to meet." I motion behind him and slip the Conroy book back onto the shelf. "I *always* meet my groups by the local authors' shelf, and you know it." I cock my head. "Are you standing here on purpose, Cameron? Are you hoping I'll compliment your new sweater?" I tap my finger against my chin. "Or notice your new haircut? Did you see your mommy's hairdresser over the weekend? Did Mommy treat you to fresh highlights? Maybe splurged on a nice brunch at the country club?"

He shifts, and something flashes behind his eyes before his mask of cool, collected composure slips back into place.

Ha! I'm right. I'm right, and I can barely contain my glee over having guessed correctly. "You *did* go to the salon. I bet they love you in there. How long does it take for you to get such perfect highlights? Two hours? Three?"

He gives me a pointed look. "Is that your tour group over by the tea table? There are only three of them, so they must be yours."

My jaw tightens as I follow his gaze to what looks like a married couple and their teenage kid standing next to a display of locally grown Charleston tea. They probably *are* a part of my group, but they aren't the only ones. I fold my arms across my chest. "I have a full tour today, thank you very much." *For once.*

That's one thing I can't spar with Cameron about. A maxed-out tour is rare for me. He, on the other hand, is booked solid weeks in advance. I hate how good he is at this job. How easy he makes it look.

"Wow, well done," he says, his tone dripping with condescension. "I was going to offer you the ten people on my waiting list, but since you're all booked up . . ."

I bite my lip. He has ten people on his waiting list?

Ten people who are so excited to do a Charleston walking tour with the illustrious Cameron Hunter that they'll show up to the Historic Foundation Gift Shop on the off chance that someone else doesn't show?

Technically, I could take those ten people. I tell myself the smaller group size is what makes my tours special. Fewer people to shout over, more time to answer individual questions. But the truth is, most guides do groups twice that size. If I had people clamoring onto my waiting list, I would probably schedule larger tours too.

But no one else needs to know that my smaller group size is anything but completely intentional. Especially not Cameron.

I pride myself on thinking I'm pretty tough. I built my tour guide business all on my own. Studied to pass the ridiculous four-thousand-page certification test. Watched endless YouTube videos that taught me how to build a website that includes an integrated scheduling calendar. I made a name for myself—even if a small one—in an industry that is extremely competitive.

I'm maybe not as successful as Cameron.

Okay, I'm absolutely not as successful as Cameron. But I'm making it. Surviving.

The two hundred bucks adding those ten people to my group would guarantee is tempting, but I have my pride.

"I don't need your leftovers, Cam."

His jaw clenches. I'm pretty sure he hates it when I call him Cam.

"If that's how you see it," he says with a shrug. He stands up straight and pushes his phone into his pocket. "By the way, I'm reversing my tour this morning." He moves toward the front entrance of the gift shop. His tour groups always congregate under the live oak out front.

I follow behind him. "What do you mean?"

"I'm heading down Meeting Street first," he says over his shoulder. "Then I'll hit the Four Corners and head down Broad Street from there."

"But that's the direction I go. You normally hit Four Corners last."

He turns to face me. "I do. But now I want the Abernathy kitchen house to be last."

I scoff. "Don't we all. Vivian Abernathy will *not* let you cross her property with a tour group."

He smirks, and my stomach tightens. *No way.* "You didn't," I say, the expression on his face telling me he absolutely did. He'd managed to get the one thing the rest of us thought was impossible.

"I did. She gave me her permission in writing, even." He glances at his watch. "I'd love to stay and chat about it, but"—he looks out the front window—"man, there are a lot of people outside. I think they're all here for me."

It's bad enough that he's managed to convince the city's most elusive widow to let him cross over her very private property with twenty tourists twice a day. The Abernathy mansion's kitchen house is one of only a handful in the city that hasn't been gutted and renovated. For over a century, it's remained untouched; it's nothing short of a miracle that it still reflects a glimpse of what life was like for the enslaved people that worked in the kitchen and lived in the quarters above. But he can't just *change* his route. Not on such short notice. There are a lot of tour guides in the city, so groups cross paths all the time. But we all know to keep our distance, to respect the routes others take, and not infringe on someone else's territory.

Unless you're Cameron freaking Hunter, apparently.

"Cameron, you can't change your route minutes before your tour starts. What am I supposed to do?"

He shoots me a droll look. "It's not a big deal. When we get to Four Corners, I'll go east on Broad Street and cut over to Church. You can stay on Meeting until St Michael's Alley. If you take five extra minutes at the cemetery, that'll give me time to get past the Heyward-Washington house and down Tradd Street toward Rainbow Row. We shouldn't cross paths again after that."

I swallow my retort. His plan will work, but that doesn't mean I like him deciding my routes just to suit his. Still, I shouldn't be surprised. This is Cameron. Entitled. Spoiled. Rich as sin. Acting like he owns the whole damn peninsula.

For all I know, he actually does. Maybe that's how he convinced Mrs. Abernathy to let him walk through her gardens. They probably met at the yacht club, sitting at the table reserved for people who own bazillions of dollars of downtown real estate.

"Why do you do this?" I ask, the words coming out sharper than I intend.

He narrows his eyes and folds his arms across his chest.

My gaze flits to his forearms, and I'm momentarily distracted by the way they flex with the motion. The curve of his muscle leads me upward to his well-defined biceps and the way they strain against the sleeves of his shirt.

"Why do I adjust my tours to better serve my guests?"

I purse my lips and shake my head. "Why are you even a tour guide in the first place?" I've never had the gumption to ask him before, but I can't be the only person who wonders. "You obviously don't need the money."

He studies me for a long moment without answering, long enough that I start to feel twitchy under his scrutiny. "Is it only about the money for you?" he asks.

For me, it mostly *is*. Being a tour guide is a means to an end. A way for me to save money while also networking with people who might help me get my foot in the door of the industry I *really* want to be in. But I'll never admit that to Cameron.

"You don't know as much about me as you think," he says, his tone cool and detached even while his expression is heated, charged with something I can't quite define.

"I don't think—" I start to say.

"Yes, you do." He cuts me off. "You think you've got me all figured out."

His accusation makes me pause, but only for the briefest moment. Because I *do* have Cameron figured out. It isn't exactly hard. Not with the way he struts around looking all high and mighty, rubbing his success in my face like my bank account isn't reminder enough of how well I'm *not* doing.

I shrug. "It's not like you make it very hard. You wear your privilege as blatantly as you do your overpriced cologne."

Cameron shakes his head, his lips tilting into an annoying smirk. He steps closer, close enough for me to feel the warmth radiating from his expansive chest. He leans down, accentuating just how much he towers over me. "You have to get pretty close to notice someone's cologne, Darcy," he says, his lips near enough to my ear to send goosebumps racing across the skin on my neck.

For a split second, something sharp and visceral pulls me toward him—the man is dead sexy even if I do hate him—but I shake the sensation away before it can truly take root. This is *Cameron* we're talking about.

I take a giant step backward and scoff. "Not with you, I don't. Maybe you ought to dial it back tomorrow morning. Try not to assault the tourists."

He chuckles, his blue eyes dancing. "You only wish tourists loved you half as much as they love me." He looks over my shoulder. "You sure you've got a full group today? Your bookshelf is looking pretty lonely."

I follow his gaze. I'm *supposed* to have a full group. It's still ten minutes before we're scheduled to leave, but I generally ask everyone to gather fifteen minutes ahead of time. "I'm sure they're all just running late," I say, hoping against hope it's true.

"Right," he says, still wearing that ridiculous smirk.

I huff. "Whatever. Go find your people. And you better stay on your side of the street at Four Corners. City Hall is mine, Cameron. That's *my* corner."

He backs toward the door and holds up his hand, cupping it around his ear. "I'm sorry, what was that? Were you saying something else?"

I shake my head, watching as he adjusts the sleeves of his sweater then pushes into the cool January air.

Chapter Two

Darcy

I turn and stomp back to the checkout counter where my friend Rachel, who works at the gift shop, is organizing a display of sugar-dusted key lime cookies. She doesn't even try to hide her grin as I drop my head onto the cool glass countertop. "Y'all are better than the movies," she says, her tone lilting with laughter. "I wish I had some popcorn."

"Shut up," I say, my voice muffled by the hair that's fallen over my face. "I hate him so much."

I stand up straight again. "Do you know what he did? He changed his route. Right now. Or, I mean, five minutes ago. But still. He changed his route, and now I have to change mine. *And* he somehow convinced Vivian Abernathy to let him cross her property and show her kitchen house."

"Abernathy," Rachel says. "Is that the house with the enormous garden? And the greenhouse?"

My heart squeezes with longing. Most of the Abernathy garden is hidden by a tall hedge, but what's visible from the street is stunning. A narrow greenhouse sits at the back, running the full length of the property. I can only imagine—and I have, numerous times—the flora and fauna hidden inside those walls. "Yeah. That's the one."

"Girl, are you really surprised? With those baby blues, he could charm his way into any house he wants." She opens a package of key lime cookies and offers me one. "Here. Eat a cookie. It'll make you feel better."

I take the cookie, munching as I look toward the local authors' shelf where my pathetically small group is gathering. A three-person tour is hardly worth the money unless they leave me an enormous tip. I angle my head, trying to catch a glimpse of their shoes. You can tell a lot about a person's tipping habits based on their shoes.

"So, speaking of gardens," Rachel says while she reaches for her own cookie, her eyebrows raised suggestively.

Were we talking about gardens? My head is still buzzing with thoughts of Cameron and his baby blues, his freckled forearms and the way they flex when he tosses his bag over his shoulder.

The gleam in Rachel's eye finally shoves my Cameron thoughts to the back of my mind. I'm always up for garden talk, but she looks like she's up to something.

She slides a brochure across the counter. "These were dropped off this morning."

I glance over the flyer, an advertisement for Charleston's summer flower show. A bright banner across the front announces that booth space is up for rent.

"You should do it," Rachel says, her finger tapping on the banner.

I can't stop myself from laughing. "Right. With what money? It's a thousand dollars just to rent the space. Not to mention what I'd have to spend on flowers to fill the booth."

"I know, I know," she says. "I knew you'd say that. But something else happened this morning, too."

I start to shake my head. I love Rachel for trying. That she believes I could eventually turn my love of urban landscape design into an actual career is sweet, but I'm an amateur garden enthusiast with a history degree. I'm hardly qualified for something like this.

"Just hear me out," Rachel says. "There was a woman in here earlier this morning from *Southern Traditions and Travel.*"

"The magazine?"

She nods. "She was with Bethany and Dave. I didn't catch all the details, but it sounds like they're wanting to do a feature on Charleston walking tours."

Bethany is the head of the Charleston Historic Foundation, and Dave has been giving tours for more than thirty years. His business—Churchtown Tours—even makes Cameron's look like small potatoes, so it makes sense he would be who the magazine wants to highlight.

"They obviously want to talk to Dave, because he's Dave," Rachel says, pulling my attention back to her words, "but they also want to feature a younger tour guide as well, someone they can highlight alongside Dave to keep things fresh. I mean, Dave is successful, but he's also . . . old."

Dave *is* old. Charming and lovely and sweet as all get out. But he can hardly call himself a tour guide anymore. Mostly he manages *other* tour guides. I can't blame him. Leading three-mile walking tours twice a day, especially in the heat of summer, isn't an easy gig.

"Have they decided who?" I ask, sensing where Rachel is headed.

She shakes her head. "I couldn't tell by their conversation. Bethany said there were several possibilities. But Darcy, just think. If you were featured in *Southern Traditions and Travel,* your business would go crazy. More business means more money, and more money . . ." She lifts her shoulders and grins, her eyebrows dancing.

"Means I could enter the flower show?" I say, doubt filling my tone.

"Why not? You've got the skill. You just need the opportunity. As soon as people see what you're capable of, you'll be hired by half of Charleston to do their window boxes."

A tiny flicker of hope sparks in my heart. The window boxes that adorn the houses and businesses that fill downtown Charleston are an iconic part of the city. But they're largely designed and filled by elite landscape designers hired by Charleston's wealthiest homeowners.

That isn't exactly my social circle. Short of going door to door and handing out flyers like a girl scout selling cookies, I've yet to discover a way to get my foot in the door.

"Would that even be fair?" I eventually say. "To be featured as a tour guide just so I could use the boost to get out of the tour business?"

"Whatever. People change careers all the time. And you're good at what you do. It's not like you'd be ripping people off. You give them a good tour, they pay you good money, you use that money to do something else you'd rather be doing. There's nothing unfair about that."

"Except, someone else who wants to give tours long term could likely use the boost more."

She shoots me a look. "Someone like Cameron? Yeah, his business really seems to be hurting."

I clench my jaw. Rachel knows how to throw a punch.

"You know it'll be him if you don't do anything about this," she says. "The golden boy of Charleston. Everyone's favorite tour guide. Plus, if anybody looks like he belongs in a magazine, it's him."

"Now you're just playing dirty."

She grins. "Do you know Bethany well enough to reach out? Make sure she knows you'd like to be considered?"

I nod. "I think so. My dad found her this really old curio cabinet last summer that she went ballistic over. Every time she sees me, she mentions it."

I know as much about my father's antique furniture business as he knows about flowers. Which is exactly nothing. But if it would give me an in to bring up the magazine feature, I could always call Dad to see if he has something else Bethany might like.

"You should do it," Rachel says.

She almost has me convinced. But as much as I like the idea of beating Cameron at something I know he'll want, the odds really aren't in my favor. He's better at this job than I am, fair and square. And even if I do get the feature, there's no guarantee I'll get enough of a boost for it to make a difference. I'd need thousands of dollars to outfit a booth for the flower show, not to mention all the start-up costs of getting ready. Marketing. A website. A business license.

I shake my head. "I love that you believe in me this much, but the booth fee has to be paid by the end of January. I don't have it, Rach."

"What if I pay half?" She folds her arms across her chest, her dark eyes serious.

"I can't let you do that."

"Yes, you can. I owe you anyway for when you got your friend to fix my car for free."

It wasn't actually free to fix her car. I asked my brother, Tyler, to pay for it, and because he's the best big brother in the world who trusts me completely and knew I wouldn't have asked if Rachel didn't deserve it, he agreed on the spot. But I'll never tell her. Rachel would die if she learned Tyler paid for the repair.

"You don't owe me anything."

"Why are you being so stubborn about this?" She props her hands on her hips. "This could really work, D. You deserve this chance. My art has been doing great the past few months. I have the money saved, and I want to spend it on this. When your business takes off, you can pay me back."

I bite my lip. Could Rachel be right?

A magazine feature would be incredible exposure.

And beating Cameron Hunter? Well, that would be icing on the cake.

But the idea of finally taking a step toward my actual dreams? That's bigger than Cameron.

"What's the worst that could happen?" Rachel asks as if guessing the trajectory of my thoughts.

"I could fail," I say pointedly. "I could pay the entry fee for the flower show and then not get the feature. I could get the feature and then not gain any new business. I could get the feature, get the new business, and then completely bomb at the flower show, embarrassing myself in front of a whole bunch of people I would much rather impress."

"Whatever. You would not embarrass yourself," Rachel says so matter-of-factly, I almost believe her.

"I might."

"You won't. I've seen your stuff. You're just scared."

"You've seen my sketchbooks. Those are just pictures. Anyone can draw pictures."

"Not anyone," she shoots back. "You've got vision, and you know it. You just need the chance to show people what you can do."

The thing is, I do know it. Deep in my gut, the truth lives there like a tiny beating heart. But vision isn't enough for success. I also need business sense and a lot of working capital and a hefty helping of luck.

At least now, my dream is still alive. If all those things don't line up, and I fail, where will that leave me?

But then, if I don't even try, is that any better?

I am a lot of things.

Extroverted to a fault. Chronically late. Horrible at sleeping or implementing even the most basic self-care routines. But I am not a coward.

Rachel takes a deep breath. "You're going to do it," she says, hope filling her voice. "I can see it in your expression. You're going to do it."

I laugh. "You're horrible."

She smiles wide, her hands shaking in front of her in a tiny, celebratory cheer. "You need me, and you know it," she says in a sing-song voice.

She isn't wrong about that. I've known her less than a year, but as soon as I moved downtown into a tiny third-floor apartment across the hall from Rachel, she quickly became one of my closest friends.

"Fine, yes. I do need you. Tonight. Dinner. I'll buy," I finally concede.

"Those sound like marching orders," she says.

"Oh, they are. If I'm going to get this feature over Cameron, I need a plan. And you're going to help me come up with one."

She hands me the bag of key lime cookies. "Here. Start with these. Give them to your tour group. And this time, *ask* them to leave you a five-star review when the tour's over."

Reviews have always been important to me, but I've never done much to solicit them. Follow-up emails, even just asking people to review on Google and Trip Advisor . . . no matter my extroverted nature, I've never felt comfortable doing it. Maybe because I'm afraid I might get bad reviews. And what sucks more than asking for a review that ends up being a bad one? Or maybe it's just that my heart has never been committed to leading tours long term.

This job is supposed to be a stepping stone. Nothing more.

But now there's something bigger on the line. Something that could boost my business in a way scrambling for Google reviews never will.

I square my shoulders and look toward my tour group. The middle-aged couple and teenage kid have been joined by seven women, all looking close to my own age. One of them is wearing a sash across her chest that says, *"I'm getting married today. Treat me like a queen."*

I breathe out a sigh of relief. January isn't exactly prime wedding season in Charleston, but the weather is mild enough, there's almost always someone getting married. I've never had a bridal party book a historical walking tour before—don't brides want to spend their wedding day getting spa treatments and massages?—but as long as she's a bride willing to write me a glowing five-star review, I hardly care.

From now on, every tour has to be perfect. It's a logical first step. *Southern Traditions and Travel* won't feature anyone they haven't thoroughly vetted, so making myself look as good as possible on paper can only help.

The second step?

Figure out a way to knock Cameron Hunter out of the running.

Chapter Three

Cameron

Losing a parent, especially as a kid, impacts people in different ways.

For me? I became a chameleon.

You want to talk about yachting? I know just enough to make you think, after a few more conversations, I might invite you to spend the weekend gliding through the Atlantic on my cabin cruiser. (Insider tip? I don't actually own a yacht.)

You want to talk college football? I can be a Gamecock if the need arises. But I'll cheer for Clemson just as quickly.

Investment banking? I don't know enough to convince anyone to trust me with *their* money, but I know enough to sound like I'm making good decisions with my own.

You know what tourists like?

Native-born sons of Charleston. Pastel colors. Deck shoes. A sweet-tea-drinking charmer who says yes ma'am and no ma'am and can talk about the storied mansions that line the city's streets like he grew up in them himself.

Well, let's just say I know how to deliver. I fit in everywhere, because I belong nowhere.

It isn't like I'm completely pretending. My childhood home in Walterboro isn't that far away. It's still Lowcountry. Still tied to the water, still impacted by the culture, the history of this ancient place. But it isn't downtown Charleston. Not by any stretch.

No, I don't lie to people.

But I don't have to.

The right image and a few well-placed nuggets of information, and people tell the lies themselves—weave my story into whatever feels the most romantic, the most magical. The most charming.

That's exactly what Darcy Marino has done. She's filled in the blanks.

Minus the charming.

And the magical.

Definitely minus the romantic.

I didn't really mean for our relationship to start out this way. For a split second, I even thought we could be friends. More than friends. With her dark hair and eyes, she immediately caught my attention.

But it's too late for that now.

She took one look at me, and I could see it plain as day in those enormous brown eyes.

She thinks she knows me. Thinks she has me all figured out.

But she's wrong. They're all wrong.

Even before she died, my mom having brunch in a fancy Charleston club? That's almost as laughable as the idea of her caring a lick about her kid.

I make eye contact with Darcy as she reaches the corner across the street, looking to where my tour group has gathered at the intersection of Meeting and Broad, right at the heart of historic downtown.

She clearly isn't happy, but that's no surprise. Because I'm standing exactly where she told me not to be, at the base of the curved marble staircase that leads up to Charleston City Hall.

Undeterred, her gaze turns to steel, and she leads her smaller group across the intersection anyway, stopping maybe ten feet to my left. It isn't enough buffer. There's no way we can both address our groups without speaking over each other.

I watch her curiously. I honestly expected her to just pick a different corner. But she's—

"This intersection of Meeting Street and Broad Street is often referred to as the four corners of law," she says, her voice loud and confident.

So that's how it's going to be.

Members of my group look my way, clearly wondering if they're supposed to be listening to her or me.

I clear my throat and scramble forward. "Behind me, and up this impressive staircase, you'll find Charleston City Hall, constructed in the Adamesque style between 1800 and 1804," I say before Darcy can continue.

Her jaw visibly clenches, and she shoots me a quick glance before she plows on where I left off, her voice even louder this time. "Across the street, you'll see the Charleston County Courthouse, originally constructed in 1753 as a provincial capitol building, then rebuilt in 1792 for use as a courthouse. Then across from the—"

"From the courthouse," I say, railroading her words with my even louder voice, "you'll find St. Michael's Episcopal Church, constructed between 1752 and 1761."

Darcy huffs beside me, then moves to the second step of city hall, placing herself slightly above me. By this point, our tour groups are watching us both, likely confused over whatever this little song and dance is supposed to be. "And finally," Darcy almost yells, "on the southwest corner, you'll see the United States Post Office and federal courthouse, built in 1896. Each of these buildings represent local, state, federal, and ecclesiastical law—"

I step up beside her. "The four corners," I say, clapping my hands together with a finality that makes the woman in the front of Darcy's group jump.

"What are you doing?" Darcy says through gritted teeth, her face still stretched into a smile that looks more like a grimace. "I told you this was my corner."

"I like to tell my groups about Trumbull's Revenge, and that's inside City Hall. This is always where I stand," I say, enjoying the way her cheeks are flushing with what I can only assume is red-hot rage.

"But you're the one that changed things up. You have to respect the system." She puts her hands on her hips. "You're just doing this to bug me."

I grin easily, crossing my arms as I drop off the step and onto the sidewalk, making us eye-level. "And clearly it's working." I lean a little closer. "You might want to stand down, Tinkerbell. Your group's looking worried."

"Tinkerbell?!" The word blusters out of her loud enough that a pedicab driver passing by swerves and almost crashes into a drainage grate.

"Easy, easy," I say, my hands held out in front of me like I'm soothing an aggressive animal. It's a wonder she hasn't hit me yet. At this point, I'm even annoying myself. "Trumbull's Revenge is a good story if you want to let your group listen in."

She huffs. "I know the story."

I cock my head. "The true one?"

She pauses. "Of course the true one," she says, but there's doubt hovering behind her eyes.

"You sure about that? Maybe just listen this time. See if you learn anything."

Man, I am insufferable.

Darcy closes her eyes for a long moment, her hands balled into fists at her sides. "I hate you, Cameron Hunter," she says softly, even as she moves off and motions for her group to face me.

Her words hit me harder than I expect, bringing a pinch of discomfort, even disappointment. She offers her group a few words I can't hear, then turns to face me herself, her arms folded across her chest and her face set in a firm scowl.

The hard thing about history is that sometimes, the truth is, well, *boring*. The story of Trumbull's Revenge, popular in Charleston's oral traditions, goes something like this. In 1792, John Trumbull is commissioned by the city of Charleston to paint a portrait of the honorable and esteemed George Washington. After the completion of the painting, officials in Charleston are unhappy with the outcome and request he try again. Not so pleased with the request, Trumbull attempts the painting again according to the councilmen's specifications, along with one major adjustment; this time, the rear end of Washington's horse is prominently featured next to the president and is perfectly poised, with tail lifted, to drop a load on the illustrious city of Charleston, visible in the background of the painting.

"It's a good story," I say, looking from my tour group to Darcy's. "And the painting really *does* seem like the horse's rump is getting a little too much attention. But the facts surrounding who requested that Trumbull paint a second portrait and why are murky. There is no record that the original painting ever made it all the way to Charleston. We *do* have records that indicate one man, William Loughton Smith, saw the painting while visiting Trumbull's Philadelphia studio and expressed his concern that the waiting city council might prefer a portrait of Washington in Charleston, rather than in battle, as the first painting depicts."

My eyes settle on Darcy as I talk. Her scowl is gone now, and she's fully engaged in this extended version of the Trumbull story.

"We also have record of George Washington himself praising Trumbull and the final painting that arrived in Charleston in a letter written to General William Moultrie. Would Washington have approved if the painting had truly been created out of spite? Was his approval his own way of casting judgment on Charleston? We have the facts that history gives us. But the rest is just conjecture. I would encourage all of you to circle back to City Hall when you've finished your tour—it's open to the public and you can stroll through and see the portrait—and decide for yourself what John Trumbull might have been feeling."

Darcy eases up next to me while we wait for the crosswalk light to change. "I didn't know that," she says without looking at me.

I shrug. "It's more fun to tell the story everyone knows," I say, not unaware that this might be the first time we've ever exchanged words that aren't dripping with venom. "And most people don't necessarily care if they're getting the absolute truth. They want to be entertained, and the possibility that John Trumbull was exacting revenge on the city *is* entertaining."

She shakes her head. "Yeah, but . . . this is history we're talking about. We should be telling the truth."

"It might be the truth."

"Might be. Is that good enough?"

"Maybe not if you're lecturing in the Harvard history department. But for a twenty-five-dollar walking tour? I doubt you have anything to worry about."

The crosswalk urges us forward and we lead our groups across Meeting Street. I motion for my group to move down Broad Street, but before I'm more than a couple steps away, Darcy calls my name.

"Cameron."

Something . . . unexpected hitches in my heart at the sound, and I turn, weirdly anxious to know what she has to say.

"I'm glad I heard your version of Trumbull's Revenge." The wind lifts her hair from the nape of her neck and tosses it across her cheek. The weather isn't terrible, but the wind coming off the water has a chill to it that makes me wish I had more than just the thin sweater tied around my shoulders to keep warm. The thing is more accessory than actual winterwear. What I wouldn't give for my faded gray hoodie and a beanie right about now.

Darcy looks warmer than I am, with her fitted jeans and puffy vest. Warmer, and . . . beautiful. It's not the first time I've noticed—it's impossible not to notice—but this time, there are *feelings* attached to the observation that knock me off-kilter.

I clear my throat. "Thanks."

"But I still hate you for stealing my corner," she adds pointedly. "And I *will* find a way to get you back."

Beautiful like those colorful poison dart frogs, then. Or a jellyfish. A lightning storm on the beach. That flower, wolfsbane, that looks beautiful on the outside but inside, carries enough poison to send a grown man into cardiac arrest—

"Are we . . . supposed to go this way?" A member of my group steps forward, knocking me out of my trance as he motions down the sidewalk. I turn to face him, glancing backward long enough to see Darcy moving around the front of St. Michael's with her group.

I have got to get my head back in the game.

"Right. Yes," I say. "Follow me."

***

I don't see Darcy for the rest of my tour. Which isn't unexpected. It's a big city, and the point of taking differing routes is so we don't run into each other.

But that doesn't stop her words from echoing around in my brain. *I hate you, Cameron Hunter.*

Darcy Marino has made how she feels about me perfectly clear.

Which is why it's so unsettling when I find myself looking for her around every single corner.

I shouldn't care where she is or what she's doing.

I shouldn't, but I very clearly do.

Chapter Four

Cameron

The next morning, I meet my best friend, Jerome, at the historic foundation offices on East Bay Street. Just beyond, the harbor sparkles in the January sun, a deep blue/gray against a cloudless sky. I've added an extra layer to my tour guide ensemble this morning—a Burberry quilted jacket my stepmom found at a consignment store in Mt. Pleasant for a tenth of what it originally cost. She's amazing at finding deals on high-end things and has made multiple contributions to my effort to "look the part."

Jerome tugs on my scarf when I arrive on the sidewalk just outside the foundation's front doors. "Look at you," he says, his tone lilting in a way that screams sarcasm. "Don't you look fancy."

I swat his hand away. "Shut up."

"I swear, I will never understand this reverse psychology thing you have going on with your tours. Wouldn't people leave you more generous tips if you didn't look like you live in the governor's mansion?"

"They're not tipping me because they think I need the money. They're tipping me because they have a good time on their tour. And this"—I gesture to my clothes—"is all part of the experience."

Jerome rolls his eyes. "Whatever. I'll never not think this is stupid. *You* are what makes your tours amazing. Not your clothes."

Maybe. But I grew up knowing the only opportunities bound to come my way are the ones I find myself. I've learned how to play the game. Walk the walk. Talk the talk. Even if there's truth in what Jerome said, if what I'm doing is working, I'd rather not rock the boat and mess it up.

"Have you seen my calendar lately?" I ask dryly. "Not a single opening until the first week in April."

"Okay, okay," he says, his smile wide. "I won't argue with you. Wear your fancy shoes and your stupid scarves if you have to. As long as you talk about those numbers when we meet with Bethany Morgan in—" He glances at his watch. "Right now, actually. Let's go."

He opens the heavy wooden door and ushers me inside.

"Wait, what? Why are we meeting with Bethany Morgan?" He was vague in his text about who and why we were meeting, only saying I needed to meet him here and I could thank him later.

"Technically, *I'm* meeting with Bethany Morgan. She has a few questions about the education center and since I've asked for the historic foundation's seal of approval, I offered to come by and discuss it with her."

"Haven't you had this conversation with her before? More than once?" Jerome's vision of a Gullah Education Center in the Lowcountry is something he's been talking about since college, so much so that his research for the project turned into his PhD dissertation.

"Three times," Jerome says. "But she says she has more questions; what else am I supposed to do?"

"I'll put money on one of those questions having something to do with her daughter's grade in your history class."

"Oh, absolutely," Jerome says without missing a beat.

"So, what? You brought me along for moral support?"

"I brought you along because I just found out from Dave Vanderhorst that *Southern Traditions and Travel* is doing a feature on Charleston walking tours. They're featuring Dave and his company, but they want someone else. Someone younger." He eyes me pointedly. "Someone with a fresh, hip vibe."

"I have a fresh, hip vibe."

He nods. "Exactly. So you're here to make sure Bethany Morgan knows you're interested in being featured."

Jerome doesn't give me time to disagree with him. Not that I would. This is just his way. Always looking out for his friends.

He smiles at the receptionist sitting behind an enormous and probably ancient desk. "Good morning, Rebecca," Jerome says in his most charming voice. "We're here to see Bethany. She's expecting us."

Jerome looks like a slightly taller version of Leslie Odom Jr., and he has the voice to match, all jazzy and smooth.

In high school, I would have hated him. He's the kind of guy who makes everything look easy. He's brilliant. Athletic. Artistic. But even aside from all that talent, he's also a genuinely nice guy. When we met my freshman year of college, as roommates and fellow history majors, he helped me settle in and find my footing enough that I had no choice but to swallow my crippling jealousy and respect the guy.

Sometimes I'm still a little jealous. But my best friend is a charming, smooth-talking black man with a voice that sounds like angels flapping their wings and the body of an Olympic athlete.

Everyone is jealous of Jerome.

His wife is the perfect complement to his superhuman status, because of course she is, and his two-year-old daughter, Evie, is the cutest kid on the planet, tied, of course, with my two little half-brothers.

Evie calls me Uncle Cameron, and I am all in with her. Even if I have to nurse my ego a little whenever I leave Jerome's and go back to my lonely house in Park Circle.

"Bethany just jumped on a phone call," Rebecca answers, "but I'll let her know you're here. I'm sure she'll be with you shortly."

As we wait, my mind plays out what a magazine feature could mean for my business. I'm busy enough already. Too busy, really. I've been debating the last few months about whether I can justify hiring a few tour guides to work for me. Take my one-man show to the next level. A magazine feature could give me the nudge I need to just do it already. Expanding the business means more money, and more money means more opportunity to help Dad pay down his growing pile of medical debt.

Jerome nudges me with his elbow. "What's happening with your hair?"

"What? What's wrong with my hair?"

"It's sticking up in the back. Here, just . . ." He reaches toward the cowlick on my crown and starts smoothing it over even as the door to Bethany's office swings open.

I swat his hand away. "Stop it, stop it, I've got it," I say, hoping I actually do. I give the errant hairs a few more intentional swipes, then square my shoulders, smiling as Bethany approaches.

"Jerome. Good to see you," she says, extending her hand first to Jerome, then to me.

"Thank you, same to you," Jerome says, his voice in full-charm mode. "You remember my friend and fellow historian, Cameron Hunter."

"We've met once before," I say, hoping I'm lodged somewhere in her memory.

"Right. At the symphony gala, wasn't it? You're the new tour guide."

"It's been two years," Jerome answers for me. "And I'd say his business has grown to the point that he's outpacing everyone but Dave Vanderhorst."

"Well done," Bethany says, her tone genuine. "That's no small feat."

She looks back to Jerome. "My daughter's been raving about your history lectures this week. I've never seen her so enthusiastic about history."

Jerome smiles warmly, but I don't miss the flash of irritation in his eyes. "She's an excellent student."

I imagine a good chunk of Jerome's students rave about a lot more than his lectures, but now probably isn't the time to bring that up.

"Thanks so much for stopping by," Bethany says, her eyes still glued to Jerome. "Come on in."

We follow her to her office and take the two seats opposite her desk.

"Did you know Cameron has been working with me on the education center?" Jerome says, leaning back in his chair, his posture saying he's as comfortable in Bethany's office as he is anywhere.

"Is that right?" Bethany says, eyeing me curiously.

I nod. "My master's degree is in business and nonprofit management. I'm writing grant proposals, pitching donors. It's all behind the scenes work."

"He's downplaying the significance of his contribution," Jerome says. "He's an incredible asset. Exactly the kind of person Charleston should be proud to see representing her."

Bethany narrows her eyes. "I sense you have a purpose."

"We've learned of the magazine feature *Southern Traditions and Travel* is doing," I say.

"Ah," she says. "Word travels fast."

"It would mean a lot if you could recommend me to the magazine," I say. "I believe I've built the business to justify the attention."

She taps a pen against the desk and studies me closely. "Do you intend to stay in the tour business? Even if you're working with Jerome at the education center?"

"I do. I'm building a business that will last, even when I'm no longer the one with boots on the ground, leading the actual tours. I have a passion for history, ma'am. *Accurate* history. There are a lot of good tour guides in this city. There are also a lot who are good storytellers but not very good historians. I'd like to improve the industry in that regard—make sure we're separating fact from fiction and folklore."

Jerome reaches over and pats me on the back. "What did I tell you, Bethany? He'd be perfect for the feature."

She smiles warmly. "You do make a compelling case for yourself. Ultimately, it isn't my decision to make, but I'll be sure to pass along my recommendation should the opportunity arise."

"Thank you. That would mean a lot," I say.

Jerome clears his throat. "Now. You had questions about the education center," he says.

Bethany smiles. "Right. But before we get to that." She holds up a finger as she speaks. "I was hoping we might discuss Madison's grade on her last paper."

I suppress the urge to chuckle as Jerome deftly handles Bethany's overzealous concern. She goes on and on about difficulties at home, including a recent divorce and a sick dog. She even mentions their broken air conditioner. It's a wonder her daughter is even making it to classes at all.

I eventually tune them out, scrolling through a few texts on my phone, responding to the pictures my stepmom, Maggie, sent over yesterday of my little brothers at their latest t-ball practice. The season just started—they've only had one practice—but they look like professionals, suited up in their t-shirts and baseball pants, their matching grins as big as the oversized hats on their heads.

I'm almost more uncle than big brother to my half-brothers, my dad's second attempt at having a family after he raised me completely on his own. The oldest, Maddox, is only five. Almost young enough to be *my* kid. If I'd been willing to have a kid while still in college, anyway, which Jerome nearly did, so the idea isn't that crazy.

Scratch that. The idea isn't that crazy *for Jerome*.

For me? I can't even imagine being in a serious relationship with someone. Kids are nowhere close to being on my radar.

Something tightens in my chest, like a rubber band stretched to maximum capacity, and I rub the spot just above my sternum. So the idea of kids is a little on my radar.

But I have to meet a woman first.

An image of Darcy Marino, her face scowling, her hands propped on her hips, flashes into my mind, and I almost laugh. She's the last woman in Charleston that would ever give me a chance.

I'll never be anything but Darcy's nemesis. The rubber band stretches tighter. Why does that thought disappoint me so much?

Jerome shifts, and I tune back into their conversation fast enough to recognize it's ending. I say a few appropriate pleasantries, then follow Jerome outside.

"That went well," Jerome says as we move into the chilly January air.

"All you have to do is open your mouth for things to go well." This is always the case with Jerome.

"Hey, how's your dad?" he asks, deflecting my praise by changing the subject.

A knot of discomfort forms in my gut, but I resist the urge to deflect right back. Jerome has been beside me for too long. I don't like giving him answers to questions like this one, but I know him well enough to know he won't let me ignore him.

"Good. Better this week. Just finished his last round of chemo."

Jerome nods. "That's great news."

I shrug. "It might be. They'll do a scan in a couple of weeks and see how everything looks."

"And Maggie?"

"She's holding up. Her mom is in town this week." A reality that seemed weirder when I was only eighteen, Maggie is only ten years older than I am. But she's only eight years younger than my dad—he was seventeen when he had me—so their relationship isn't all that weird. I don't really think of her as my stepmom because I never lived at home after she and Dad got married, but I do think of her as family.

"Tell them I said hello, would you? Angie was asking about them the other day."

My reply freezes in my throat as the very woman I was just thinking about appears on the sidewalk in front of us.

Darcy stops directly in front of me. "Cameron," she says pointedly.

"Darcy," I say back, matching her frosty tone. I almost call her Tinkerbell but think better of it with Jerome listening.

I should introduce her to Jerome. But that would be the polite thing to do, and Darcy and I established a long time ago that we are not polite. At least not to each other.

Unfortunately, Jerome is. He bumps me with his shoulder a little harder than necessary and extends his hand. "Jerome Dawson," he says.

Darcy nods. "The professor." The animosity immediately melts off her face and I'm suddenly . . . transfixed. And intensely jealous that the warmth now visible in her eyes is directed at Jerome instead of me.

I met Darcy over a year ago, at a social thrown by Charleston's department of tourism, and the hostility runs all the way back. What did I do to make her hate me so much?

"Have we met?" Jerome says.

"No. I'm Darcy Marino. But I did attend a lecture you gave last summer through the Gullah Geechee Heritage Commission. The one on horticulture." She lifts her hands to emphasize her words. "It was fascinating. Truly. I really loved it."

Horticulture? That . . . isn't what I expect. Darcy likes plants? Growing things? Or . . . just farming, maybe? It occurs to me that I don't know anything about her except that she has a razor-sharp tongue and an explosive wit. And that she hates my guts.

Jerome is saying something else about rice fields and eighteenth-century harvesting practices, but I can't make the words compute in my brain. Something is happening to me. Something Darcy-related and I don't really like it.

". . . Cameron knows all about that," Jerome says, looking my way.

"I . . . I'm sorry, what?"

But Jerome plows on without any explanation. "I've got class in a few minutes," he says. "Darcy, great to meet you." He nods in my direction. "You still coming tomorrow night?"

Tomorrow night? I barely stifle a groan when I finally remember. Tomorrow night, I'm going on a blind date with Jerome, Angie, and a woman Angie knows from work. I like dating. I'm open to dating. I just don't like *blind* dating.

It is the inevitable reality of having married friends. As soon as the people close to you say I do, every other interaction you have with them for the rest of your life will circle back to the fact that you are *not* married like they are and *what* are you planning to do about that?

But I can't say no to Angie. More like Jerome can't say no to Angie, and he will never let me live it down if I bail and force his hand. "I'll be there," I finally say.

He disappears down the sidewalk, leaving me with a no-longer-warm-and-friendly Darcy.

She narrows her gaze at me, her lips pursed, her expression

searching. "So what brings you here this morning?"

"Here, on the sidewalk?" I ask with feigned confusion.

She heaves a sigh. "Here," she says as she points to the building behind us. "What were you doing here?"

My hunch is that she thinks she already knows. She's just trying to see how much I'll admit on my own.

"Nothing consequential," I lie. "Just chatting with Bethany. She and I are old friends." Another lie, and a risky one. I wouldn't put it past Darcy to march right into Bethany's office and verify whether she and I are old *anything*.

She studies me a beat longer. "Just chatting?"

"Mm-hmm," I say. "Just chatting."

Suddenly, we're locked in a staring contest. She pushes her hands into the pockets of her coat, and I do the same. She purses her lips and furrows her brow, and I mirror her expression.

She scoffs, and I repeat the sound.

"Oh my word, are you twelve?"

I grin. "I don't know what you're talking about."

She looks away, her hand slipping over her dark hair and pulling it forward onto one shoulder. "You are impossible," she says. "You know that, right?"

She shifts like she's planning to move around me and go inside, and I suddenly don't want her to leave. Not yet.

"We were talking about the magazine article," I blurt out.

She stills and looks back at me.

"Have you heard about it yet?" I say.

She nods. "Possibly."

"That's why I'm here. To tell Bethany I want to be featured along with Dave."

Her eyebrows knit together, as if she can't quite figure out why I would admit it so plainly.

I'm not even sure why I admit it.

Every tour guide in the city, especially those who work independently and not with a larger company, will want to be featured. And everyone will be trying to figure out how to make a good impression on the people who might have a little bit of pull.

If we're playing a game of poker, I just showed Darcy my hand.

"That's why *I'm* here," she says carefully. "I know Bethany as well."

I shrug. "Then may the best tour guide win."

Her shoulders drop the tiniest bit and for a split second, I see a vulnerability in her eyes I've never seen before. "I really need this," she says simply. "I have . . . *reasons.*"

"You don't think I have reasons?"

She hardly looks convinced. "Cameron, you're already crazy busy. You don't need the boost this feature would give."

"Maybe it isn't about booking more tours for me."

"Then what is it about?" she asks.

"What is it about for you?"

She shakes her head, her lips pressed into a thin line. "I asked you first."

The only answer I'm comfortable giving Darcy is the least complicated one. I want to grow my business. But I get the sense what she's really asking me is why. Because in her mind, I don't need money. I don't even need a job.

I could tell her I wasn't born with a silver spoon in my mouth. That I've never lived anywhere near a Charleston peninsula mansion, and half the reason I work so hard is because paying for college by myself, both undergrad and my master's degree, left me with a mountain of student loan debt. I could tell her how much debt my dad is in because of not one, but two bouts of osteosarcoma. Tell her that even though he hates taking money from me, he does it anyway because he has two little boys he's trying to take care of, and they're more important than his pride.

But would any of that matter? Or would she still despise me anyway? I've always assumed Darcy treats me the way she does because she thinks I'm spoiled and rich. Annnd . . . okay, also because I act like a jerk around her. But she started it. She made the first assumption.

The image I put off when I'm downtown is carefully crafted and very intentional; I have worked hard at blending in, at belonging. This is largely the reason I'm so good at what I do, both when it comes to tours and when it comes to fundraising for Jerome. I know how to make people comfortable. How to speak the language of my audience. Most of the time, this means people like me.

Only Darcy seems to hate me for it.

Maybe because she sees through it?

Every time I see her, I grow more certain that I'd like to learn more about Darcy Marino. Of course, I'd prefer she like me. But if hate is all I can get for now, I'll take that, too.

"What do you say we raise the stakes a little bit?" I say, intentionally ignoring her previous question.

"What do you mean?"

I cross my arms over my chest. "If I get the magazine feature, you do something for me. If you get it, I'll do something for you. Winner's choice."

A tiny vertical line appears between her brows, and I feel a sudden urge to reach up and trace it.

"Fine. But we declare what we want *now*. And there are no takebacks. And no changing your mind once the terms are set."

"You drive a hard bargain."

"I just don't trust you," she says plainly. "I need to know exactly what's on the line."

"Fair enough," I say. "If you win, what do you want?"

She hesitates a moment, drawing the side of her bottom lip between her teeth. She takes a deep breath, then squares her shoulders as if she's preparing for battle. "I want you to introduce me to Vivian Abernathy."

I hesitate.

That . . . is not what I expected. Vivian was pretty clear that she wouldn't be letting other tour groups cross her property. I had to practically beg to get permission just for myself, and that was only after I promised to help her figure out the paperwork to get her kitchen house registered as a historical landmark so none of her children, who apparently don't care quite as much about the preservation of history as she does, can alter the structure once she's gone. "Darcy, I don't think—"

"I don't care about the kitchen house," Darcy says quickly. "I mean, I do, but I don't care if she won't let me take tours across her property. This doesn't have anything to do with that."

"Okay."

"I just want to see her garden." That same vulnerability I noticed before is back in her eyes. "And her greenhouse."

"Oh. That's it?"

"Could you do it?"

"Easily," I say. I could probably walk her over this afternoon and get her permission to spend every afternoon in the garden, though Mrs. Abernathy would probably talk her ear off. She's not nearly as intimidating as people think she is. You just have to get through her prickly exterior.

"Good." There's a note of something new in Darcy's voice, something hopeful. So Darcy likes gardens. Greenhouses. *Horticulture*, I remember, thinking of her earlier comment to Jerome. I've finally learned something real about her.

She glances at her watch. "I've got to see Bethany before my tour starts. What do you get if you win?"

I only hesitate a second before saying the first thing that pops into my mind. "I get to take you to dinner." The idea comes out of nowhere, but the second the words are out of my mouth, I realize how much I want just that. To spend time with her. To get to know her.

But then she laughs. Out loud.

It's almost as much of a hit to my ego as hanging out with Jerome.

"Oh," she finally says. "You're actually serious."

"Just one dinner," I say, fighting to keep a mask of neutrality in place. I barely resist the urge to take it all back and disappear into the storm drain at our feet. There are tunnels all over this city. I could find one that will lead me away from this place. Anywhere would be better than here, where the signs of just how hilarious Darcy found my proposal are still evident on her face.

She huffs another laugh. "But . . . why? We hate each other."

"Are you in or are you out, Tinkerbell?"

"Do I get to pick the restaurant?"

"Absolutely not. My prize. My choice."

She frowns but holds out her hand anyway. "Fine," she says, slipping her palm into mine. Her skin is soft and warm, and I'm tempted to hold on a beat longer, but she yanks her hand away and shoves it back into her coat pocket. "But only if you stop calling me Tinkerbell. Where did that come from anyway?"

I don't remember the first time I called her Tinkerbell. But my reasons should be obvious. Darcy is an extremely tiny person. If she's taller than five feet, it's only by an inch or two. But she's got such big opinions, the sassy fairy from *Peter Pan* seemed like an appropriate moniker.

"Really? You need to ask?" I hold my fingers out in front of me, stretching my thumb and pointer finger to measure five or six inches. "You're this big, Darcy. Fairy-sized."

"Hahaha, so funny. And original. I never hear short jokes." She takes a step closer, close enough that I have to drop my chin to my chest to maintain eye contact. "You are so going down, Cameron Hunter."

She spins around and disappears through the brick façade of the historic foundation offices, leaving me with what I'm positive is a stupid grin on my face. "I'm looking forward to it," I say to myself as I move down the sidewalk. "Probably more than I should be."

Chapter Five

Darcy

Are you in or are you out, Tinkerbell?

Cameron's words repeat through my mind as I walk toward the gift shop, an echoing reminder of how infuriating he is. Who does he think he is?

And the idea of me having dinner with him? As if I would ever.

I've seen enough of the kind of man Cameron is to cement my certainty that I would *never* voluntarily go anywhere with him. Especially not to dinner.

I push through the doors to the historic foundation gift shop, still fuming. My conversation with Bethany was short. She was kind, but clearly resistant to offering any kind of specific reassurance. She admitted I wasn't the only tour guide to seek out her recommendation, and the most she could promise was that she would let her contact at the magazine know I was interested.

It was something, at least. But that meant the magazine would get the same heads up about Cameron.

Last night, Rachel and I combed over Cameron's reviews on Google and Trip Advisor. He has twice as many as I do, with a glowing four-point-eight stars out of five average. The only one-star review he's ever gotten complains about the weather.

I realized then that I have my work cut out for me, but my little run-in with Cameron this morning—it complicates everything.

I make eye contact with Rachel as she bags up a package of stone-ground grits for an elderly woman wearing a bright pink velour tracksuit. The sight makes me grin despite the foul mood Cameron has put me in. I hope I'm gutsy enough to wear bright pink when I'm old.

The second the woman has paid and turned away, I move to the counter, fiddling with the pineapple magnets on display to justify me hogging all of Rachel's counter space. I'll move if someone needs her, but there is mission-critical information on the line, and I only have thirty minutes until my tour group shows up.

And until Cameron shows up.

I groan at the thought, and Rachel's eyebrows go up. "What's up with you?"

I breathe out a sigh. "Everything just got way more complicated."

"What? Why?"

"Cameron knows about the magazine feature."

"That's not too surprising, right? I'm guessing most tour guides do by now."

"Right. But he also went to see Bethany this morning."

Understanding dawns across Rachel's face. "Oh."

"Yeah." I'm not even sure how to tell her the next part. Probably best to just . . . admit everything at once. "And also I ran into Cameron, and now it's turned into this whole competition thing, and if he wins he gets to take me to dinner, and I don't even know how to feel about that." I scoff, still baffled by the whole idea. Cameron.

Me. Dinner.

"The good news is that if I win, he's going to introduce me to Vivian Abernathy," I continue, "and I'll finally get to see the inside of her greenhouse."

Rachel holds up her hands. "Wait, wait, hold up. First of all, the way you just said *inside of her greenhouse* all breathy and hopeful almost sounded sexual, so you should probably work on that before you go and give someone else the wrong impression. Unless you're changing teams and going for elderly widows. Second of all, did you just say Cameron wants to take you to dinner?"

"It's not the widow that has me excited. It's the *flowers*," I say, happy to skip right over the Cameron dinner conversation.

"Yeah, but not that kind of excited. My feedback still applies."

I roll my eyes. "Not everyone automatically thinks of sex."

"When people talk like you just talked? Yeah, they do. But whatever, it doesn't matter. Talk to me about Cameron."

I force out a breath. "What is there to say? It can't mean anything. I mean, this is *Cameron* we're talking about. I'm sure he's just trying to mess with me. Throw me off my game."

Rachel studies me for a long moment, then her lips curl into the biggest, stupidest grin.

"Orrrr," she says, dragging out the word, "he likes you." She picks her hands up and does a little dance, shaking her shoulders and hips while singing, *"He liiikes you."*

"Shut up," I say quickly, glancing toward the door. Cameron could literally show up any minute. "Do you really have to dance about everything? Besides, he does *not* like me. I'm telling you. He probably just wants to embarrass me somehow. Or, I don't know, add another feather to his hat full of conquests."

"His hat full of conquests, huh?"

"Exactly."

"I'm still not sure your opinion of him is totally justified," Rachel says. She pulls a stack of paper toward her—shiny brochures highlighting one of the mansions the city owns and keeps open to the public. She shifts them to me. "Here. Make yourself useful. We need to fold them into thirds."

I pick one up and start folding. "My opinion is absolutely justified. You see the way women flirt with him. It's gross to use his tours to meet women. It's probably the only reason he even leads tours."

Rachel rolls her eyes. "Men that look like Cameron Hunter do not need help meeting women. And he's too good at his job to only be doing it for that."

"What is happening to you? Just last night you were helping me brainstorm ways to sabotage his tours. Are you seriously switching sides on me?"

She holds up her hand. "Hey. We talked about that word. *Sabotage.*" She whispers it like we shouldn't even say it out loud. "You want to get the magazine feature over him. You are not trying to ruin his career."

"Right, right, I know. Nothing truly disparaging, blah blah blah. Still. Where's your loyalty?"

She purses her lips. "Of course my loyalty is to you. But you haven't been on a date in a hundred years, Darcy. And this guy just admitted he wants to take you to dinner."

"Cameron admitted he wants to take me to dinner. *Cameron.* I would rather eat with . . . with . . ." I actually can't think of anyone worse. Cameron is at the very bottom of my list. I have seen way too many women fawn over him while he eats up the attention to be even a little bit interested. Throw in the clothes, the attitude, the privilege. All the snarky little comments dripping with condescension and judgment. He is not the man for me. No way, no how. "It doesn't matter," I finally say. "Because he's not going to win."

"Fair enough," Rachel says. "Fair enough."

We fold a few more brochures in silence. "So, what's your first move?" she asks. "Have you decided?"

After hours of discussion the night before, we came up with a few basic ground rules. I can't write Cameron any bogus reviews. That's slander, and as much as I don't like the guy, I won't stoop so low.

But I can make it difficult for him to give five-star tours. Thwart his route. Change mine up to mess with his, at least as much as I can without messing up my own tour in the process. Just little stuff to mess with his head. *Like asking him out,* a voice in my head says. I'm growing more and more convinced that's probably all his dinner invitation was. Which makes me more annoyed. Because that means he believes he's just that charming. That a single dinner invitation will throw me off.

I could play his game the same way. Except Cameron Hunter is patently unflappable. Always polished. Always put together. Always serene and charming and confident. It's maddening.

To actually get under his skin? It would be supremely satisfying.

A little niggle of doubt makes its way into my brain. I am not a prankster by nature. I'm maybe the opposite of a prankster. April Fool's Day has always been my least favorite day because the thought of making other people uncomfortable to get a laugh has never felt like fun to me. Most pranks are just mean. But I push away my hesitations.

Cameron is always making my life more difficult. Messing with my head. Taunting me. Teasing me. Making fun of my small groups. My small stature. My small paychecks.

I think of the flower show booth rental I paid the night before at Rachel's urging. She coerced me into accepting her five-hundred-dollar contribution, which is amazing, but also doubles the pressure I feel to make this work. I can't waste time worrying about Cameron's feelings. I need to get that magazine feature, no matter the cost.

***

My first move ends up finding me before I manage to come up with it on my own. It's Thursday morning and for whatever reason, Cameron has shown up to the gift shop decked out in a suit.

Let's not talk about the overly long moment I stand motionless in my customary spot by the local authors' shelf and stare at the inconceivable glory that is Cameron Hunter wearing a tie and cuff links. Even from across the room, I can see how the bright royal blue of his tie makes his eyes pop.

He says something to Rachel, who smiles and laughs.

"Traitor," I mumble softly.

Cameron turns and heads toward me, a bag slung over his shoulder. My eyes are on my phone, my ankles crossed casually as if I hadn't even noticed him come in, by the time he reaches me.

"Tinkerbell," he says in greeting as he passes by.

I manage to keep myself from looking up, but my lips twitch—stupid lips—and he must have seen it because he chuckles softly.

I ignore him—I am nothing if not determined—and he continues toward the bathroom.

"Cameron," Rachel says from the front of the gift shop. "Can you help me a sec?"

He drops his bag by the bathroom door—the gift shop is mostly empty at this point so I would have done the same thing—and returns to help Rachel lift an oversized porcelain platter onto the top display shelf.

I watch, confused, until Rachel shoots me a look over her shoulder, looking pointedly at Cameron's bag. She mouths the word *shoes*, and I finally figure out what she expects me to do.

"Right there," she says to Cameron. "Good. Maybe shift it a little to the left?"

Okay, so *Rachel* finds me my first move. The woman thinks on her feet better than anyone I know. During dinner the other night, we had a highly entertaining conversation about possible ways to mess with Cameron's shoes, but we dismissed them all as impossible because how would we ever get his shoes off his feet?

But here we are.

With Cameron's back turned, I sneak over to his bag. He's wearing a suit and dress shoes—shoes he for sure can't walk three miles in. Which means his customary Sperrys are probably in the bag.

I ease the zipper open, wincing at the noise it makes, but Rachel is talking loudly, bless her, and Cameron doesn't seem to notice. Sure enough, his shoes are right on top.

I slip them out one by one and tug on the inside soles of each shoe until they pull free, then push the shoes back into the bag. He'll still be able to walk three miles, but his shoes will be a lot less comfortable without any insoles.

I'm back in my same spot when Cameron passes by again, his insoles shoved into the backpack sitting at my feet. We make eye contact, and he narrows his gaze just slightly, but I feign nonchalance and look back at my phone.

"What are you up to?" he asks pointedly, crossing his arms.

"What are *you* up to?" I say. "You're a little overdressed for a walking tour."

"I had a meeting this morning."

My eyebrows go up, despite my best attempt to mimic Cameron's unreadable demeanor.

"Not with the magazine," he says.

I scoff. "That isn't what I was thinking."

He takes a step closer. "Yes it was."

"Was not," I say back like we're third graders in some sort of recess battle.

He stops right in front of me, his big body looming in a way that feels more enticing than intimidating. He's close enough for me to make out the ring of dark navy that outlines the bright blue of his eyes. To feel the heat of him, to catch the faint scent of . . . *not* cologne. I've noticed Cameron wearing cologne before. He smells clean. Masculine. There's a hint of something I recognize, but it's not strong enough for me to identify what it is. A sudden urge to lean closer, to push up on my toes and press my nose into the skin above his collar overwhelms me, and I take a step back, bumping the bookshelf hard enough for a Conroy novel to tumble over my shoulder.

I scramble to catch the book as Cameron chuckles.

"You okay, Tink?" he asks, a gleam in his eye. "You look flustered."

"You wish you could fluster me," I say. I turn around, intentionally bumping my shoulder into his chest, and shove the book back onto the shelf. *Sorry, Pat. I love you.* I take a deep breath, hoping it will help clear my head before I face him again, but Cameron is still close enough that the breath I manage is man-scented and mesmerizing. I want to climb this man like a baby sloth. Wrap my arms around his neck and hang on forever.

He can have the magazine feature. He can have all the clients. All the tours. If only he'll just let me—

No.

NO, NO, NO.

I cut the thought off and force my gaze to stay fixed on the light blue flowers that cover his tie. I'm too afraid to look up. To see whatever expression is on his face.

What even is this? He mentions dinner one time and suddenly I surrender all my good sense to some primal need to—*nope.* Not going there. My ovaries are not in control. *Not. In. Control.*

I am a strong and powerful woman who does not need a man to whisk me away and ride me into the sunset. Especially not this man.

I suddenly wonder if Cameron rides horses.

I bet he does. Rich people do that, don't they? They ride horses and sail sailboats and drink Arnold Palmers out on the veranda. He probably wears those tight little pants . . .

"Hey, um . . . Darcy?"

My head snaps up, and I see Rachel standing a few paces away. Her eyes are wide, a question clear in her expression. "Can you, um . . . I have a thing. For you to . . . read. About . . . the dungeon."

Cameron takes a step away from me and clears his throat. He doesn't even look back as he grabs his bag and disappears into the bathroom.

I give my head a good shake. I need to go outside and cool off. Let the January breeze blow away whatever just happened. Because . . . *what the everlovin' H just happened?*

Rachel folds her arms and stares at me, not even trying to hide her smile. "You want to talk about it?"

"Shut up."

She laughs. "What even was that, D?"

"Nothing. It was nothing. He was just . . . teasing me. Like always."

"Yeah. Then you bumped into him—obviously on purpose—then your eyes got all weird, and you touched his tie."

"What? I did not."

"Oh, man. This is too good."

"I *did* touch his tie, didn't I?"

"Uh-huh," she says gleefully, obviously enjoying this conversation way too much. "We got to get you out more. You need some action, girl. And fast."

I press my palms against my cheeks. "I don't even know what happened. He just . . . he smelled so good and then . . ."

"Did you find his shoes?" she asks.

I look over my shoulder toward the bathroom. "Oh. Freak. I need to get out of here. Once he figures out—" I grab my bag from where it still sits next to the bookshelf. "Can you tell my group to meet me outside? I'll be in Washington Square Park next to the statue. Please?"

She nods. "Of course. Go. But we aren't done talking about this."

I push through the gift shop door, relishing the cool air as it hits my still-flaming cheeks.

Rachel will never let me live this down.

But she's probably right. I do need to be dating more.

Because nothing but desperation would have me feeling anything close to attraction when it comes to Cameron freaking Hunter.

Chapter Six

Cameron

"Where is she?" I say, dropping my shoes onto the glass counter in between the pineapple magnets and a sample plate of key lime cookies.

Rachel looks up, her expression benign, but she's eyeing my shoes with enough glee, she has to know what Darcy did. "Where's who?" she asks innocently.

Funny. *Very* funny. "She took off, didn't she? Is she meeting her group outside?"

"I have no idea what you're talking about, Cameron. Are you asking if *Darcy* is still here? She's with her group already. Everyone showed up early, so they got an early start." She looks out the front windows to where my own group is gathering under the tree. She raises an eyebrow. "Something wrong with your shoes?"

"You know what she did to my shoes," I say.

"I don't, actually." Rachel nudges my Sperrys out of the way and adjusts the magnet display, an obvious effort to keep herself busy and avoid eye contact. "And you still haven't told me who we're talking about."

I'll never tell Rachel, and I definitely won't tell Darcy, but I'm actually kind of impressed. Stealing the insoles out of my shoes isn't detrimental enough to keep me from doing my job. It's just annoying.

I drop the shoes onto the floor and slip them on, wincing when my feet rub against the exposed, scratchy bottom. "She's clever," I say. "I'll give her that. Though after three miles without insoles in my shoes, I may not think so anymore."

Rachel barks out a laugh. "She took your insoles? I thought she'd just take your laces." Her hand flies to her mouth and her eyes go wide.

I shake my head in mock exasperation. "A willing accomplice."

She eyes me warily. "An innocent bystander."

I glance at my watch. My group is likely wondering where I am, but I technically have another four minutes before the hour. I lean onto the counter and ply Rachel with my most charming smile. "Tell me why Darcy wants this so much."

She holds up her pointer finger, wagging it in front of my face. "Uh-uh. Don't try and pull that Prince Charming act on me. I'm not telling you anything about Darcy."

I tap my chin with my pointer finger, undeterred. "I get the sense it isn't just about growing her business. There's another reason."

She shakes her head, her long dark hair swinging forward enough to hide her expression.

"Is she saving for something specific? A new car? A house?"

Rachel starts to roll her eyes but stops herself, as if remembering too late she isn't supposed to give anything away.

"So, not a car," I say.

Finally, Rachel huffs and folds her arms. "Tell me why you care so much."

I stand and push my hands into my pockets.

Most of the time, whenever I'm in Charleston, I'm wearing a mask. Pretending to be whatever the people around me need me to be. But for a split second, I let the mask fall. My gut tells me if I really *do* want to get to know Darcy better, Rachel is an important ally.

"Because I like her," I say simply.

Rachel lifts her gaze to mine, her surprise clear. "You have a funny way of showing it."

True. "She started it."

She rolls her eyes completely this time, not even trying to hide the gesture. "And you could end it with one conversation. You're adults, Cameron. Just do better."

My watch beeps with an incoming text and I glance at it long enough to see it's a message from someone in my group, asking if they're waiting under the right tree.

"You know it's more complicated than that," I say, suddenly desperate to have Rachel on my team. Or at least not actively working to thwart my efforts. "Darcy is more complicated than that."

"That's the understatement of the year. But still. I don't know what you want me to tell you. I'm not saying anything Darcy wouldn't say to you herself."

My watch beeps with another incoming text.

"But if Darcy spent some time with me, away from our jobs, away from this . . . competition between us, she might get to know me and change her mind."

Rachel shrugs. "You know what else might change her mind? You could just let her have the magazine feature."

Maybe, but there's too much on the line for me to do something like that. "That's not going to happen. I've got a lot riding on this decision too. But even if I didn't, I don't have any power over who the magazine decides to feature."

A guy sticks his head into the gift shop, momentarily drawing our attention. "Hey. Are you Cameron?"

"Yep. I'll be right there. Sorry to keep everyone waiting."

"It's cool," the guy says. "Just wanted to make sure we're in the right place."

I backtrack to the bathroom, ignoring how uncomfortable my shoes are now, and grab the duffle I left next to the sink. I haul it back to Rachel's counter. "Do you mind if I stash this behind the counter until after my tour?"

She takes the duffle, but the look in her eyes says she still isn't sure if she can trust me.

"Listen. I'm going to be at the Darling tonight with some friends. If you can convince Darcy to show up, I'll buy you both dinner."

Tonight was supposed to be my blind date with Madison, the woman Angie and Jerome want me to meet, but Angie texted this morning to tell me Madison canceled. I'm still having dinner with Angie and Jerome—they already booked a babysitter and don't want to waste the night out—I'll just be third-wheeling like I normally am. Not that Angie and Jerome care.

Rachel only raises an eyebrow.

"Seven o'clock," I say. I tap the counter before heading toward the front door of the shop. I look back to see Rachel still watching me.

"You really like her?" she asks.

I shrug. "I don't know her. But I'd like to get to know her."

She studies me another moment, her eyes narrowed, then finally sighs and puts her hands on her hips. "I'm not making any promises," she says.

I grin. "But you'll try?"

She nods. "I'll try."

***

Three hours later, I'm reconsidering my desire to spend even a minute with Darcy Marino.

My feet are killing me.

The memory foam insoles inside my Sperrys might be thin, but I will never underestimate their power. Not after limping my way through three miles of a walking tour without them.

I'm impressed with Darcy's ingenuity. She couldn't have planned ahead; I've never changed clothes at the gift shop before. The only reason I did today is because Jerome and I attended a breakfast this morning with Charleston business executives to schmooze our way to a few more donations for Jerome's education center. Sometimes, it feels like we have the literal breath of angels buoying up our efforts. Other mornings, it feels like we're facing a brick wall with nowhere to go but up and no equipment to help us get there.

But this morning, things went well.

Then I talked to Darcy—an exchange that was memorable even if we didn't say anything important. She looked guilty, that much was obvious, and rightly so. By that point, she'd already messed with my shoes.

She also looked . . . *enticing*. Alluring. A million other words to describe someone who has suddenly caught my attention in a big way.

Now to rehab my reputation. I'm not exactly sure how to accomplish such a feat. A decent start will likely be letting Darcy see a little more of the real me. The me I pretend to be when she's around? I don't really like that guy either.

After a quick trip home to swap out my shoes, an afternoon tour that secured me tips enough to at least cover drinks at dinner tonight, and an hour of killing time at the coffee shop down the street, I pace outside the Darling Oyster Bar where I'm meeting Jerome and Angie, nerves dancing in my gut.

I haven't texted Jerome to let him know I've possibly invited someone else to join us. He's heard me complain about Darcy before. If he figures out I'm trying to see her on purpose? I'll never hear the end of it, and I'm not ready for that level of best-friend awareness. But if she happens to be here, and I see her, it'll seem casual. Coincidental. It might even seem rude if I don't invite her and Rachel to join us.

I sigh and run a hand across the back of my neck, not wanting to mess up the hair I just styled in the coffee shop bathroom.

It's possible I'm overthinking things.

I'm definitely overthinking things.

"Hey, are you Cameron?"

A tall blond woman stops in front of me on the sidewalk.

My eyebrows go up. She's attractive, wearing a light blue dress and heels that make her a little taller than me, which is saying something since I'm over six feet. "Yes?"

She smiles wide. "I'm Caroline. Angie's friend."

My mind whirrs, tracking back through all the conversations I've had with Angie over the past few days. Madison canceled, but Angie hasn't mentioned Caroline.

"She . . . didn't tell you I was coming?" Caroline says, obviously reading the confusion that must be clear on my face.

"Sorry, I . . . we haven't talked all day."

"Right. This was pretty last minute. She told me your other date canceled and asked if I wanted to come. But if you were expecting to have dinner with just your friends—"

"No," I say quickly. "No, it's . . . fine. Great." Because it has to be fine. No way I'm sending home a woman that one, is friends with Angie, who I absolutely find terrifying, and two, was willing to show up on a blind date last minute. There's a hope in her eyes that I don't have the heart to squelch, no matter how much Darcy has been filling my thoughts the past few days.

"Hey! You're both here!"

We both turn to see Jerome and Angie coming toward us. Angie reaches out and gives Caroline a quick hug, then turns to me. We hug and she shifts me slightly, angling me away from Caroline, and grips my forearms. "Sorry I didn't tell you. It fell into place last minute. You don't care, right?"

"No, it's fine. She seems nice," I lie. Except, she *does* seem nice.

"She just went through a horrible breakup," Angie adds, "and I had to beg her to come, so you better be on your best behavior."

I swallow.

Angie's grip tightens. "You can do that, right?" she asks. "You can be nice?"

I nod because I don't have another option. Angie isn't actually asking me a question. "Right. Nice. Got it."

I shake Jerome's hand while he eyes me suspiciously.

I give my head a slight shake and try to smile convincingly enough that he won't ask me any questions.

His expression says he'll still ask me what's up later, but for now, he moves to the restaurant door and opens it so Angie and Caroline can precede us in. I follow behind him, hoping against hope that Rachel couldn't convince Darcy to come.

My hope lasts less than thirty seconds.

Rachel and Darcy are already sitting at the bar.

I turn my back to them, hoping it'll seem like I'm just really excited to face my date. Maybe they won't see me. Maybe they won't notice that I'm here with a woman whose expression says she's very excited about getting to know me.

The hostess leads us to our table seconds later—Angie called ahead to make a reservation—and we pass directly behind Rachel and Darcy. Darcy doesn't look up, but Rachel catches my eye over her shoulder, her eyes narrowed in obvious confusion. I can't blame her. I told her I was having dinner with friends. But Jerome and Angie are obvious in their status as a couple. They're holding hands, Jerome leading Angie through the restaurant, and Caroline is walking beside me. This doesn't look like a group of friends. It looks like exactly what it is. A double date.

I hang back as we approach the table and motion for Jerome to come over. He helps both women into their chairs, then approaches me, his eyebrows raised. "What's up?"

I look toward the bar. "The two women at the bar. I know them."

Jerome looks over my shoulder. "Oh, right. That's Rachel Grant. The artist. And . . . wait, is that the tour guide? The one who hates you so much?"

I infuse my voice with a nonchalance I don't feel. "Darcy Marino."

Jerome's expression shifts. "Right. She enjoyed my horticulture lecture. You know, I was surprised when I met her the other morning. She wasn't what I expected."

"Really? How?"

"I don't know. Based on your description, I thought she'd have fangs. Talons, maybe."

"Very funny."

He looks back at the table, where Angie is eyeing him with an expression that clearly says, *Get yourself over here right now.* "Why are we talking about this?" Jerome asks.

"I don't know. Should we . . . invite them to join us?"

He all but laughs. "Are you serious? This is a date, man. You want to make a *positive* impression on Caroline. How would inviting Darcy Marino to join us help with that?"

Angie clears her throat loudly.

"No, you're right," I say. "It was a dumb idea."

He grips my shoulder with his hand. "Are you okay? You seem off."

"Yeah. Great. I'm . . ." I look toward the table. "Let's do this."

Chapter Seven

Cameron

I watch Rachel and Darcy out of the corner of my eye as the evening wears on. At least, I try to. For having just endured a breakup, Caroline makes every effort to monopolize my attention and seems very comfortable flirting. As in *let me feed you bites of this appetizer* comfortable. After I refuse the bite, she puts down her fork, but that backfires because it frees up her hand to sneak under the table and grip my leg, just above my knee. The fork was way better.

I can only hope that, to someone observing from the outside, my lack of interest is obvious. The death glares Angie keeps shooting me across the table make me think it probably is.

I keep looking for an opportunity to escape, to make a break for the bathroom so I can say hello to Rachel and Darcy and offer Rachel some sort of explanation, but Caroline hasn't stopped talking long enough for me to breathe, let alone leave the table.

I finally manage to get up just after the appetizer plates are cleared away, but I'm still standing in front of my chair when Angie swears from her place across from me. I turn and follow her gaze to a woman striding across the restaurant toward us. "Who's that?" I say.

Angie shoots me a panicked look, then her eyes dart over to Caroline. "That's Madison."

Madison . . . as in the other woman I was supposed to date tonight?

I repeat Angie's swear. "What am I supposed to do now?"

Madison walks right up to me, offering Angie a little wave. She loops her arm around mine and presses her body into my side like I anticipated her arrival and stood up just for her. "Cameron, right? You are just as delicious as Angie said you are."

My mind temporarily hitches on the fact that Angie said I'm delicious—I will never let her live that down—but it's a temporary blip of pleasure in what is quickly turning into the most awkward night of my life. Because now I have two dates.

With two women I don't want to date.

While the woman I *do* want to date watches the entire thing.

Because she is watching.

Watching as Madison leans up and kisses me on the cheek.

Watching as Caroline clears her throat and stands up, eyeing Madison like they're on opposite corners of a cage fight, waiting for the referee to signal the start of the match.

I'm not at fault. Both women have to know I wasn't the one that invited either of them to dinner.

But Darcy doesn't know that. And the expression on her face screams her disapproval. Maybe even her disgust.

Angie also stands, holding a steadying hand out to Caroline. "Madison. I thought you couldn't make it tonight."

"I didn't think I could. But the thing with my family ended early," she says, her arm still hooked on mine.

I scratch my nose—which doesn't itch—and extricate myself in a way I hope doesn't seem obvious. Something is about to go down, and I want to look as innocent as possible.

"Turns out my brother's fiancée is a complete nutso," Madison continues. "After she fought with my mom for fifteen solid minutes about whether the sweet potatoes topped with marshmallows are vegan, my mom stormed out, then *she* stormed out, then Dad went to comfort Mom, and of course, Paul went to comfort Jasmine. That left me with the bill—*rude*—but I was happy to pay it because it meant I could come here. You did say I should stop by if things ended early, and listen, after stalking pictures of this hunk on Instagram all week"—here, she runs her hand up my arm suggestively, curling her fingers around my bicep—"I couldn't wait to see him in person."

Angie grimaces. "Except you told me things definitely wouldn't be ending early." She looks awkwardly at Caroline, who is standing with her arms folded tightly across her chest, her expression sour. "So I found Cameron another date."

Madison finally looks Caroline's way, her gaze moving over her in blatant assessment. She must not feel very threatened because her lips lift into a smirk. "I suppose we can both stay and let Cameron choose. I'm not intimidated."

Caroline scoffs just as the waiter shows up with two large platters. "Who's ready for some oysters?" he says.

"I am," Jerome says, his eyes dancing. "With so much entertainment, I've worked up quite the appetite."

"Shut up, Jerome," Angie says under her breath.

The waiter looks at Madison. "Do I need to grab another chair?"

"Yes, please," Madison says at the same time Caroline says, "Absolutely not."

"Listen, you b—"

"Enough!" Angie says, loudly enough for everyone in a four-table radius to hear. Forks still and heads turn, eyes glued to the showdown happening at our table. Only Jerome seems completely impervious to the commotion surrounding him. He fixes himself an oyster, topping it with minced garlic, olive oil, and a splash of cocktail sauce. My mouth waters just watching him, and I suddenly wish we'd made it through the oysters before the drama started. No one does oysters like the Darling.

"This is my fault," Angie says, her calm and commanding voice slicing through the tension. "If we can all behave like adults, we can have a nice dinner, enjoy some drinks, and laugh about this tomorrow. What do you say?"

Caroline eyes Madison, then moves to my other side. She wraps an arm around my waist and puts her other hand on my chest. She's already had a few drinks tonight, and I get a distinct impression that fully sober, she might not be behaving so forwardly. "I'm fine with that," she says, her voice alarmingly husky. "I'd like to behave like an adult with Cameron."

Madison steps closer, her hand going to my shoulder. "We're going to need that other chair," she says to the waiter, who is still staring stupidly at what has to seem like the worst episode of *The Bachelor*. Or maybe the best episode? All we need is for someone to start throwing oysters.

Only, I didn't sign up for this. I don't want women vying for my attention. At least not these women.

My eyes lift to see Darcy standing beside the bar. She's putting on her coat, and as her body shifts, she catches my eye, one eyebrow arched in blatant disapproval.

"Actually, you know what? Madison, you can take my chair. I'll just—" I disentangle myself—again—and move away from the table. "I'll be right—"

I don't finish the sentence because I'm not sure I will be right back. This is a mess of Angie's making. She can referee whatever is brewing between Caroline and Madison on her own.

Why these two women feel any right to fight over me in the first place is another conversation altogether. If anything, the experience has reinforced what I was already growing to realize. Darcy has caught my interest in a big enough way, I don't really want to date anyone else. Not until I play this out. See if there could be something between us.

I pause on my way to the bar to let a hostess lead an enormous party to their table. By the time they've all passed by, Darcy has disappeared. Rachel is still at the bar, signing the credit card receipt of their bill.

"Rachel." I stop next to her and lean on the bar. "Please let me explain."

She chuckles and shakes her head. "This ought to be good."

"It isn't what you think. Tonight was supposed to be a double date. The first woman canceled, which is why I invited you and Darcy to join us, but then Angie found me a new date without telling me, and then the first date ended up showing up anyway."

Rachel purses her lips, her expression saying she doesn't believe a single word I've said.

"Come on. Why would I have done this to myself on purpose?" I argue. "The entire night has been a disaster."

Her expression softens. "Yeah. Especially if you were hoping to make a good impression on Darcy."

"She was watching?" I'm not sure why I even ask the question. Of course she was watching. The entire restaurant was watching. One lady in the corner was even recording. There will probably be videos up on TikTok by the end of the night. *Dummy tries and fails to date two women at once...*

"Why do you think Darcy doesn't like you?" Rachel asks, crossing her arms, her expression serious.

The question takes me by surprise. "I don't know. Because I'm good at my job? Because she thinks I'm rich and stuck up?"

Rachel's eyes narrow. "She *thinks* you're rich? As in, you aren't, she only thinks you are?"

"That's not . . . I'm not saying . . ." For all my posturing, I won't lie to people. I take a deep breath. "I don't know why she feels the way she does," I say again.

Rachel studies me closely. "Cameron, Darcy likes everybody. Honestly. She's the most extroverted person I know. But she also *sees* people. Right to their core. I think you're a mystery to her. It bugs her that she can't figure you out."

"I don't understand. Why am I a mystery?" I ask the question, but I already know the answer. I work very hard to keep people from seeing the real me. Self-preservation, and all that. I've been burned too many times.

She shrugs. "You've been coming in the shop a long time, and I don't know a thing about you. Darcy doesn't either. Nothing but what she sees on the outside."

"And what's that?" I ask, dreading the answer.

Rachel shakes her head. "You really need to ask? Tonight, she saw a man who looks like he can't keep up with his own social calendar and is comfortable dating multiple women at once. But generally? You're too perfect, Cameron. Too polished. And Darcy sees through it."

My jaw tenses, but I don't say anything. How can I? Rachel isn't wrong.

"I've got to go." She moves the strap of her bag up her shoulder. "Take my advice, all right? Let this thing go. Whatever it is you think you might be feeling, I don't see Darcy changing her mind."

"But she doesn't really know me," I manage to say.

Rachel scoffs. "And why is that?"

After she leaves, I almost don't go back to my table. But I'm still hungry, and after tonight's drama, Angie and Jerome are absolutely buying my dinner. And Madison and Caroline's dinner, too.

Madison really did take my chair and when I approach the table, she and Caroline are leaning toward each other, their heads close. Caroline says something I can't hear, and Madison bursts into laughter. I look to Angie who only shakes her head and lifts her shoulders.

I was gone from the table less than five minutes, but these women look like best friends.

I drop into the extra chair the waiter placed at the end of the table. Madison is on my right, and Jerome is on my left. I lean toward him. "What happened?"

"They bonded over their mutual dislike of oysters," he says softly. "One said she only agreed to come because Angie promised you were a catch, then the other admitted she stopped and had a cheeseburger on her way to the restaurant. The other responded that she stopped and got Chick-fil-A, they both started laughing, and they haven't stopped talking since."

"There's other stuff on the menu," I say, as if that's the most important point to make. But seriously. Having a fast-food burger over anything on the Darling menu? It's practically an unforgivable offense.

The women finally pull Angie into their conversation, something about one of Caroline and Angie's mutual coworkers, and Jerome leans closer to me. "You want to tell me how long you've been obsessing over Rachel Grant?"

"I'm not obsessing over Rachel Grant."

He shakes his head dismissively. "I've given this a lot of thought. You moved your tour start from Washington Square Park to inside the gift shop. You changed at the gift shop after our meeting this morning, instead of at the actual breakfast, which makes me think you wanted to walk past her all decked out in your suit. And tonight, you suggested we invite her to join us, even though she had the tour-guide terror with her."

I nearly choke on my water. "Tour-guide terror?"

"I came up with it myself. Catchy, right?"

I roll my eyes, debating how honest I ought to be with Jerome. He's not entirely wrong. He's mostly right. He just named the wrong woman.

"It's not Rachel," I finally say. I grab my drink and drain it before setting the glass aside, doing my best to avoid Jerome's searching gaze.

He slowly starts to chuckle. "Wait. *No.* It's her? The tour guide?"

I don't say anything, and his laugh grows.

"But she hates you."

"I know. And this little show tonight"—I tilt my head toward the women at the other end of the table—"is really going to help me change that."

The waiter comes before Jerome can respond, refreshing our drinks and taking everyone's order. Both of my dates—should I even still call them that?—mostly ignore me, the occasional glances they send me thick with disdain. As if this entire debacle were my fault. *Whatever.* I'm not interested in either of them anyway. I hope they become best friends and joke about the disastrous blind date that led them to each other.

After a particularly scathing glance from Madison, I nudge Jerome under the table. "You know you're buying tonight, right?"

"Oh, absolutely," he says without missing a beat. "I need you to be honest with me though."

I sigh. He's using his big brother tone—the one that magically appeared as soon as he became a father. He's only older than me by a few months, but in the couple of years since Evie was born, he turned into a full-fledged adult. Sometimes, I think I'm still just a practice adult.

I squirm in my seat, and my jaw clenches.

Jerome nudges my refreshed drink toward me. "Come on. One personal question. You can handle one."

It is one of the greatest frustrations of my life that as easily as I talk about history or politics or anything else, the minute someone wants me to get even remotely personal, I shut down. As in, construct massive walls and make sure other people stay firmly on the other side of them. Not with my family. There are no walls with them. And over the years, Jerome has managed to figure out ways to make me talk. But generally, I'm not great at letting people see the real me. As evidenced by the accusations Rachel threw at me minutes ago. "Fine. Go. One question."

"Are you sure you actually like Darcy, or do you just not like that she dislikes you?"

This question isn't too terrible. Easier than when Jerome asks about my dad's health. Or hints that my history with my mom might be a reason to get some therapy.

I think about my interactions with Darcy. I always enjoy the banter. The teasing. If I didn't, I wouldn't intentionally place myself in her path; I don't *have* to start my tours inside the gift shop. And there's no denying our chemistry.

Still, I am very good at making people feel comfortable. It's become something of a superpower over the years. Jerome thinks I want to make her like me just to prove that I can, prove that I'm charming enough to do it.

Something crystalizes in my brain, bringing a jolt of shocking clarity.

Jerome's got this one wrong.

"I don't like that she doesn't like me," I finally say. "But that's not why I want her to. I'm not trying to prove anything to anybody."

He studies me carefully. "It's been a long time since you've wanted to be real with anyone."

He's right. Not since college.

Jerome saw me at my worst—saw me struggling to shake off the dust of my small-town roots for the first time and fit into a more cultured city scene.

A pang of embarrassment pulses through my chest. I will never forget standing outside the Theta Sigma Pi fraternity house, nerves dancing, knees shaking. My rented tux didn't quite fit, the jacket too tight across my shoulders, but that didn't matter. I was in. Accepted into the most prestigious fraternity on campus. Except, I wasn't really. In the afterglow of a successful informal rush, I'd opened up to the girl I was dating, told her about my family back in Walterboro, about my mom who had died a few months before.

It didn't take long for word to spread. Turns out, Theta Sigma Pi thought I was one of the Hunters that grew up over on Church Street, kin to one of our state senators, a part of one of the old Charleston families. Apparently, that sort of thing was important to the fraternity. The backwoods of Walterboro? That just wouldn't cut it.

I stood on the street for two hours that night, the line of guys pledging dwindling until I was the only one left. Jerome found me a few hours later, still sitting on the curb across the street from the now-darkened frat house. The next day, the girl I was dating stopped answering my texts.

I'm not ashamed of who I am. That doesn't mean I haven't learned when to keep my mouth shut. Not everybody needs to know everything about me. Especially when I'm trying to make it in a city like Charleston. Which is a big part of why Jerome has never seen me in a serious relationship with anyone. There's a long string of women I've dated casually. A few weeks, a couple of months, tops. But I always bail before things get too serious.

But Darcy is different. "Jerome, if she doesn't like the guy she thinks I am, maybe that means she *will* like the guy I really am."

"You hardly know this girl, man," he says. "You sure you know what you're doing?"

I let out a hopeless laugh. "I don't have a clue what I'm doing. I just . . . get the sense that she's different. That with her, it'll be worth the risk."

I glance toward the other end of the table and notice for the first time that all three women have disappeared.

"They went to the bathroom," Jerome says. "You didn't notice?"

My shoulders fall. "I must really be out of it."

"Look. Why don't you ask for your food to go? I'll take care of Angie and the others. You go home and get some sleep. We can talk about this tomorrow."

Tomorrow.

I have plans tomorrow.

My stomach clenches.

It was an impulse move—one I made while still nursing my sore feet right after my insole-less tour this morning. A way to get Darcy back. To mess with her as thoroughly, maybe more thoroughly, than she messed with me.

For a moment, I half-wonder if it's still a good idea.

I take Jerome's advice and duck out of the date early. As I drive home, an uneasiness settles on my shoulders. If Darcy thinks she isn't seeing the real me, tomorrow isn't going to help.

But I'm in this thing. This little competition with her. And if Rachel is right, and Darcy isn't going to change her mind about me, then I can't give up and let her win.

I try and muster up the spirit of competition that's been spurring me forward. The exposure, the boost in business, the growth, the money.

They matter. They have to matter.

There's too much on the line for them not to.

But that doesn't stop me from thinking about Darcy. About the way she smiled at Jerome, all kindness and light. A new motivation flares up, this one almost as bright, *brighter*, than my desire to win.

I want one of those smiles for myself.

Chapter Eight

Darcy

One person still hasn't shown up for my Saturday morning tour. Everyone else has checked in and is milling around the gift shop, waiting for us to get started. It's still five minutes to ten, so technically, we aren't running behind, but I like it better when everyone shows up early, and we can chat and get to know one another. There aren't too many adjustments I can make to fit my audience, but if there are kids in the group, I might change up the stories I share, or if someone looks like the distance might be a struggle, there are shortcuts I can take to reduce our mileage.

So far, this group looks pretty adaptable, so unless the one missing person is—

"Darcy Marino?" A voice rings through the gift shop. Slightly nasally, much louder than it needs to be, and unnervingly familiar.

"Darcy Marino?" the voice calls again. "I'm looking for a Darcy Marino."

I step around the corner and audibly gasp.

Because Cameron Hunter is standing in front of me. Except, not the Cameron Hunter I'm used to. This version is wearing jeans pulled *ALL THE WAY UP* to his waist. That has to be doing unmentionable things to his . . . *unmentionables*. A t-shirt featuring an image of the periodic table and the words "Talk Nerdy to Me" is tucked into his jeans. A thin, brown belt is fed through his belt loops and he's wearing white Reebok sneakers that look like he pulled them out of his grandfather's closet. He has on a baseball cap—the only part of his ensemble that looks like something a guy his age would wear—and enormous, black-rimmed glasses. To top off the entire look, he's wearing a fanny pack with a College of Charleston logo on the side, and he has a Members Only jacket that looks like he pulled it off the set of *That Seventies Show* draped over his arm.

"Are you Darcy Marino?" Cameron says, his voice still too loud for the small gift shop.

I can't respond. Not without laughing. Or cursing. And there are too many members of my tour group watching for me to do either.

Cameron tugs on the waist of his jeans, hitching them even higher, and I wince on his behalf. I have a wedgie just looking at him. He strides over and stops directly in front of me. "You're Darcy?"

I nod. "I'm Darcy."

He nudges his glasses up his nose with his knuckle, then holds out his hand. "Aloysius. Aloysius Butts at your service. I'm so excited to begin our tour."

Oh no. Oh *hell no,* he is not going on my tour. I look over my shoulder, unhappy to see most of my group watching our exchange. But I shouldn't be surprised. Cameron practically bellowed my name when he came in. He literally caught everyone's attention. I take a small step forward. "Right, let's get you checked in over . . ." I nudge Cameron around a display of postcards. "You are not going on my tour," I whisper hiss.

"Oh, but I am," he says in his fake nasally voice. "I'm a paying customer. Booked yesterday and everything."

I take a slow, deep breath.

"You know, I was surprised to even find an open spot on a Saturday morning. Saturdays are really busy. I tried to book with this other guy, Cameron Hunter, do you know him?" He raises his voice. "But his tours are booked out for *weeks!*"

I grip his arm. "Stop it." I look back over my shoulder and drop my voice into a whisper. "Right now. Stop it."

He smirks. "Are you going to let me go on your tour?"

"Absolutely not. If you keep this up, I will out you so fast—"

"Go ahead and try," he whispers in his still-altered voice, cutting me off. "I've got a picture ID to prove I'm Aloysius Butts and have logged more time than you'd guess practicing this ridiculous voice. The only person you'll make look foolish is yourself."

I close my eyes, needing a moment to breathe and an excuse to stop staring at Cameron's arms, which, despite his dorky ensemble, are looking incredibly well-defined in his t-shirt. It's distracting as all get out.

Why is he even doing this? Except, I know exactly why he's doing this. I did make him walk three miles without insoles in his shoes.

With my group waiting patiently, I make a mental catalog of all the things I want to think about when I'm alone and free to dissect exactly what's happening with Cameron and his ridiculous wardrobe. The jeans. The fanny pack. An actual picture ID as Aloysius Butts? He has to be joking about that part.

Rehearsed persona or not, I can't let him hijack my tour.

I am calm. Collected. Completely in control. I reach up and adjust my lucky hat—I'm going to need it today—and take one more cleansing breath. I open my eyes, shooting lasers at Cameron. "You know, after your exhausting night last night, I'm surprised you're even up for a walking tour this morning. Juggling *soooo* many women. I can't imagine the strain."

His jaw tightens, but beyond that, he doesn't break character. "There's more to that story than you think. Not that you'll ever ask. You're much happier just making judgments, aren't you?"

"Oh, I know the full story," I say. "Rachel told me what you said. I'm just not idiot enough to believe you."

"I told her the truth."

I scoff. "Says the man with a fake ID in his wallet?" I turn away, ready to gather my group and get this nonsense over with, but I turn back one last time. "This isn't going to work, you know," I say, arms folded across my chest. "Your biceps are a dead giveaway you're pretending to be something you're not."

He only smirks. "Nerds can have muscles too."

I scoff. "You don't look like a nerd."

"No? What do I look like, Darcy?"

Curse the man for even making his nasally fake voice sound sexy. My nostrils flare, and I purse my lips. He's trying to rile me up. Trying to distract me so I tank my tour. But I won't let him win. I take a step closer. "You aren't going to ruin this tour for me," I say. "If I can handle Cameron Hunter, I can handle *Aloysius Butts*."

I turn back to the rest of my group and clap my hands to get everyone's attention even as I hear Cameron mutter under his breath, his voice perfectly normal this time, "I bet you can."

***

"Sorry about that," I say to everyone. "There was a slight mix-up with Mr."—I clear my throat—"Butts's booking, but we've got it all sorted out, and now we're ready to get going."

I lead my group out of the gift shop and into Washington Square Park where we stop at the foot of the large statue of George Washington. It's a great statue, but mostly I like to stop in the park, one, because the swooping branches of the live oaks overhead keep the park shaded all day long—a benefit in the summer months—and two, the park sits beside the Ravenel mansion, a house with a more storied history than most.

"The George Washington statue directly behind me," I say as my group gathers around me, "wasn't installed until 1999, though the park has long borne the name of Washington Square Park—a tribute to the general when it was named in his honor in 1881." At this, Cameron's hand shoots into the air, and he dances on his toes like a first grader hoping to answer the next question. "The paving stones under your feet and the planting beds that edge the park are as old as the park's name, and—"

Cameron starts making a grunting noise to accompany his flailing hand.

I sigh. "Do you have something to add, Mr. Butts?"

He grins. "A question, actually. Is it true George Washington had wooden teeth?"

I'm prepared to be annoyed, but it isn't a terrible question. "No. That's a myth. He did wear dentures though. By the time he gave his inaugural address in 1789, he only had one natural tooth remaining. But his dentures were not made of wood. They were likely made of ivory, gold, or perhaps even other human teeth." Cameron nods in approval as I answer. Maybe this isn't going to be so bad after all.

I direct everyone's attention to the Ravenel mansion behind us and launch into a history of the house, then spend a minute talking about the architecture. The wide front porch, the privacy door at the end of the porch that faces the street, and the kitchen house at the back of the property.

"Wait, wait, I know this one!" Cameron says, flailing his hand in the air again.

Okay. Maybe it *is* going to be bad.

"You know what, Mr. Butts?"

"I know why the houses don't face the street," he says. "It was for tax purposes. Less street frontage, lower taxes."

Several people in the group start to nod, clearly liking his explanation.

"Actually, that isn't true," I amend. "That's also a myth. Taxes were the same no matter how much street frontage your home took up. Mostly the houses were positioned this way because that's the way the lots were originally configured." I shoot Cameron a pointed look, knowing *he* knows as much, even if Aloysius Butts doesn't. "A boring explanation, but the most logical one just the same." I look at the group at large. "It's likely lots were configured this way to take advantage of the breezes coming off the ocean. Homes like the one behind me are only one room wide, with windows on either side. The narrow alleys in between homes channeled the breeze through and cooled off the entire house, rather than only hitting the rooms that face the street."

Before we leave the park, I tell the story of Anna Ravanel and her brief and tragic love affair with Edgar Allen Poe—a story that always wows tourists, especially when they hear that Anna's ghost is rumored to wander the Unitarian church graveyard where she was buried after her untimely death. But knowing Cameron is watching, I lean a little more into the "legend" part of the story, better identifying the parts of the story that are more city lore than actual fact. Usually, I do the opposite, playing up my storytelling to make even the most skeptical tourist believe that if they go to the graveyard at night, they'll more than likely see the ghost of Anna Ravenel searching for her lost love. But there's something satisfying about sticking more closely to the facts. About honoring history instead of only relying on fantastical stories that may or may not be true. Cameron taught me that, and for a second, I want to forget about everyone else on the tour and ask him how *he* tells the story of Anna Ravenel. Ask if he even tells it at all.

We share a look as my group files out of the park and heads down

Broad Street; approval is evident in his warm gaze, and it sends a pulse of heat through my body.

It suddenly occurs to me. *I want his approval.*

I don't *want* to want his approval, but I do. And I've never been so annoyed to realize as much.

***

Never mind. I take it back. I don't want Cameron's approval.

I want to throw him in the Cooper River.

That one little something that happened as we left the park pales in comparison to the rest of the tour. To how incessant he is with his questions. His weird facts. His long-winded stories that have nothing to do with Charleston history at all.

Is it true Rainbow Row was painted weird colors to help drunk sailors find the right boarding house?

Is it true that Charleston doctors made their pregnant patients drive over the cobblestone streets to try and induce labor?

Is it true there are hundreds of unmarked graves under streets and other buildings?

Only that last one is true, and it's a valid question, except with Cameron steering the conversation, we end up on a totally unrelated tangent about homemade gravestones for deceased pets.

The whole thing makes me furious.

Almost as furious as I am when Cameron tells a story about a float trip down the Ashley River where he saw an alligator with a bird on its nose.

That's the entire story.

An alligator. A bird. Aloysius Butts observing from his kayak.

And it took him ten agonizing minutes to tell it.

I part ways with my group at the Dock Street Theater—another intentional calculation based on summertime tours. The theater is open to the public, so we're able to walk around and, when it's hot outside, cool off in the air conditioning. True story. People who aren't overheated and cranky leave bigger tips.

I'm in the theater lobby saying goodbye to the last two members of my group when Cameron emerges from the bathroom. His jeans have dropped to a normal position on his hips, his fanny pack is slung over his shoulder, and his hat is flipped around backward.

He's still wearing the grandpa sneakers and the nerdy t-shirt, but that hardly seems to matter. I'm . . . struck. This dressed-down Cameron looks . . . right, somehow. Like I'm catching a glimpse of who he really is, and every other time I've seen him in all his Charleston finery, he's been playing dress-up.

The impression is fleeting, and I immediately question it. I *know* Cameron. I know what he is. And it isn't . . . this.

I angle my body so it's easy for him to see what I'm doing, pointedly counting my tips. "Not a bad haul, really," I say as he approaches. "Considering how hard you worked to make me bomb, I'd say this"—I fan the money out and wave it in front of his face—"is pretty impressive."

"I'll admit," he says playfully, "you held your own. But the true test isn't in the tip. People tip because they're facing you. They feel obligated. We'll see what they say when they leave a review."

"Probably something along the lines of, 'I had a great time despite the idiot on our tour who wouldn't stop talking. Luckily, Darcy is an expert and knew exactly how to handle him.'"

He smirks. "You've mentioned that a few times now, Darcy. You handling me. Some dormant fantasy you want to tell me about?"

More like a not-so-dormant fantasy.

I roll my eyes. "You wish." I tuck the money into a pocket on the inside of my jacket. "You owe me a story, by the way."

He raises his eyebrows. "I do?"

"Aloysius Butts? Yeah. You totally do."

Cameron doesn't shy away from eye contact. Maybe it's because he knows his eyes are *notable,* and he likes to maximize their impact. Or maybe it's just his confidence. Either way, the look he's giving me now has my cheeks warming up. It's flirty, but also . . . intense? Like he's thinking about something big. "Maybe one day," he finally says. "But that day is not today." He reaches up and flicks the bill of my hat. "What's with the hat?"

I adjust the hat and scowl. "What do you mean what's with the hat?"

"Just wondering if it has a story. You wear it every tour."

"I do. It's my lucky hat. It's how I tell people to identify me when we meet up. My brother Tyler gave it to me when I first started out."

"Sounds like it's pretty special to you."

"It is. Plus, I look cute in a hat," I add warily. He's up to something. The flirty glint in his eye has shifted to something a little more calculating. "What's up with *your* hat?"

He pulls it off his head and gives me a glimpse of his hair all tousled and mussed. So different than the perfectly styled, parted look he usually wears. And so, *so* sexy. "I've had it since high school," he says. "But I think I like yours more." He reaches up and grabs my hat, replacing it with his.

I am momentarily distracted because his hat smells like him, and just how good Cameron Hunter smells is a well-established fact. It helps that it's late January—easy weather for walking three miles without working up a sweat. If we were having this conversation in August, I'd have panicked if he stole my hat. Three miles outside in Charleston summer heat and humidity? Nobody should touch *anybody.* Much less steal clothes off their body. Everyone is sweaty in that kind of weather.

But who knows? Cameron probably made some deal with the devil to keep him from sweating. Or maybe it's one of the classes only rich people get. *How to sweat and still stay classy.* Makes me think of my best friend from high school who was a Charleston debutante. She had a debutante ball and everything. Big white dress. Formal introduction into society. One of the classes she took in preparation included how to handle bodily functions discreetly and with poise.

Apparently, Southern women should *not*, under any circumstances, fart in public. Even in front of their family. Which is a far cry from what I heard from my mama's mama. She'd always smile and say, "Honey, there's a lot more room outside your body than there is in."

I snap my attention back to Cameron to see that he's now wearing my lucky hat, and he's slowly backing toward the door of the theater.

"Cameron Hunter, don't you dare take my hat."

He grins. "Sorry, Darce. I need collateral."

"Darce? You do not get to call me Darce." Only Tyler calls me Darce.

My heart swells with a sudden desire to see my big brother. He's living up in North Carolina with his fiancée, Olivia, which is amazing, but I miss having him around. He's great at keeping me grounded. It occurs to me that I haven't even called and told him about signing up for a booth at the flower show. It'll be big news because he doesn't even know I was considering it. I intentionally didn't tell him, because if I had, he would have immediately signed me up himself, paying the fee without a second thought.

Letting Rachel help is one thing because she'll let me pay her back. But Tyler wouldn't. He'd just do it and never give it another thought. Mom would probably do the same thing; only Dad would look at me sternly and tell me to keep saving my money until I can make it happen on my own.

Which is precisely what I want to do. A task that will be much easier if I have my lucky hat.

"Collateral? Really?"

He only smiles and pushes out of the theater.

I chase him outside. "Cameron," I say one more time.

"I'll take good care of it," he says. "I promise." And then he leaves me standing there, watching him stroll down the street with *my* lucky hat on his head.

I heave a sigh. That man. I pull his hat off my head and look at it a little more closely. There's an image of a cougar on the front and the letters CC stitched along the side. It feels familiar, but I can't immediately place why. He said he's had it since high school—

I pull out my phone and do a quick Google search of the CC Cougars.

"Colleton County High School," I say to myself, eyes scanning the results. I click on the high school web page to confirm, and the logo featured on the hat fills the screen of my phone.

But that doesn't make any sense. Colleton County isn't too far, but it *isn't* downtown Charleston.

I assumed Cameron went to Porter-Gaud—Charleston's premier private school—like every other yacht club socialite in the city. But . . . Colleton County? The only town in the county big enough to have a name is Walterboro, and it's tiny.

I walk back to the Historic Foundation gift shop, my thoughts racing.

I assumed Cameron attended Porter-Gaud. Assumed he spent time at the yacht club, came from old Charleston money. But he led me to a lot of those assumptions. It's not like I was shooting blind based on appearances alone.

Cameron Hunter wants me to think he was peninsula-born and bred.

But why? What game is he playing?

And since he obviously switched our hats on purpose, does he want me to figure out he's from Walterboro? Is he trying to tell me something?

The thought makes my heart stutter, and my stomach does this weird flip-flop thing.

Which leads to the most important question.

Do I *want* Cameron to be telling me something?

Chapter Nine

Darcy

"But that's just it," I say to Rachel, my chopsticks hovering in the air.

It's Sunday night, the day after Cameron crashed my tour; we're on either side of the coffee table in my living room, a selection of rolls from our favorite sushi place spread out between us. A movie is cued up on my television, but we haven't stopped talking long enough to start it.

"He stole my hat on purpose and gave me his. What is that if not him trying to send me a message?"

Rachel shrugs. "It only feels like a message because you made an assumption about where you thought he grew up. Now you know differently. It could be as simple as that."

I lean back onto the couch and huff.

"Or," Rachel continues, "he did grow up downtown and bought the hat at a thrift store as a part of his costume." She takes a big bite of sushi, her eyes closing as she chews. She nudges the container toward me. "Here. Try this one. It's the best one."

I take a piece even as I consider the validity of her suggestion. He *was* in costume—parts of it completely ridiculous. The shoes, for example, had to have come from somewhere. A thrift store. A garbage can. He could have picked up the hat at the same time. "Oh, man," I say, swallowing my bite. "You're right. This is the best one."

"You know, he could be rich as sin and from Walterboro. There are rich people all over the Lowcountry."

"I know. But Charleston rich is different. And Cameron screams old money. The way he dresses, the way he talks, the way he . . . swaggers."

Rachel eyes me curiously, almost like there's something she isn't telling me. "That's all pretty superficial stuff, Darcy."

"No. My judgments are *not* superficial. He's been nothing but a jerk to me. I'm judging his actions, not his appearance. Plus, you saw him the other night at the Darling. He doesn't deserve your defense."

"He had an explanation for that," Rachel counters. "And it seemed logical. Why would any man set himself up to have two dates at the same time?"

"Maybe one of them wasn't supposed to show up until later."

She bites her lip, hesitating for a minute before she levels me with a stare. "Darcy, Cameron asked me to bring you to the Darling that night. Said if I could convince you to show up, he'd buy us both dinner."

I still. "What?"

"Right after he realized you'd stolen the insoles of his shoes."

"Why would he do that?"

"Because he likes you, you dummy. He was hoping to spend time with you."

I scoff. "Me and two other women, apparently."

She picks up the tray of sushi and scoots back onto the couch, clearly unwilling to share the last of the roll we were both enjoying.

"You know what I think? I think you like him back. And all this *hating* is you trying to convince yourself you don't."

I purse my lips. Rachel is too intuitive for her own good. Or for *my* good.

"Okay, fine. I find Cameron... intriguing. Definitely handsome."

"And sexy. Don't forget sexy."

"Also sexy," I amend. "But I still don't trust him."

Rachel nods. "That's fair. Explain why."

"I don't think his feelings are real. I think he's pretending interest to mess with my head. To woo the competition into not being competition at all. Plus, I get the sense that he's hiding something. He's always so calm and collected. So completely put together. He doesn't even seem like a real person half the time. Who is he really? The fact that he's from Walterboro and not Charleston only makes me more convinced. Cameron Hunter is a man with secrets."

"But if you get to know him, you'll learn what those secrets are. And maybe they aren't anything nefarious. Maybe he's just a private guy."

"Maybe. But I can't risk finding out until after this thing with the magazine is over."

"Because you think he might be playing you?"

"Exactly."

"Okay, but what about before the competition started? Before you knew he wanted to take you to dinner. You've always been bugged that you can't figure him out. Why do you think that is?"

I hold up a hand. "Stop. Don't even try and convince me that means I like him. All he has ever done is irritate me."

She breathes out a little huff and shakes her head. "Whatever you say."

A sound bumps behind us and together we look toward the closet at the edge of my living room.

My apartment and Rachel's are the only two on the third floor of the ancient house our landlord converted into six ridiculously tiny living spaces. I can't speak for the other four apartments, but Rachel's looks as cobbled together as mine does. Our floorplans are mirror image: a minuscule galley kitchen with a single bathroom hidden behind a stackable washer/dryer combo, a bedroom barely big enough to hold a queen bed, and no closet to speak of, except for a narrow space off the living room that looks more hallway than closet. It's ten or so feet deep, with an unexplained brick wall at the back that stops three inches shy of the ceiling. Even the weird closet/hallway is mirrored in Rachel's apartment, right down to the brick wall. We've experimented enough to discover it isn't the *same* wall. As far as we can tell, the two walls are on either side of the same space, a hidden room someone has intentionally walled off.

Trust me. It's as creepy as it sounds. There's a window on the front of the house that we're pretty sure leads into the space, and we hear weird noises coming from that general area all the time.

Rachel is positive the house is haunted and is hiding secrets behind the brick walls.

I keep insisting there's got to be a more logical explanation. Old houses make noises. And every house in downtown Charleston is old. Old, and full of weird nooks and secret passageways. Why shouldn't ours be?

"She's been active lately," Rachel says.

I roll my eyes. Rachel has lately taken to calling the ghost a *she*.

I think *she* is probably our air-conditioning units. Or old pipes expanding and contracting with changes in water temperature.

"Don't roll your eyes. I heard distinct shuffling the other night. Like slippers moving across the floor."

"It was probably *my* slippers," I say.

"You don't own slippers."

"Socks, then. You aren't going to convince me we have a ghost."

She's maybe already convinced me that we have a ghost. Charleston is just that kind of city—so rich with history that even the most skeptical start to doubt once they've spent a little time here.

Still, I cling to my logic. I like it better. I live *alone*. Logical explanations are what keep me sleeping at night.

"I know, I know. Just like I'm not going to convince you Cameron is actually a nice guy."

I stand and gather our trash. "I'm so glad we agree." I hold out the bag our food was delivered in, and Rachel drops in her chopsticks and the empty tray she nearly licked clean.

"So what's your next move?" she asks. "Do you have any ice cream? I need something sweet after all that salty."

"There's Ben and Jerry's in the freezer. Grab me a spoon too."

I pause on my way to the kitchen trashcan when a loud thump sounds on the other side of the wall. *Not a ghost, Darcy. Not. a. ghost.*

We meet back at the couch and settle in, the ice cream on the cushion between us. Rachel sets a third spoon on the coffee table before taking her first bite.

I eye her curiously. "You worried about losing your spoon?"

She shakes her head. "It's for her. I want to make sure she knows she's welcome."

"You're ridiculous."

She grins. "I'm imaginative. And intuitive." She raises her voice. "And friendly to all spirits no matter where they dwell."

I can't argue. Rachel *is* imaginative and intuitive. She has the heart of an artist and the brain to match. If benefiting from all that means I have to go along with her ghost stories, I'm all in.

"So my next move," I say, wanting to run my plan by her. It's been buzzing in my brain since Cameron stole my hat earlier this morning, and I need someone to tell me whether or not it's too ridiculous to have any merit.

"Right. Yes. Lay it on me."

I finish a bite of ice cream before digging in. "So I was thinking I could give him a dose of his own medicine. Find a way to distract him on his tours like he distracted me."

"Okay," Rachel says. "Keep going."

"And since *he* isn't hesitating to flirt in the name of winning—"

"I don't think that's what he's doing," Rachel says, cutting me off.

I shoot her a look, and she holds up her hand. "Fine, fine. Agree to disagree. Please continue."

"I'm going to send him a series of text messages while he's on his Monday morning tour."

"Texts?" Rachel asks.

I grin. "*Sexy* texts."

She laughs as she shakes her head. "What does that even mean? Did you like, write them yourself?"

"Oh, definitely not. I am not that talented. I mean, I wrote the first few. Those are pretty benign. The rest are lines from steamy romance novels."

"Oh. Oh, that's mean. Brilliant, but mean."

"Right? He wears a smart watch, I know that much, so the texts should come up on his wrist even if he doesn't get out his phone."

"If your goal is distraction, that should do it," she says as she digs through the ice cream.

"Hey, no mining," I say as I reach for the pint.

She holds it higher, out of my reach, as she scoops out an enormous chunk of fudge-covered waffle cone. She finally surrenders it back, and I stare at the crater-sized hole she left in the ice cream. "How big was that chunk?"

"Ri-wee bwig," she says through her bite, her hand covering her mouth.

I start mining for my own piece but end up settling for a generous swirl of caramel.

"Do you worry he might take the texts seriously?" Rachel finally asks.

"Absolutely not," I say. "First of all, he doesn't know my number, so he'll have no way of knowing the texts are from me. He's probably going to think he's getting spammed. Or that someone thinks he's someone he's not."

She nods but still seems skeptical. "How do you even know his number?"

"It's on his website."

She shoots me a look. "Isn't *your* number also on your website?"

"It isn't. It only goes out in a confirmation email after people book."

"An email Cameron would have gotten when he booked?"

A wave away her concern. "It's in tiny print, buried in the Frequently Asked Questions, as a solution for people who can't find our meeting spot. Cameron would have had no reason to read the answer because he knows exactly where I meet my groups."

"Sounds like you've given this a lot of thought."

"I have. Plus, even if he did see my number, why would he have programmed it into his phone? Who does that? He's never called me before."

Rachel rolls her eyes. "Um, someone who likes you?"

"Whatever. He doesn't like me. I'm positive he's not going to recognize my number."

She sits up straighter. "Fine. But I still have more questions. How are you going to send him all those texts while you're leading your own tour?"

"I downloaded an app that lets me schedule texts ahead, but I'm not doing a tour tomorrow morning anyway. Tyler and Olivia are going to be in town for Olivia's wedding dress fitting with Dani."

Rachel gasps. "I always forget you have a personal connection to Dani Randall. You're almost related, right?" Dani Randall is one of

Charleston's latest claims to fame. Her clothing design company—which she opened on King Street only a couple of years ago—has exploded. She just opened additional stores in New York and Los Angeles and signed a deal with Nordstrom for an exclusive, limited-edition line available only in their stores.

"Not quite. Her twin brother Isaac is best friends with Tyler."

Rachel waves away my explanation. "Best friends. Siblings. It's practically the same thing. Do you think she'll do a wedding dress for you?"

"I best find a man first," I say, though I can't help but hope Dani's "friends and family only" policy regarding custom wedding dresses will extend to me. Tyler isn't technically family, and his fiancée is getting one. Surely his baby sister will qualify as well. Besides, Dani loves me. Whenever our brothers hung out when we were growing up, she looked out for me. Kept the boys from pushing me around too much.

Rachel laughs. "If you play your texts right, you may have a man by Monday afternoon. Just go ahead and have Dani measure you up."

"Very funny." I stand and stretch, the movement interrupted by my phone, which starts ringing from the counter in the kitchen. I move to answer it and say over my shoulder, "I won't mean a single one of the texts I'm sending. This is *Cameron* we're talking about."

It's not the entire truth. I spent time this afternoon crafting a list of text messages to send to Cameron that will never, under any circumstances, be seen by anyone but me. Well, and Cameron. Obviously. The list is digital, stored in the cloud, and password protected. And the minute I'm finished with it, I will delete it forever.

But even as I crafted the list, blushing my way through a few Kathleen Ayers romance novels to mine out the most perfect lines, I couldn't ignore the obvious. The first text on the list reads: *I dreamed about kissing you all night long.*

Annnd...that dream totally happened a few nights ago. My

back pressed up against the local authors' shelf in the gift shop. Cameron's lips on mine. His hands tangled in my hair. I woke up with a start, my heart pounding, the sensation of his imagined touch still dancing across my skin.

But it was a dream. *Only* a dream. My brain's messed-up way of processing how annoyed I felt to see Cameron out with two women at the Darling. But my brain got it wrong. I wasn't annoyed because I wanted to *be* one of those women. I was annoyed because Cameron is smug and entitled and thinks he can do whatever he wants.

The ringing on my phone stops just as I pick it up. I've got one missed call from Tyler. I carry it back into the living room. "Hey, that was Tyler. I'm going to take a quick walk and call him back. Give me fifteen and then we'll watch the movie?"

"No problem," Rachel says, "but I'm finishing your ice cream."

I grab my Vans from the shoe rack that sits beside my front door and slip them on. I don't grab a hoodie, but as soon as I'm down the stairs and outside, I wish I had. It's February already, but winter is still hanging on to the nighttime hours, and the fifty-degree air feels cool against my exposed arms.

Tyler answers on the first ring. "Hey!" he says, his tone warm.

I smile. North Carolina has been good for him. "Hey yourself. Where are you? Are you in town?"

"Not yet. We stopped to eat in Columbia. You're on speaker."

"Hi, Darcy," Olivia says.

"Hey."

I haven't spent a lot of time with Tyler's fiancée, but I didn't need a lot of time to know she's perfect for him. My only complaint is that she doesn't live here, and they intend to settle in North Carolina for the foreseeable future. Still, Tyler's roots in Charleston are deep. His family is here. His best friend, Isaac, and Isaac's wife, Rosie, are here. Tyler has so many reasons to visit. He and Olivia have only been engaged a few months, and they've already been down three or four times.

"So what's up? How are you? I feel like we haven't talked in weeks," Tyler says.

"And whose fault is that?" I say. "I'm blaming Penelope."

Olivia chuckles. "It is definitely Penelope's fault."

Olivia's family owns a farm and orchard in North Carolina, and Tyler worked there for a few months last summer. Penelope is a goat he rescued after she was rejected by her mom right after she was born. She bonded to Tyler in a big way, following him all over the farm, his red bandana tied around her neck. Because she is literally the cutest thing on the planet, Tyler started posting videos and photos of her on the internet and now Penelope has a following almost as big as Isaac's. Which is saying something because Isaac's following—his YouTube channel—is his job.

"Don't be knocking Penelope," Tyler says. "You've been busy too. What's new?"

"Um, nothing really."

Sure. Nothing. Just a competition with my nemesis to be featured in a travel magazine that could potentially boost my business enough to make it possible for me to create a display at a flower show that might launch the career I actually want instead of one that mostly feels like treading water—a competition that is *not* made less complicated by KISSING DREAMS.

"Your tone does not sound like nothing is going on," Tyler says.

I sigh and turn onto Church Street, where the houses get larger and more expensive, and stop to admire my favorite flower box in all of Charleston. It's been refreshed recently, still with winter plants, but ones that will appreciate the rise in daytime temperatures sure to hit us over the next couple of months. Ruby kisses bromeliad fills the center of the box, surrounded by diamond frost euphorbia, and a sweet potato vine that spills over the edges and reaches toward the sidewalk below. The contrast of the red in the bromeliad and the vibrant green of the sweet potato vine is eye-catching, but it's more than just the color that makes the design work. The euphorbia is wispy and light, which softens the stiffness of the single stem bromeliad. And the way the vine curls around the other plants makes it all seem as though it could have sprouted up spontaneously, just like this, out in the wild. It is intentionally messy, not perfectly precise, and I love it with my whole soul.

I'm half-tempted to knock on the door and ask the home's owner if they refill the boxes or outsource the job to someone else, but experience has taught me this isn't the best tactic. Living in a town so consistently full of tourists, most homeowners don't readily answer knocks from strangers. If I lived in one of these houses, I likely wouldn't either.

But I have to tell Tyler something. My silence will only increase his determination to grill the truth out of me. Instead, I settle for a half-truth. "Okay. There's one thing. Rachel convinced me to sign up for a booth at a flower show happening this summer."

"Hey! That's amazing," Tyler says. "And a big step."

"I know. But I haven't figured out how I'm going to—" I stop myself, only because I know Tyler will offer to pay for the flowers I need to properly outfit a booth. But it's so much more than flowers. It's business cards and signage and a website and all kinds of things I haven't even begun to think about. And Tyler will want to pay for all of it. At this point, I'm not confident enough in the possibility of success to let him stick his neck out like that. Right now, if I don't make it, I'll owe Rachel five hundred bucks. That's manageable. But allowing Tyler to foot the bill for a whole bunch of start-up costs?

Nah. I'm not there. "—how I'm going to find the time to get everything done," I finish, changing my trajectory mid-sentence. "I'm still leading fourteen, sometimes fifteen tours a week."

"I'm sure you'll be able to figure it out," Tyler says.

"Oh, hey, I took your ideas to the florist in Asheville, and she loved them," Olivia says. "She asked if you were looking for a job."

"You'd love Asheville," Tyler chimes in.

"Not if there's ever snow on the ground, I wouldn't. You know I'll never leave this place." I reach out and finger the sweet potato vine in the window box in front of me. Maybe I'll leave Charleston at some point. Never say never and all that. But the city, the culture, the climate, it all holds my heart in a big way. It would take a lot to make me say goodbye.

"Just the same," Olivia says, "I'd love to use your designs at the wedding. The florist said she'd love your help the day of to implement everything, if you're up for it."

Floral arranging isn't exactly what I want to be doing long term. While arranging is ornamental, making flowers beautiful in the short term, I'm more interested in urban landscape design. Creating beautiful spaces that will stay beautiful. Window boxes, especially, but also flower beds, gardening spaces, that sort of thing. Still, drawing up some designs for Olivia's flowers scratched at my creativity in a satisfying way. Even if Tyler bribed her into asking me to do it, which I'm pretty sure he did, I enjoyed the process. "Of course. I'd be happy to help."

"And you'll be at the fitting with Dani tomorrow?" she asks.

"Oh, absolutely. I'm excited to see the dress, but I also haven't seen Dani in a long time."

"Perfect. And wear something comfortable because we'll do your bridesmaid fitting at the same time."

"Wait, are you serious? She's doing *my* dress?"

"Her friend, Chase, is. He's a designer up in New York, and from what Dani tells me, is just as incredible as she is. When he offered to design them, Dani said we weren't allowed to refuse."

"That sounds amazing," I say, even as I try not to dwell on what a custom-made bridesmaid's dress from an elite New York City designer is going to cost me. I spend most of my life wearing a baseball hat and Vans—as many miles as I walk in a day, comfort is paramount—but I love to get dressed up. Still, no amount of excitement is worth swallowing a three or even four-digit price tag. I'm currently in more of the hopefully-I'll-find-something-for-less-than-fifty-bucks-on-the-clearance-rack economic bracket.

"The dress is a gift, Darce," Tyler says before I can add anything more. "Not from us. From Dani. I mean, all the bridesmaids are getting a deal. But she told me specifically. She wants your dress to be a gift."

I swallow, simultaneously appreciating the gesture and resenting it. I have a lot of successful friends. Friends who are living their passion and making money doing it. Even Tyler has finally found his groove filming for a boutique ad agency in Charlotte. I'm the only one not *making it*. Still working to get any semblance of a career off the ground. Not Dani. Not Tyler. Not Olivia. Not even Rachel. Her presence in Charleston's art scene is new, but she's finally getting the recognition she deserves, making the money she deserves.

And I'm . . . sending naughty texts to a man who despises me in an effort to win a magazine feature promoting a job I don't actually want to keep.

"I . . . that's . . . really sweet."

Tyler sighs. "I know you don't want to take it, but don't think of it as charity, all right? It's a gift. Dani loves you. She wants to do this for you."

Maybe that's true. But there's no way she isn't motivated by the fact that she knows I can't afford the dress on my own. She means well, but it still makes me feel like a failure.

But tomorrow isn't about me. It's about Olivia. Her wedding. I can't let my wounded pride cast a sense of unease over everything.

"I'm grateful," I finally say. "Truly. I'm sure the dress is going to be beautiful."

"And I'll see you at the house tomorrow after the fitting?" Tyler asks.

"Of course. You think I'd miss the drama of Dad and Phil hanging out together?" My parents are amicably divorced. They split up when Tyler was a junior in high school and ceased any and all communication that didn't have to do with either of us. Which mostly worked. But now that Tyler lives out of town, whenever he comes back to Charleston, we all get together for a meal so he has time to see everyone. Mom. Dad. Mom's new husband, Phil. Me. Tyler. And now Olivia, bless her, who is an excellent buffer when stuff starts to get weird.

I sense that Tyler is reading between the lines, understanding that my feigned enthusiasm is nothing but an effort to cover up my singed ego. But he knows me well enough not to push. Especially not with Olivia listening, and for that, I'm grateful.

We say goodbye and I make my way back to my tiny, third-floor apartment. When I first signed the lease, I'd never been so proud. So excited to be living on my own, making it in a city that is notoriously expensive, surrounded by million-dollar homes and the flowers that fill my sketchbooks and my heart. Who cares that my floors slope dangerously to the left, my air conditioning only works half the time, and a ghost knocks things around at night? I'm living my dream.

But after years of barely scraping by, adding extra tours to make the rent, sharing groceries and takeout with Rachel to cut corners, the weight of Dani's charity—I refuse to call it anything else—feels especially heavy. I know Dani and the rest of Tyler's circle of friends aren't people who judge, who would ever make me feel less-than.

But to them, I've always been the little sister struggling to keep up.

This just feels like more of that.

I pause at the top of the stairs when a familiar thump sounds from the landing in between my apartment and Rachel's. There is nothing but a smooth stretch of plaster between our front doors, but beyond that wall is whatever we can't see at the respective ends of our living room closets—the secret, walled-off space Rachel believes is the home of our ghost.

I've heard the thump dozens of times and always dismissed it as our old house making noise.

But I'm probably going to be living in this tiny apartment forever.

Long after Rachel leaves. With the way her star is rising in the art world, I can't imagine she'll endure the quirkiness (a kindness, that word) of our third-floor apartments much longer.

Maybe I should give the ghost a name.

And get a cat.

Multiple cats.

Who will sit with me on Friday nights while I watch the garden channel and eat all the waffle-cone chunks out of my Americone Dream Ben and Jerry's all by myself.

Rachel is still on my couch, the empty Ben and Jerry's container on the coffee table in front of her. "What happened to you?" she asks as I mope my way into the living room.

I drop onto the couch with a huff. "I'm having a pity party, and I don't want to talk about it," I say.

"Understood." Rachel reaches for the remote. "You still want the romance? Or do you want to watch something with explosions?"

This is Rachel's specialty. Part of her magic imagination and intuition. If I tell her what I need, she will absolutely pick the perfect movie. "I don't want explosions. But maybe something funny? That will give me hope that love exists in the world even for people who are down on their luck and have crappy jobs and look like they are very likely going to die alone with their cats?"

She raises an eyebrow. "All that, huh?"

I only nod.

She thinks for a second, her eyes narrowing until she snaps her fingers and smiles. "Got it."

When the opening credits roll for Marilyn Monroe's *How to Marry a Millionaire*, I start to laugh.

"This is one of the main reasons I love you," I say to her.

She smiles and settles in as she props her feet up on the coffee table.

"Also, the ghost's name is Matilda."

She eyes me, her expression curious. "Matilda?"

I nod. "I feel like it fits."

"Okay. Matilda it is."

Chapter Ten

Darcy

I'm wedged in between Isaac's wife, Rosie, and Dani's best friend, Chase, when the first text auto-sends to Cameron. I don't see the text send, but I know what time I scheduled it, and I watch the seconds tick toward ten thirty-five with rapt attention. So what if I feel a little sick?

It's fine.

I'm fine.

Everything is *fine*.

Olivia is on a raised platform in the middle of the room at the back of Dani's shop, facing a three-sided mirror that fully reflects her unbelievably gorgeous dress. Olivia told Dani she wanted a dress that looked like nature. Soft lines, flowing fabrics, curling vines and flowers cascading over the entire thing. The look on Olivia's face says everything. Dani nailed it just like we all knew she would. She hovers around Olivia now, adjusting the hem, a collection of pins in her mouth and a measuring tape hanging around her neck.

The measuring tape is the same bright pink as the one she always wore when we were kids—she was constantly making things—and I suddenly wonder if it's the same one.

I glance at my watch. Cameron is ten or so minutes into his tour now—likely making his way down Broad Street. I itch to check my phone, to pull up the texts and reread them, but with Rosie and Chase sitting so close, there's no way I'm risking it.

Olivia's nearly done anyway, and then it'll be my turn.

A twinge of embarrassment snakes up from my belly, making my throat feel tight as I think about the brief conversation I had with Dani when I first arrived.

She gave me a hug, holding me extra tight while she whispered in my ear, "Please don't worry about the dress. I know you. I know you won't want to take it. But getting a business off the ground is hard work. Every penny counts, so you should save yours."

I managed to smile and nod and whisper a thank you. Because what choice do I have? I can't afford the dress, so I'm in no position to complain about her giving it to me.

I did, however, feel a renewed sense of determination to impress *Southern Traditions and Travel* and get the feature story over Cameron. I've grown too complacent over the past few months. And I won't grow my business if I don't start doing things differently. If I don't start fighting for what I want.

"Okay. I think I'm finished," Dani finally says. She steps away and Olivia turns her body from side to side, admiring Dani's creation from every angle.

My heart squeezes.

I want that kind of happiness. To be a bride. To be loved as much as I know Tyler loves Olivia.

Chase and Rosie hop up from the sofa and move to Olivia's side, and I jump at the chance to pull out my phone. Only the first text has sent, but the next should go any minute.

My Cameron kissing dream pops unbidden into my mind. I normally forget my dreams but this one is as potent, as vivid, as any kiss I've actually experienced. I can even conjure up the way he tasted—like tangerines and salty air. Rachel is supposed to be the one with an amazing imagination, but my brain was very thorough in filling in all the details of a kiss that has never even happened. That *will* never happen.

The second text sends while I'm watching. *Right now, I'm imagining sliding my hands over your biceps, feeling the curve of your shoulders.*

It's hard not to laugh. I am not a sexy text kind of woman. I don't know how anyone can be. If some guy sent a text like this to me? I'd throw my phone across the room and hide in the living room closet with Matilda.

"Darcy? You ready?" Chase asks.

I drop my phone into my purse like it's a hot coal and smile. "Yep. Ready."

Rosie and Olivia's mom have both disappeared into a changing room with Olivia, leaving Chase and me alone. I take off my hoodie and step onto the platform Olivia just vacated so Chase can get my measurements. He works in silence for a few moments, giving me the chance to study him through the mirror.

I don't know a lot about him. Just that he's from New York and is Dani's best friend. His dressed-down look, jeans and a V-neck sweater worn with a pair of stacked white sneakers, looks polished and hip on his lean frame, and I get the sense that this man is *always* fashionable and put-together. I suddenly feel a tiny bit sloppy in my leggings and tank top, but Olivia said to dress comfortably. I push the insecurities away. It's not like I need to worry about impressing Chase anyway. He's wearing a wedding ring and isn't giving off anything but a warm and friendly vibe. "Your shoes are fantastic," I say.

"Thanks. I don't get to wear them too frequently because I have daughters, and they are messy. I'm too terrified to wear white shoes around them." His gaze drops to my shoes. "Yours are also great."

I glance down at my Vans, white with a deep blue stripe up the side. "It's a weakness," I say. "You'd think my tiny paychecks would cure my love for amazing sneakers. Alas . . ."

"You know what they say," Chase says. "Happiness is fleeting. Unless you have amazing shoes."

I chuckle. "That's what they say, huh?"

"There are studies to back it up and everything," he jokes. "Lift your arms for a sec?" He waits while I lift them, then bumps them up a few more inches so they're perfectly level with my shoulders and measures my torso from my armpit to the line of my waist. "So Olivia wants bridesmaids in jewel tones. Deep shades of blue, purple, and green. Do you have a preference?"

"Um, should I have a preference?"

He raises an eyebrow. "Most women do."

"Yes, but Dani tells me color is your gift. So what if you tell me what color is going to make me the most beautiful?"

He smiles. "I knew I liked you." He crosses his arms, one hand perched on his chin, and studies me closely. "Honestly, with your hair and skin tone, I don't think we could go wrong. You're gorgeous. A fashion designer's favorite canvas. But I think, if I had to choose, I'd put you in purple."

"Purple it is," I say.

My watch buzzes from my wrist, and I lift it to see a text from Cameron. A single word. *Darcy???*

The sight of those three question marks after my name does something to me.

He knows it's me? HE KNOWS IT'S ME.

With my phone across the room, I can't be sure exactly how many of the texts have sent. Enough that it's obvious they're a prank?

Few enough that he thinks I'm serious? Maybe I've been more blatant than I think in my admiration of his biceps.

I close my eyes. "Oh my word," I say slowly. "Oh my word, oh my word, oh my word." Doubt suddenly fills every square inch of my body. Toes to fingertips. Even my hair follicles feel charged with uncomfortable energy.

My whole body buzzes.

I'm . . . maybe possibly going to be sick.

I lean over and press my hands onto my knees and take a deep breath.

Chase places a tentative hand on my back. "Darcy? You okay?" he says, alarm evident in his voice.

Why did I think this was a good idea? Aloysius Butts was one thing. Annoying as all get out, but mostly harmless.

But this. I'm sure I will distract Cameron, which is the goal. But what if my texts do more than that? What if they make him mad? What if they give him the wrong idea? What if he takes me seriously and he wants to—

No. NO. My brain cannot go there.

He started this. He flirted with me first.

Still, the thought of him reading my messages *knowing* I was the one that typed them up? If there's even the slightest possibility that he's taking me seriously, he can't get the rest of them.

I throw myself off the podium, startling Chase, and dive for my bag. I have to stop them. Cancel the rest of the messages.

My hands tremble as I grab my phone and pull up the app. It takes longer than usual to load; when it finally does, it's on the main log-in screen. I close my eyes. "You have got to be kidding me," I say to myself. "Password. What's my password?" I type in the only possible thing it could be, and it doesn't work. Because OF COURSE it doesn't work.

"Breathe, Darcy," I say. "It's fine. Everything is fine."

"Darcy," Chase says again. "Do you need me to get Olivia in here? Or Rosie?"

I shake my head. "Just give me a sec."

I try three more variations of my password—none of them work—and then the app locks me out, saying I can't try again for twenty minutes. The universe literally hates me.

I sigh and let my shoulders drop.

Now what?

I pull up the actual text thread with Cameron, wincing when I realize how many of the texts he's already seen. I type in a new message.

Darcy: This would have been a lot funnier if you hadn't figured out it was me.

His response comes through immediately. I have no idea how he's managing to text me while also leading the tour, but this is Cameron we're talking about. Everything else is easy for him. Why not this too?

Cameron: Oh, I think it's funnier because I DID figure it out. Your number is on your website, Darcy. This wasn't very sneaky.

Darcy: On my website is different than programmed INTO YOUR PHONE.

Cameron: You know what they say. Keep your friends close, and your enemies closer . . .

Another scheduled text pops up in the thread immediately after Cameron's message. We're finally hitting the juiciest ones.

Cameron: Oh, wow. They're still coming.

Darcy: I scheduled them ahead of time and I can't make it stop. ABORT MISSION. ABORT. ABORT. ABORT. Please promise you won't read anymore.

Cameron: Hahahaha. I promise I won't read anymore . . . until after my tour is over.

I drop my phone beside me and press my face into my hands.

So that didn't go *exactly* as I planned. But at least Cameron doesn't seem mad.

Chase drops onto the couch beside me. "You sure you're okay?"

I offer him a small smile. "I am now, I think. There's just a thing going on with this . . . you know what? It's a long story. But I'm good. In control. Do you need any more measurements?"

"No, you're done. I got what I need."

I grab my sweatshirt and pull it over my head. "Do you have to get measurements for the other bridesmaids?" I ask, needing the distraction of normal conversation to keep me from dwelling too much on Cameron's texts.

Chase shakes his head. "You were the last one. I already have Rosie's, and Olivia's other bridesmaid, Kelly, couldn't make the trip down, so we did a Zoom call and I talked her through taking them for me."

"Wait, don't you live in New York? Did you make the trip to Charleston just to measure me?"

Chase grins. "I need very little persuading to make a trip to Charleston, but Dani and I had a few other business things to work through. That's why I'm here. Are you coming to lunch?"

I nod. I blocked out the entire day to spend with Olivia, and later, Tyler. Dress fitting. Lunch at Magnolia's. Then back to Isaac's house, where Tyler and Olivia are staying, to hang out until we head to Mom's for dinner.

"How about you walk to the restaurant with me?" Chase asks as Olivia and everyone else emerge from the dressing room, Dani cradling Olivia's dress. He holds out his arm, like a gentleman preparing to escort a lady onto a Regency dance floor. "You look like you could use an unbiased third party to talk through whatever is on your mind."

"Take him up on it," Dani says. "Whatever it is. Chase is the very best listener, and his advice is always spot on."

I only hesitate a moment. Maybe it will be nice to have a man's perspective.

It's only a few blocks to Magnolia's, but I talk fast, and by the time we arrive, Chase has been fully debriefed.

I can tell he's trying hard not to laugh, but I don't get the sense he's laughing at me. Not that I would blame him if he did. I'm a one-woman comedy show with my parade of misjudgments and errors.

Chase pulls me onto a bench outside the restaurant while everyone else moves to the door. Olivia shoots me a questioning look, her concern obvious. I know Dani and even Rosie better than I do Olivia, but her connection to Tyler trumps theirs, and no one looks out for me like Tyler does. I'm sure his concern has rubbed off on her. I smile and wave her on. "I'll explain later," I say.

Seemingly satisfied, she follows everyone else inside and leaves me with Chase.

"Here's what I think," he finally says.

"Lay it on me."

"I think it's possible that Cameron is trying to mess with your head."

"Right? My friend Rachel thinks I'm crazy, but that's what I think, too."

He holds up a hand. "I didn't say that's what I think. I just said it's possible. Why does Rachel think you're crazy?"

I roll my eyes. "I have no idea. She thinks he likes me. That he truly wants to spend time with me. But—" My words cut off because Chase is smirking. "Oh, no. You too?"

He shrugs. "Look. Nothing this guy has ever done is actually hurtful. You've seen him with other women. You think he's rich and snobby. But has he ever been cruel to you?"

It only takes a moment of thought to know the answer to his question is no. Even the verbal sparring, the teasing, which I'm just as responsible for, has always remained surface level. "Not cruel," I say. "Annoying as all get out, but not cruel."

"Let me ask you a question," Chase says. "Why haven't you moved the start of your tour to somewhere else in the city?"

"Because Rachel works at the gift shop," I immediately say.

"That's fair. But you said Rachel is your neighbor, right? Do you really need to see her at work?"

My brain catches on his question. Because I could move the start of my tour. When I stole the insoles out of Cameron's shoes, I did just that. Met everyone in Washington Square Park right next door and it didn't matter in the slightest. Realization dawns, and I squirm with sudden unease. I haven't moved because I look forward to sparring with Cameron.

"Well, crap." I drop against the plaster wall behind us with a huff.

Chase grins. "A part of you likes it, right? The banter? The interactions?"

I don't tell him that *all* of me likes it.

"The same could be asked of him," Chase continues. "If Cameron truly despises you, why hasn't he moved his tour-start somewhere else? Why does he keep placing himself somewhere he knows you're going to be?"

I sigh. "That is a very good question."

"When I fell in love with Darius, he was working at a record shop in Chelsea, and I bought a dozen records I didn't even need for bands I didn't even like so I had an excuse to talk to him."

My heart does the same little twitchy thing it always does whenever I learn about real and true love stories. "That's really sweet."

"Add in Cameron asking you to dinner?" He shrugs. "I could be wrong. He really could be messing with you. But I think I agree with Rachel."

I swallow. "Which only makes me more embarrassed about sending all those texts."

"I'm sure they aren't that bad."

I shoot him a look and retrieve my phone from my bag. I unlock it and pull up the text thread. The last few messages delivered in the time it took for us to walk to the restaurant.

Wordlessly, I hand the phone over to Chase.

"*I've seen a glimpse of those muscles. I want to see—*"

"No!" I shout, interrupting him. "Don't read them out loud."

He purses his lips and shoots me some side-eye but reads the rest of the messages silently, laughing out loud more than once. "Is that last one even physically possible?" he finally says.

"How should I know? I didn't write them. They're lines from romance novels." I push out a breath, feeling more and more deflated. "I honestly didn't think he would know it was me."

Chase hands my phone back. "But he responded, and it seems like he's laughing about it. I don't think you have anything to worry about. If nothing else, I'm sure your prank worked exactly like you wanted it to. There's no way he read all those messages and wasn't distracted." He gives my knee a friendly pat. "Now come on. Let's go eat. I've heard the fried green tomatoes here are the best in the city."

"Oh, they definitely are." I pause at the restaurant door and look into Chase's bright blue eyes. "You have been an unexpected gift today," I say. "Thank you for listening."

"Of course. I hope you'll keep me posted."

"For sure."

He follows me into the restaurant, and we wait for the hostess to finish up a phone call.

"I usually talk to Tyler about stuff like this, but somehow—"

"Oh, say no more," Chase says, cutting me off. "I'm happy to have saved your brother from reading text messages like *those* written by his little sister."

I nod sagely. "Please promise you'll forget everything you read."

He wraps a brotherly arm around my shoulders. "Consider it forgotten."

***

Lunch is easy. I am always at ease among Tyler and his friends; even with him gone—he's hanging out with Isaac, Alex, and the kids—they still treat me like I belong, like I'm one of them. But to say I'm distracted would be an understatement.

Because I can't stop thinking about what Chase helped me realize.

It's very possible that Cameron really does like me.

And it's just as possible that I like Cameron back.

Chapter Eleven

Cameron

I programmed Darcy's number into my phone when I booked her tour as Aloysius Butts. And yes, I've thought about coming up with some random reason to text her.

Typed them out and everything.

But I always chicken out.

Because no matter how interesting I think Darcy is, she still thinks I'm a womanizing, privileged jerk. Still, when I was on her tour, there were moments when it felt like she was seeing me differently. It's almost as if there is the way Darcy *wants* to feel about me, and then there is the way she actually feels about me. And the two don't sync up.

But that doesn't mean I can call her up on a random Tuesday and invite her to a picnic lunch on the battery. A stroll around downtown. A trip to Jeni's Ice Cream. Dinner at the Obstinate Daughter out on Sullivan's Island followed by a long walk on the beach.

It's possible I've given this a little too much thought.

When her first text came in, I stopped in the middle of the intersection between Meeting Street and Broad and stared at my watch so long, my tour group all made it across the street, the traffic light changed, and the first car in line had to honk to snap me out of my daze.

I jogged to catch up with my group, reassuring them that I hadn't lost my mind, then carried on with the tour.

I shifted into autopilot, reciting the historical facts and anecdotes I know well enough to repeat in my sleep, while my brain kept tripping over the implication of Darcy's text. *I dreamed about kissing you all night long.*

Maybe she didn't hate me. If she dreamed about me, and then felt bold enough to tell me? It had to mean something.

Then another text came in. This one was enough to make me question. Did Darcy know what she was sending? Was this for real?

When I finally figured things out, all I could do was laugh. It was a well-played prank. But while my group wandered around Saint Michael's, admiring the stained glass designed by New York's Tiffany and Company in the late nineteenth century (the church itself is over two hundred years old but the windows are a more recent update), I sat in the back pew and let myself feel something else. Something almost like disappointment.

For a split second, I'd believed she was serious. And that second was all I needed to trigger a string of thoughts I probably shouldn't have entertained sitting in the back of a church.

I ignored the buzzing her arriving messages triggered on my watch and kept my phone well out of reach for the rest of my tour, but she'd still knocked me off my game. I didn't engage with my tour half as much as I usually do. Didn't share my funniest stories. Didn't joke around and set people at ease. I did the job, and from what I could tell, no one left disappointed. But I didn't shine. I didn't give them the experience I always try for.

Hard to do all that when I couldn't get my brain to think about anything but what it *would* be like to kiss Darcy all night long.

I run a hand across my face. *Gah.* I have got to get this girl out of my head.

Or just kiss her. Figure out if what I imagined all morning is anything like the real thing. Scratch the itch, so to speak. Make it possible for me to think about something else. Someone else, maybe?

Except, I don't really think that's true. Something in my gut tells me kissing Darcy Marino is more likely to fall in the life-changing category than the casually-walk-away-unscathed one.

I pace back and forth across my tiny living room and pause when I see Darcy's hat sitting on the mantel over my minuscule gas fireplace. The house I live in is old. Not historical preservation society old. Just normal old, built in the 1920s. It's been gutted and modernized, but the floors are original, as is the brick around the fireplace and the hand-hewn mantel.

I'm not normally home in the middle of the day. I have another tour in a couple of hours and driving off the peninsula to Park Circle doesn't make sense. Instead, I usually go to the college and eat lunch with Jerome or find a quiet corner in the downtown library to read or research and kill some time.

But after my morning, I was too restless to hang out with Jerome and I wasn't stupid enough to think I'd be able to read more than a couple of lines without my mind drifting back to Darcy.

I came home thinking the drive might help, but I'm still restless. *I need to see her.*

The thought pops into my head and a sense of rightness washes over me. I need to spend time with her. Convince her I'm not who she thinks I am.

This little game has gone on long enough. I'd rather just wish her luck and see if she'll have dinner with me anyway, no matter who the magazine chooses.

Jerome used to joke that I should make myself a set of cue cards to hand to women whenever I'm ready to take our relationship to the next level—to move past the shallow, surface stuff and get real. He knows I'll never just talk. Not about that. Cue cards really might be my only hope.

Or, I can keep dating women who only care about the surface-level stuff. Which is relatively easy to do.

The thing is, I don't think Darcy is like that. I get the sense that if we were in a relationship, she would demand more of me, go after my walls with a sledgehammer until she knows everything there is to know. I crave that level of honesty. Deep in my bones, I want it.

I'm also terrified of it.

Next to Darcy's hat on the mantel, there's a small wooden box. It's beat up and worn, the latch broken, a crack running across the top left corner. It was my mom's box—the only thing I kept of hers when Dad and I cleaned out her stuff after she left. Inside, there are half a dozen photos of the two of us together when I was a kid, the feet and hand prints the hospital made of me when I was born, and the wedding ring she briefly wore when she believed herself capable of being faithful to my dad.

Sometimes I wonder why I've kept it all these years. It doesn't even tell half the story. Not that she was strung out most of the time. Not that she left right after Dad was diagnosed with cancer. Though, in hindsight, I see her leaving for the kindness it was. I'd been taking care of her since I was six years old. Once Dad was sick, she probably realized I couldn't take care of them both.

Mom died of an overdose the summer after I graduated from high school. I hadn't seen her in four years.

It's laughable now when I think about believing that Sigma Theta Pi was interested in me. A nobody poor kid from Colleton County. My own mama wasn't even interested. That has to say something.

I'm not that kid anymore. Not when I'm in Charleston. But maybe I need to be with Darcy. Maybe that's the man she needs to see.

An inkling of an idea coalesces in my mind. I have Darcy's hat. Her lucky hat. If I offer to return it to her, she'll likely agree to meet me. But what would entice her to do more than grab the hat and leave?

I don't know much about Darcy. But I know she likes history, and I know she likes flowers. Fortunately, I'm a man who has access to both.

No, scratch that. I am a man with *friends* who have access to both.

And I'm not below begging for some favors.

One favor I can request over the phone.

But the other? If I'm going to ask anything of Vivian Abernathy, I'm doing it in person over the glass of sweet tea I know she'll insist I drink and one of the blueberry scones her live-in housekeeper, Betty, keeps stocked in the kitchen.

I glance at my watch. If I hurry, I'll have an hour to spend with Vivian before my next tour starts. Hopefully that will be long enough to charm her into saying yes.

***

I only see Darcy twice after she spam-texts me on Monday morning; both times we dance around each other like we're waiting for the other to make the first move. To say the first thing. Both times, our tour groups keep us from truly having a real conversation.

On Thursday night, I finally text her.

Cameron: Are you busy tomorrow night? I have something for you.

She immediately responds.

Darcy: It better be my hat.

Cameron: I love how you immediately go back to your hat and ignore the fact that you wrote me a bodice-ripper of a romance novel this week.

Darcy: I love how you throw in a term like bodice-ripper like it's common vernacular. Trying to tell me something about your reading habits?

Cameron: I'm a historian. I make no apologies for my broad awareness of literary terms.

Darcy: I just googled. The first documented use of the term "bodice-ripper" was in 1978.

Cameron: Historians study modern history too.

Cameron: Are you free tomorrow night or not?

Darcy: I'm free. But only if you promise to bring my hat. Time?

Cameron: Are you a night owl? I'll text where and when tomorrow.

Darcy: I am NOT a night owl. But I love a good mystery, so I'll take the bait and await further instruction.

I meet my friend Wesley outside of the Old Provost Exchange building at the end of Broad Street at ten forty-five p.m. on Friday night. We're standing in a shady parking lot to the side of the building, waiting as the last of Wesley's evening ghost tour group takes pictures in front of the barred windows along the base of the building. The windows are only inches off the ground and lead into a space referred to as the dungeon because of its use as a prison when the British occupied Charleston during the Revolutionary War. Even though it was only a prison for a couple of years, calling it a dungeon is more poetic than a belowground room with lots of different uses over the years. Especially for the ghost tours.

"You know I'm doing you a solid, man," Wesley says as he waves to the last of his group.

"I know. I owe you one."

He motions me forward. "Come on. Let's do this then. I've got somewhere I need to be."

"Right now?" I ask. "It's almost eleven."

Wesley scoffs. "What, are you eighty? It's Friday. The night is still young."

Fair point, even if my weekend habits do lean a little more geriatric. At least Darcy and I have that in common.

We arrive at the back door of the dungeon and Wesley pulls it open. I've been in the dungeon before, multiple times, but I've always gone in the front door and accessed it via the stairwell that's regularly open to visitors. Only the company Wesley works for, Dave Vanderhorst's Churchtown Tours, has permission to access the dungeon through this rear door. We step into a small, hallway-like space and stop in front of the heavy, wooden double doors that lead into the actual dungeon. One of the doors is propped open.

Wesley pulls out a key dangling from a small chain shaped like the Arthur Ravenel bridge that crosses the Cooper River to the islands beyond the harbor. There's a wooden wedge doorstop just behind the exterior door, and Wesley uses it to prop the door open. "I'm going to lock it now," he says. "Just keep it propped open until you leave, then be sure to shut it firmly behind you."

"Sounds good. But will people notice if the door is propped open this late?"

"How long are you planning on staying in here?" he asks. "I thought this was an in and out kind of deal."

"No, it is. It shouldn't be . . ." I let my words trail off because I don't know how long we'll be. I hope we'll be able to talk a little, but that doesn't necessarily need to happen *inside* the dungeon.

"Cameron." Wesley shoots me a judging look. "If you're planning on bringing a woman here for a little somethin' somethin'"—he waggles his eyebrows suggestively—"we need to have a conversation about what kind of location you think is sexy." He pats me on the back. "Newsflash. It isn't a dungeon."

"Thanks for the tip, man. I'll keep that in mind." I don't have plans to even kiss Darcy in the dungeon, not to mention anything

Wesley might be talking about. But it's fun to let him think I might.

"You'll keep it in mind? Are you bringing a woman here, or aren't you?" He squares his shoulders. "Dude, I'm putting my job on the line here—"

I quickly hold up my hands. "A woman is meeting me here, but only to talk. Your job will be fine."

He eyes me warily, but the tension lines between his brows ease. "So this woman . . . she's into history or something?"

I nod. "Or something. I don't know. It's complicated."

He finally smiles. "When are women not? All right. I'm out. If anything goes wrong, you don't know me, and I didn't have anything to do with this."

"Understood."

Wesley leaves me standing in between the exterior door and the dungeon door. The silence is heavy around me and a pulse of fear—unreasonable fear—snakes through my gut. I've never been in the dungeon at night, and the space suddenly feels much darker and creepier now that I'm alone.

It's just a room. I'm totally chill. Totally and completely chill.

So what if hundreds of people died here from the harsh prison conditions imposed by the British? It's fine. I'm fine.

"I come in peace," I say to the room at large, mostly joking. Mostly.

The basement space is divided into two halves. One half functions as a sort of museum, full of informational displays and historical artifacts detailing the room's many uses over the years. The other half is in its original state, allowing people to step back in time, walk on bricks that were laid more than two hundred and fifty years ago, and admire the Palladian arches overhead.

Several mannequins are dressed to represent the more notable uses of the space over the years. One corner houses mannequins styled to represent the three signers of the Declaration of Independence native to South Carolina, and a few other well-to-do and noteworthy citizens who were arrested and imprisoned under charges of treason. Another group depicts a rougher group of prisoners—the horse thieves, the deserters, the violent criminals.

I've been told the mannequins are animatronic and used to move, likely scaring the stink out of tourists. Luckily, they were turned off a few years back. I'm not particularly easy to spook. But down here alone? This late at night? Seeing a replica of Thomas Heyward Jr. waving at me might do me in.

I pull a flashlight out of my back pocket and use it to find one specific mannequin. This one is separate from the prisoners and represents a time before the dungeon was an actual dungeon and was a storeroom for goods coming in off the ships docked behind the building. Mr. McGregor, as the tour guides like to call him, sits at his desk, his pen poised over a list of goods eighteenth-century Charlestonians might have found useful. Wire-rimmed spectacles sit on his nose, and his mostly balding head is covered with sparse gray hair.

And now, Darcy Marino's favorite hat.

I adjust the angle of the hat and step back, hoping the night mode on my iPhone will do a decent job of catching what little light is filtering in through the dungeon's barred windows. "Looking good, Mr. McGregor," I say as I snap the photo.

My phone camera does not disappoint, and it only takes a second to send the picture to Darcy, accompanied by a brief text. *Come and get it.*

My heart pounds as I await her reply.

What if she doesn't respond?

What if she's already asleep?

What if she says no and tells me I can keep the hat?

I distract myself from my own spiraling thoughts by reading back through the texts she sent earlier this week. I let out a low chuckle. I admire her gumption. How she managed to put even half these words in a text message without cracking is beyond me.

A simmering heat stirs in my gut, growing in intensity. I want to be around her. To talk to her. Make her smile. Feel the softness of her skin . . . of her lips.

I swallow the giant lump that's suddenly formed in my throat. It's been a few minutes since I sent my text. Enough minutes that I start to think through my actions. I can't leave her hat on Mr. McGregor's head. I could possibly convince Wesley—

My phone buzzes, and a new message from Darcy pops up.

Darcy: WHAT THE WHAT. I was beginning to think you'd forgotten me. But this is maybe worse.

I grin.

Cameron: I mean, the hat looks really good on Mr. McGregor. I'm sure he'll keep it for you. At least until the staff opens up tomorrow morning. Then I imagine your hat will be lost forever.

The three bouncing dots that tell me she's responding show up immediately, and a new message pops up seconds later.

Darcy: CAMERON MY HAT CANNOT BE LOST FOREVER.

My heart does this weird twinge thing when I read my name. There's only been one time Darcy has ever said my name without venom dripping from all three syllables. And that was right after our tour groups shared the steps of City Hall, and I talked about John Trumbull and his Washington paintings. It did something to my heart then, too.

I turn around and take a selfie with Mr. McGregor, Darcy's hat visible just behind my face. I send the photo along with my next message.

Cameron: Then. Come. And. Get. It.
Cameron: It'll be fun. I'll give you a private midnight tour.
Darcy: This is crazy. I'm already in my pajamas.
Cameron: You really did think I forgot you? I asked if you were a night

owl.

Darcy: *I kept my jeans on all the way until ten-thirty before I gave up.*
Cameron: *Please?*
Darcy: *WEARY SIGH. Fine. Don't go anywhere. I'm coming.*
Cameron: *Come to the back door. Left side of the stairs.*

I wait for her outside. I wasn't exactly scared hanging out inside the dungeon, but the number of people who have claimed to see ghosts in or around the building is high. And not just tourists. Tour guides. Docents from the museum. People that wouldn't joke around about it.

It only takes Darcy ten minutes to show up, which means she must live close by—useful information that I tuck away in my brain.

She isn't still wearing pajamas, but she's dressed way down in black leggings and a giant hoodie. But then, those could be her pajamas. Either way, I'm glad she felt comfortable enough to come as she is. Her sneakers are on point, as always, gray Nikes with a shiny gold swoosh. Her hair is pulled back in a ponytail, and in the faint glow of the streetlights overhead, she doesn't look like she has any makeup on.

"Cameron Hunter, this is the stupidest thing ever."

I raise an eyebrow. "As stupid as feeling the firm roundness of my—"

"Stop!" she says quickly, holding up her palm. "Fine. I deserve it. I'll never complain about my hat as long as you promise to delete those messages and never read them again."

I grin. "Oh, I'm not deleting them. Not ever."

She sighs. "I should have been more thorough in considering the collateral damage."

"You were certainly thorough enough in the other half of your research."

She fights a smile as she studies me for a long moment. "I thought I might have scared you off for good," she finally says.

"Nah. Just had to think of the perfect response."

She eyes me. "Is that what this is?"

I shake my head. "This is not a prank, I promise." It's suddenly very important to me that she knows that. "This is just me returning your hat." *And hoping to spend some time with you.*

She nods and waves her hand in a motion that encompasses my entire person. "You look different," she finally says. "Casual."

I smirk. "Like Aloysius Butts?"

"Minus the wedgie."

"That was a very uncomfortable two hours."

"I still want the story," she says. "Unless you were lying and there's no photo ID in your wallet?"

I pull out my wallet and grab the fake ID a guy who lived across the hall of my college dorm room made for me. "The ID is real," I say, holding it out to her. "But there isn't much of a story. Just a poorly behaved college kid pretending to be older than I was."

"Did people actually buy it? That you were named Aloysius?"

"I was very convincing."

"Yeah, that seems to be your superpower." She motions to my outfit. "I like this though. The dressed-down look."

I look down at my faded hoodie and jeans. I chose the clothes intentionally, wanting her to see me in something different. "You've only ever seen me in my work clothes, Darcy. I don't live at work."

"That's fair. But you could wear whatever you want to work. Tourists don't care how casual you are. Dave leads his tours looking like the instructor for a senior sneakers class at the YMCA, and he's killing it."

"Dave has forty years of experience and reviews backing him up." I shrug. "I don't have that luxury."

She rolls her eyes. "Yeah. Your career really looks like it's hurting."

I move toward the door. "So maybe there *is* something to the way I dress." I look over my shoulder. "You ready to fight Mr. McGregor for your hat? I think he's grown to like it. It's keeping his head warm."

"How do you even have a key to this place anyway?" she asks as she follows me inside.

"I don't. But my friend Wesley works for Churchtown. He let me in."

She crowds me in a way I like, her body close enough to mine that I can feel the warmth of her. "I've never been in here at night," she says, her voice almost a whisper.

I pull the door toward the building so it's almost closed, closed enough that unless someone is really looking, they won't notice it's propped open. I pull out my flashlight, flicking it on. "I haven't either. Not until tonight."

"So you thought to yourself, *I should hide Darcy's hat in the dungeon. It's a great place to hang out after midnight. It wouldn't be creepy at all.*"

"I needed it to be somewhere you would recognize. Which you did."

"You know what else I would have recognized? You, walking up to me at the gift shop on Monday morning, holding my hat."

I smile into the darkness. This back and forth with Darcy never gets old. "But that wouldn't have been near as much fun."

She scoffs. "Who said I'm having fun?"

A thud sounds across the room, and Darcy gasps, jumping toward me and threading her arm around mine, her body pressed flush against me.

"*I'm* having fun," I say, my tone light.

"Shut up," she whisper-yells. "What was that? What was that noise?"

"We're standing in the basement of a building that was built in 1771. It probably groans and moans all the time."

"Come on." She tugs on my arm, her tone saying she isn't convinced. "Let's get this over with."

I inch forward, pulling her along beside me. Mr. McGregor is only a few yards away, but the bricks underfoot aren't particularly level.

It makes sense to move slowly. For safety.

It doesn't have anything to do with how much I like having Darcy this close to me.

"Are we only using the flashlight because you want me to be freaked out? Or can we really not turn on the lights in here?" she asks.

"Technically, we could. But the lights would be visible from the street and any passing policeman would notice. We don't really want to get noticed."

"Oh, fun. So we're trespassing. That's awesome."

"We aren't trespassing. It's fine."

"Just not fine enough for us to turn on the lights."

I chuckle. Darcy is cute when she's scared. "Are you afraid of the dark, Darcy? Or . . . maybe you're afraid of ghosts?"

She scoffs. "I am not afraid of ghosts. There's one that lives in my house, actually." Her voice wavers the tiniest bit, like she's trying to convince herself as much as she's trying to convince me.

The building groans again, and Darcy's grip on my arm tightens.

"Her name is Matilda," she whispers. "Oh, look. There's my hat. Time to go." She grabs her hat from Mr. McGregor's head and beats it against her leg for a moment before putting it on.

I've gotten what I wanted. She came to meet me. We're finally together. Without tour groups. Without women I'm not interested in. It's just us, and I don't want her to leave yet.

"Come on. You sure you don't want to look around a little bit?"

Her eyes go wide, the whites flashing in the dim glow of my flashlight. "Are you serious right now?"

"I said I'd give you a midnight tour." I smirk, angling the

flashlight so she can see my face. "Maybe you'll learn something."

Her eyes narrow and she scoffs. "What makes you think you know more about this place than I do?"

I lift one shoulder. "Prove that I don't." She'll take the bait. She's too competitive not to.

Sure enough, she drops my arm and crosses both of hers against her chest. "Gah, fine! Give me your flashlight." She grabs it out of my hand and takes a few steps away, shining the beam around the room. She's quiet for several moments, and I appreciate the opportunity to watch her, barely illuminated, as she shifts the light around the room. "Okay," she finally says, "behind that far wall, the patriots hid fourteen-thousand pounds—"

"Of gunpowder to keep the British from finding it," I finish for her. "Even when the British were using the room as a prison, they had no idea it was there. Try again."

She lets out a breath and continues her perusal. "How about this one? Instead of throwing British tea into the ocean like they did in Boston, in Charleston, city officials simply stored all the tea they received from England in here."

"For two years," I say. "Until they needed money to fund a revolution. That's when they hauled it all over South Carolina and sold it to citizens who were happy to pay top dollar for the British tea they'd been without for so long."

She purses her lips and steps closer, her arms folded tightly across her chest. "Colonel Isaac Hayne."

"Loyal to the American cause, Hayne fought in the Continental Army and defended Charleston until it fell to the British in 1780. He was paroled on the condition that he would not raise arms against the British. But in 1781, things weren't looking so hot for the British, so they demanded he sign an oath of allegiance and join the royal army. Or go to prison."

"But his family was sick," Darcy says, picking up the thread of the story.

I nod. "Smallpox."

"So prison didn't sound like a very good option. When the British promised that if he signed the oath, they wouldn't make him fight, he signed so he could care for his family."

"But then they called him up to fight anyway," I say, taking a step closer. We're close enough now that our toes touch, the beam of the flashlight she's holding illuminating us both.

"And he refused," she says softly. She holds my gaze, something sparking in her eyes that makes me feel like our bodies are having their own conversation, something entirely different than what our words are saying. "He was charged with treason and executed," Darcy adds. "Poor guy. All he wanted to do was take care of his family and stay loyal to the cause he loved."

"They say his ghost still wanders Broad Street, trying to make it back home."

She gives her head a tiny shake. "Now is not the time to talk about ghosts, Cameron. Not unless you want to be wearing me on our way out of here."

"I wouldn't mind," I say coyly.

She scowls, but there's no malice in it. This one feels playful. Flirty. "The US Constitution," she says breathily.

"Ratified upstairs by the state of South Carolina in 1788," I answer, my eyes never leaving hers.

"Stede Bonnet."

"The gentleman pirate. Captured in Charleston and held here in 1718, or at least in the building that was here before this version was built, until he was convicted and hanged for his crimes. Do you know why he became a pirate?"

Darcy smiles. "To escape a nagging wife. Though I'm guessing if her husband talked about her like that, she was happy to see him go."

I reach forward, my finger skimming down the side of her pinky.

The touch is so light, she might think it's accidental, but that's all it takes for my heart to start thumping in my throat. "Shall we call a truce?"

She shrugs. "Might as well. Because I'm all out of facts, and by the gleam in your eye, I'm guessing you could keep going a while longer."

I shake my head. "I didn't bring you here to beat you in quiz bowl."

"Well, that's good. Because I don't like losing, and I'm positive you would win." She adjusts her hat, pulling it low enough on her face that her eyes are lost in shadow. "Why *did* you bring me here, Cameron? Something tells me this isn't just about my hat."

I could just tell her.

Because I can't stop thinking about you.

Because your texts, even if they were joking, put thoughts in my head that I don't want to forget.

Because you don't know the real me, and I want you to.

A sudden surge of vulnerability washes over me. I swallow and flex my fists.

"I felt bad for taking it," I finally say. "It's your lucky hat." It isn't what I want to say. It isn't enough. But—

The metal exterior door suddenly screeches as it slides against the ground, and I immediately click off the flashlight. I pull Darcy toward me, almost throwing her into the shadowed alcove to the right of the heavy dungeon door. If someone looks inside the room, they won't see us here.

No one enters, from what I can tell, but honestly, it's hard to hear anything over the sound of my own pounding heart. Darcy is pressed against the wall, her hands gripping my forearms, her breathing as shallow as mine.

Seconds later, the door closes and latches shut.

Which means . . . *damn*. We're locked in.

It was probably a security guard circling the building. Or a policeman on a late-night patrol that saw the door wedged open and believed it was accidental.

"What was that?" Darcy whispers. She's still holding my arms, her grip even tighter than before.

"What?"

"That noise? What was it?"

"It was the door." I don't say anything else, just tug her around until we reach the exit. I try to open it, but it only takes a second to confirm the heavy door isn't going anywhere.

I lean my forehead against the cool metal. This isn't good. Not. Not. Good.

"Cameron?" Darcy says, alarm and something else—something scarier—filling her voice.

I don't move. It feels safer here, my forehead pressed against the door, my breaths filled with the scent of old brick and mildew.

"Cameron." The question is gone from her voice, replaced with a demand.

I slowly turn to face her, and she shines the flashlight directly into my eyes.

I squint and turn away, and she lowers the light.

"Please tell me there is another way out of this dungeon," she says.

"I . . ." I run a hand through my hair.

"Oh my word." She turns and heads across the room toward the door that leads to the museum upstairs and the regular dungeon entrance that's used during daytime tours.

"Darcy." I start after her. "Stop and think a second."

She whirls around. "What, think about the fact that you just got us locked inside a dungeon? There has to be another way out of here."

I put my hands on her shoulders. "There are security cameras everywhere upstairs. And the main doors are chained shut from the outside every night. We can't go up there without getting caught. Even if we do, we won't be able to get out of the building."

Her shoulders deflate a little. "But maybe if they see us on a security camera somewhere, they'll come and let us out. That sounds better than staying in here all night."

I shake my head. "I doubt there's someone monitoring the security cameras twenty-four-seven. And if we get caught, Wesley gets caught. I can't jeopardize his job like that."

"Jeopardize his job? Really? Cameron, we're not criminals. We're tour guides. We're allowed to be in places like this."

"At midnight on a Friday night? Let me just call him, all right? He has a key. He can come back and let us out."

She shrugs my hands off her shoulders. "Fine. But if he can't come, and I have to spend the night in a dungeon? I am never going to forgive you."

Chapter Twelve

Darcy

We are trapped in a dungeon. An actual eighteenth-century *dungeon*. A haunted eighteenth-century dungeon if even half the stories that have been told about this place are true.

I pace back and forth in front of the door while Cameron stands next to the window, angling his phone upward to try and get a signal. We're standing under tons and tons of stone and brick, so reception isn't fantastic. With the flashlight off, my eyes have adjusted to the light, and I can see a little more. There are streetlights on outside, and they're bright enough that a little light trickles through the windows. It isn't enough to see by. But I can at least make out the shape of Cameron a few feet away from me, pick out the blur of his movements.

Aside from the uncomfortable realization that I'm likely spending the night on a very cold brick floor, I'm not sure what to make of the dressed-down Cameron who invited me here tonight.

There was no question that I would come. When his message came in yesterday, I knew the second I read it I would show up. Mostly because I'm curious. Interested in spending time with him now that Chase has given me some clarity regarding my potential feelings.

I'm maybe going to have to revisit Chase's theory after I'm no longer trapped in a dungeon. Because right now, all I really want to do to Cameron is punch him.

I look again around the dim space, my thoughts spiraling further and further out of control. I force in a breath, but the smell of damp, musty brick is heavy in my nose, and I'm aware of it now more than ever. I breathe out slowly, counting as I do so, and will myself to calm down. I've never done well with small spaces. Even though the dungeon isn't small, I still feel trapped, and my body is reacting just like it did when I was stuck in the elevator of my college dorm for three hours. Or locked in Tyler's closet during a childhood game of hide-and-seek.

"I can't get a call to go through," Cameron says, his shadow appearing next to me. "But I've texted him, and he should respond soon. I know he's not asleep."

"He might be," I say. "I would be if you hadn't hoodwinked me into coming here."

"I didn't hoodwink you. You knew exactly where I was, and you still came willingly."

I huff. "But I didn't know you were going to get us locked in. Is that actually what happened? Did you do this on purpose?"

"Yes, Darcy. I planned the whole thing. I even made a deal with a ghost to move the doorstop and lock us in."

"I wouldn't put it past you. You've done everything else you can think of to mess with me. Why not lock me in a dungeon? Or is *that* what you were planning? Were you going to lock me in here by myself?" I'm not being rational. I realize this as the words are coming out of my mouth. But it's after midnight. I'm not rational after midnight when I'm in my apartment, warm and safe and far away from scary dungeons.

Cameron responds by laughing, of all things. Except it isn't a laugh that sounds fun. It's more caustic. Biting. "I can't win with you, can I? Do you honestly think I would have locked you in? Darcy, I brought you here because—" His words cut off and he sighs. "Just forget it."

I'm not doing particularly well. I'm sweating in weird places, and my heart is racing. But I'm with it enough to recognize I'm not being fair to Cameron. I take a slow deep breath and try to reorder my brain. The door *was* propped open when we came in. I saw the doorstop shoved under it myself. And Cameron couldn't have shut the door on purpose because he was standing with me when it closed.

Still, how does a door randomly close by itself? If I don't blame Cameron, who do I blame? "Do you think it was a ghost?" I ask, my voice small. Small, and still leaning toward irrational. *Get it together, Darcy.*

"I don't think it was a ghost," Cameron says, a little of the fight draining from his voice.

"Then what was it?" My hands are trembling, and I ball them up and shove them into the pocket of my hoodie. I'm fine. In control. Everything is *fine.*

"A security guard, probably. Or a policeman?" Cameron says. The tone in his voice reminds me of the way he talks to me whenever we're sparring in the gift shop. It's cool and collected—almost too cool. Is he pretending to be in control right now? "Maybe a breeze blew it closed?"

That wasn't an entirely unreasonable thought. There is water *very* close to Charleston, and Broad Street is at the edge of the peninsula. This part of the city is always breezy. "Right. A draft. A breeze off the river. That . . . that makes sense."

"Hey," Cameron says, stepping closer. "Are you okay? You sound like you're shaking."

I let out a little laugh. I do feel mildly hysterical, but I'm not sure talking about it is going to make me feel any better. "I'm managing," I say weakly.

Another thud—this one the loudest of all, like someone has dropped something heavy on the floor above us—echoes through the room. I lurch toward Cameron with a yelp, throwing my arms around his waist. "Just kidding. I'm not okay. I don't like the dark, and I don't like ghosts, and I don't like being out after midnight. Why can't I just be an old lady who likes her flowers and her books and is allowed to go to bed by ten p.m. every night?"

Cameron's arms lift and wrap around my back, pulling me even closer. His sweatshirt is soft, and his arms are strong, and he smells like clean air and safety.

And I am absolutely never letting go.

"Darcy," he whispers into my hair. "Breathe."

My lungs collapse as I force out the breath I don't realize I'm holding.

"You're fine," he says softly. "We're fine."

We stand that way, all tangled up in each other, for a long moment. Long enough for my breathing to stabilize, for me to decide I really like the feel of Cameron's hand moving up and down my back.

"You okay?" he finally asks.

"I am, but if you loosen your grip, I might not be."

He chuckles. "I don't know how you handle sharing your apartment with Matilda."

"Matilda is friendly," I say, nestling even further into his hoodie. "And could still be my air conditioning unit. I only need the possibility of a logical explanation to be fine."

"Well, I mean, upstairs is also air-conditioned," he says.

I finally lift my head. "True. That actually helps."

His arms tighten around me like he doesn't want to let me go even if I am feeling better. "I'm glad."

"So I guess we have some time to kill?" I ask.

"Wesley should respond soon."

I nod, suddenly appreciating this moment for what it is. "In the meantime, I think . . . we should talk about you."

Cameron stills and takes a long, slow breath, and I sense that talking about himself might be a bigger deal for him than it is for me. I've always been a pretty open person. Golden retriever puppy, and all that.

"How about we move over to the bench under the window?" Cameron says softly. "There's a little more light there."

"*Then* we can talk about you?" I ask, unwilling to let him off the hook. He got us into this mess, after all, even if I have calmed down enough to realize it wasn't intentional. "I think it's fair to say you owe me."

"You seem awfully curious, Darcy," he says. He relaxes his arms a bit but doesn't fully let me go. "Are you trying to tell me you're interested in me?"

"I'm trying to tell you I need you to distract me from the fact that I'm trapped in a dungeon with no cell service and no bathroom."

His shoulders drop. "I hadn't thought about the bathroom."

"We do have the buckets the prisoners used," I say.

"Hey! You're making jokes. That's a good sign."

I push on his chest, noticing how firm it feels under my palms. "Shut up."

He grabs my hand and laces our fingers together before clicking on the flashlight and leading us to the bench under the window. It's a narrow bench, so we wind up facing each other, straddling the bench with feet planted on either side. Once we're situated, he turns off the light.

"Okay. What do you want to know?" he says, a hint of resignation in his voice. Resignation . . . or maybe fear?

There are dozens of questions I want to ask. About his family. His money. His reasons for being a tour guide. How he knows Jerome and why the two of them keep going places together dressed like they're walking the red carpet. Why he wants to take me to dinner. If he's really just messing with me or if his interest is genuine.

But I don't start with any of those. "Did you really graduate from Colleton County High?"

He's quiet a long moment, so long that I begin to wonder if he's going to answer at all. But then he breathes out a weary sigh. "Go Cougars," he finally says.

So Cameron Hunter really is from Walterboro. It doesn't matter. Not at all. It's just different than what I thought.

"Why did you let me think you grew up downtown?"

"Why did you assume I did?"

"Because you said . . . and then you . . . but you always . . ." I can't finish a sentence because I don't have a good reason. I just assumed. Wrongly, apparently. But I'm still not sure my judgment wasn't justified. "You want people to assume that about you though. I was wrong, but you wanted me to be."

I wish I could make out his facial expression, but the darkness is obscuring everything but a blurry outline of his head. When he turns to the side, I can almost make out the shape of his nose, but I definitely can't see his eyes.

"I don't mind when tourists make assumptions about me. They like thinking of me as someone who knows Charleston inside and out. But I've never wanted you to assume anything."

"Then why have you never corrected me?"

"Does it really matter that much? Where I grew up?"

I think on his question. It doesn't matter. Not to me. But I'm sensing that it does matter to him. Why else would he keep his own heritage hidden? And whether or not it's intentional, that's exactly what he's doing. "I think it does," I say. "But only because where we're from is a part of us. Is your family still in Walterboro?"

"Yeah," he says simply. "They are." He clears his throat. "It's my turn to ask a question."

I swallow the words on my tongue. Which is probably better anyway. I was going to ask him if Walterboro money is as powerful as Charleston money, but that's a question Darcy-from-a-week-ago would have asked. I need to muzzle her for now. Give my more reasonable, less feisty side a chance to make some judgments based on fact and reality instead of suppositions and the thrill of besting Cameron in an argument. Still, I can't help but notice how cagey he is when it comes to talking about his family. What else is he hiding? Or maybe hiding from?

"Go ahead," I say. "Ask me anything."

He doesn't hesitate. "Why do you want to see Vivian Abernathy's greenhouse?"

It's a tricky question with a tricky answer. Actually, the question itself isn't tricky. It's admitting the answer out loud that's the hard part. There is one very good way to keep yourself from ever having to fail. You don't ever try. Every time I speak my truth to another person, I am that much more accountable. The way Rachel roped me into signing up for a booth is evidence of that. She knows what I want and didn't ease up until I did something about it. It's precisely the reason I waited to tell Tyler about it and left out all the things I still need to make it happen.

"Because I love flowers," I say simply. It's the truth, simple as it may sound.

"I don't buy it," Cameron responds. "There are flowers all over the city. Why hers?"

"Because she has a greenhouse. And her window boxes are spectacular, and last summer she had wishbone flowers instead of regular petunias and she had a mother of thousands, which no one ever picks. Her greenhouse makes me think she fills them with plants she grows herself, and . . ." I sigh. "I'm just curious."

"Mother of thousands?"

"Kalanchoe daigremontiana. It's a succulent."

"This sounds like more than curiosity."

I shrug, even though I know he can't see me.

"She does design them herself," he says. "Her window boxes. Though she's eighty-seven years old, so I'm sure she has someone who helps her."

I try and fail to stifle my gasp. "I want that job," I say without thinking.

"So, definitely more than curiosity?"

Something about the darkness, about the calm in his voice, makes me loosen the hold I have on my dreams and suddenly, words are spilling out of me like the water cascading out of the pineapple fountain in Waterfront Park.

"It's more than curiosity. But I was already halfway through college before I figured it out. I dated a guy whose parents owned a nursery out in West Columbia—I was at U of SC—and it only took one stroll through their rose garden to hook me. Roses were their specialty, and they had a hundred different varieties. I'd never seen anything like it. It was too late for me to change majors—or maybe I was too scared to—but I started working at the nursery part time and . . . I guess here we are."

"Here you are . . . using your degree like you thought you would?" he asks.

"Not even close. I mean, I guess I'm technically using it. I have a degree in history, but my original plan was to teach high school."

"That never worked out?"

"I never tried. Every time I came home and spent any time downtown, I saw all the window boxes and thought . . . there have to be people who design all of these. That fill them with flowers. I'm sure a lot of rich people garden, but I'm guessing more of them pay other people to garden. So I figured, if I was also downtown, and I could get to know the right people, maybe I could work my way in. But then, I don't know. I started doing the tour guide thing and that means hanging out with tourists all the time. Turns out, people who live downtown avoid tourists like they avoid grits in a Northerner's kitchen. Plus, I have nothing to qualify me but the fact that I really like flowers. That's not much to go on. Especially when there are landscape artists who have been working in this city for decades."

"How long has it been?" His tone is open, curious, and completely without judgment.

"Almost four years. Which is three years longer than I wanted it to take."

"What's holding you back?"

I bristle at the question, but his next words smooth out the sting quickly enough.

"That came out wrong. What I mean is, what are the obstacles? Aside from the very tightly knit community of wealthy elite that make up most of the peninsula's residents, which, I'll give you, is incredibly hard to break into no matter the industry."

He sounds like he's speaking from experience, and I make a mental note to come back to that. He and Jerome are up to something.

"Money, mostly. Plants are expensive. And experience. I need people to see that I'm good at it so they'll give me a chance, but they can't see that I'm good at it until someone gives me a chance."

"*It* being . . ."

"Designing. Gardens. Flower boxes. Deciding what plants fit where, then knowing how to take care of them."

"So is that landscape architecture then?"

"That's what I would have studied in school had I known to do it. But a lot of people break into the industry without a degree. They work at nurseries or florist shops and build out from there. And I probably could too if I were willing to leave downtown. But . . ."

"This is your dream?" he says.

I suddenly wish we were sitting closer. The conversation is keeping my brain occupied, too occupied to think about Colonel Hayne's ghost or whatever else was thumping around upstairs, but the dungeon is still chilly. My mind flashes back to the way Cameron held me earlier, his hand tracing circles on the small of my back.

It would be weird to ask for that again, but I can't keep myself from inching forward until our knees are touching.

"Yeah," I say. "I love this place. I don't want to work anywhere else."

"Your family is here?"

"Not downtown, but yeah. My parents are divorced, but they're both still local. My brother just moved a few hours up the highway, but he and his fiancée visit all the time, so I can't complain."

"Your brother," Cameron says. "Is he . . . famous? Or . . . something?" He suddenly sounds nervous, like he said something he wishes he could take back.

I smile. "Cameron Hunter. Did you stalk me on social media?"

"I felt justified in staking out my competition," he says, and my heart squeezes. For a moment, I'd forgotten about the magazine feature, about the rivalry that buzzed between us even before we knew there was something we might actually win.

I suddenly wonder how I'm here. *With Cameron.* Thinking about him wrapping his arms around me and hugging away everything that is wrong in my world. I slide my hands down to my legs until my fingertips are resting against his knees.

"Tyler isn't famous," I say. "Not really. But his best friend is. Isaac started *Random I,* his YouTube channel, when they were sixteen. Tyler acted as his cameraman. He worked with Isaac up until a year or so ago when he decided to do his own thing."

"He's got a pretty decent following too, though."

"And most of them are middle-aged women wooed by his pretty face and all the baby goat pictures he posts."

"There is nothing wrong with liking baby goat pictures," he says defensively.

"Says someone who follows his account?"

"I don't follow his Instagram account," he says. "I follow him on TikTok."

I laugh softly until I feel a nudge against my finger. Cameron slowly traces the top of my pointer finger then slides over, his touch feather-light as he continues across my knuckles and down my ring finger.

At least, I *hope* he's the one touching me.

"Please tell me that's you and not Colonel Hayne," I whisper into the darkness.

He chuckles and laces his fingers through mine so our hands are palm to palm. "It's me," he says, his voice low.

"Can I ask you a sincere question?" he says, squeezing my hand gently.

"Okay." I'm keenly aware that at the beginning of our conversation, I hoped to learn more about Cameron and so far, we've only been talking about me. He's good at listening, but something tells me this is how he prefers it.

"Why do you want the magazine feature so badly if you'd rather be doing something else?" he asks.

It's a fair question. One I've asked myself before. The answer is as simple as the question. "Because I need the money. I just paid the rental fee to have a booth at this flower show that's happening this summer. Rachel helped me pay it, so I need to pay her back, but it'll take five times the rental fee to get the flowers I need to create a booth people will notice. Not to mention marketing materials. Business cards, a website, all of it. If the feature gives my business a boost, I'll make more and will hopefully be able to save enough to have what I need."

He doesn't drop my hand, but something between us still changes. His fingers stiffen the slightest bit, and he pulls back, though he doesn't let me go. I wish again that I could see him, read his expression so I can guess what he's thinking. "Why not apply for a business loan? Or borrow money from your family?"

They aren't terrible questions, but there's a faint undercurrent of judgment in his tone. I pull my fingers free. "I don't have the credit or the experience to justify a loan. And my family paid for my education. The education I'm not using the way I thought I would. I can't ask them for more. If I'm doing this, I'm doing it on my own."

"That's fair," he says. He finds my hand in the darkness and holds it loosely. "Darcy, I'm sorry. I didn't mean to sound rude."

"You didn't sound rude. Just . . . judgy."

The silence stretches long enough that I pull my fingers free *again*. "Because you were judging."

He makes a sound like he's trying to say something, but nothing comes out but a strangled sigh.

"Just say it, Cameron," I say. "You might as well. I think we've proven ourselves more than capable of arguing with each other."

"It just seems a little selfish to want a magazine feature for something you don't want to keep doing. Why build a business you intend to quit?"

I ignore the fact that I asked Rachel the exact same question when she convinced me to rent the booth in the first place. I'm allowed to ask those questions about myself. Cameron isn't. "How is it any less selfish than *you* wanting the feature when your business clearly doesn't need the boost? What would be the point? Unless tourists are with it enough to schedule their walking tours six months in advance, the feature won't bring you any new bookings."

"Only if I intend to be a one-man show forever. But that's not the goal. I want more than that."

"Then why don't *you* get a business loan? Or ask your family for help?"

He scoffs. "My family is in no position to help. And it isn't just about me. There are bigger things at stake here."

"Oh, please," I bite out, angry that he's placing his goals so high above mine. "You may not be from the peninsula, but you can't fake rich."

The sound of keys jangling against a metal door echoes through the room, then a voice calls out. "Cameron? You in here?"

Cameron sighs. "Over here." The flashlight clicks on, and he shines it at the door. He stands from the bench and offers me his hand. I take it begrudgingly, hating that even as mad as he made me, I still crave his touch.

He holds my hand until I'm on my feet, then keeps a hand at the small of my back as we walk across the uneven bricks to the door. He and his friend banter back and forth about how we managed to lock ourselves inside in the first place, but I don't pay close enough attention to hear what they're really saying.

I'm too distracted by my swirling emotions.

There is truth in what Cameron said. I know that much. Which is probably why it stung to hear him say it. But regardless, it's still not his place to decide. No matter what my end goals are, I am as entitled to a fair shot at the magazine feature as he is.

"Darcy?"

I startle and look up at Cameron who is standing a few feet away, his arms loose at his sides.

"Sorry. Did you ask me something?" He did. I can remember now that he said something. I was just too caught up in my own head for it to register.

"Do you need a ride home?" he repeats.

I only live a few blocks away. I walked to get here, and riding home in Cameron's car doesn't sound fun. But walking home alone with a brain full of ghost stories sounds less fun. "It's only a few blocks, but . . . yeah. If you don't mind, that would be great."

He turns silently and walks to the only car left in the small parking lot beside the dungeon. I follow behind, waiting while he unlocks the door to a Honda that looks like it's as old as I am. It's clean, and obviously well taken care of, but it isn't fancy. I slide into the passenger seat and tuck my hands into the pocket of my hoodie, watching as Cameron climbs in and starts the car. He still hasn't made eye contact, and I get the sense the avoidance is very intentional.

We don't talk outside of me pointing out the few turns necessary to get me home. He stops in front of my house and finally turns to look at me. "Sorry the seats aren't leather," he says coolly. "I left my rich person car at home tonight."

I close my eyes and wince. "I . . . probably deserved that."

He offers me a small grin. "You definitely deserved it."

His smile breaks the tension between us and I sigh, leaning back in my seat. "So. Not from the peninsula. *Not* rolling in old family money," I say slowly.

"Not a member of the yacht club," he adds. "And I've never been to a salon. Whatever highlights you think I have, they're natural. I get my hair cut by a barber in West Ashley named Leroy."

I chuckle. "Tell Leroy he does good work."

"I'm sorry I judged you," he says simply. "I don't get to decide what's right for your business."

"Funny thing is," I say, "neither of us gets to decide who the magazine features. Maybe it won't be either of us."

He scrunches his forehead. "I don't know. I think it will be. Of the guides working on their own, you're the only one who comes close to—" His eyes go wide, and he bites his lip.

My jaw drops. "You were going to say I'm the only one who

comes close to being as good as you."

He grimaces. "I was . . . not going to say it exactly like that."

I roll my eyes. "You're horrible." I reach for the door handle. "Thank you for returning my hat even though you trapped me in a dungeon to do it."

"I'm calling it a happy accident."

I shoot him a questioning look and he lifts his shoulders in a shrug.

"I like spending time with you, Darcy."

He doesn't pull away until I'm safely inside, the door closed behind me. I watch through the sidelights that frame the front door as his car eases away and turns left at the corner, moving out of sight.

The night was not what I expected. *He* is not what I expected.

The sting of his judgment flairs back up; he apologized for judging, but apology or not, he still clearly believes he deserves the magazine feature more than I do.

Which only serves to remind me that I cannot assume Cameron's motives are pure.

But I want to assume. I want Cameron to be good to his core, his interest genuine.

And I don't know how to feel about that.

Chapter Thirteen

Darcy

I am no less confused when I wake up the following morning.

Cameron isn't rich.

He isn't a yacht club socialite.

He didn't grow up in downtown Charleston or attend Porter-Gaud with all the other society boys.

They are minor details, really. But they are foundational to everything I thought I knew about Cameron. If he isn't an entitled rich boy, then what is he? Who is he?

And why doesn't he want people to know? There have been dozens of opportunities over the months and months of teasing and sparring between us when he could have challenged the assumptions I've made about him. When I've joked about him looking a little wind-blown, like he just stepped off his cabin cruiser, all he'd have to say is, "Darcy, I don't own a yacht."

Instead, he's only ever rolled his eyes. Which, granted, isn't an admission of truth. But neither is it a denial.

I finally climb out of bed and stretch, debating whether I should call Tyler and get his opinion. He's good at reading people and always has good insight, but I don't want him to make any negative assumptions about Cameron.

I ignore the implications of this—why do I care what my brother thinks if I don't like the man myself?—and pad across the hallway to Rachel's apartment. I knock twice. "Rachel! You awake?"

I hear shuffling inside, then a muffled groan before the door swings open to reveal a giant comforter with legs, the swirl of Rachel's braids piled on her head poking out the top.

"Whoa, tough morning?"

The comforter slides down to reveal her eyes. "Nah. Tough night," she says, her voice muffled. She turns and walks toward her bedroom.

"Have you not been to sleep yet?"

She collapses onto her bed and crawls up to her pillow. "I started on a painting and lost track of time."

I peek out into the living room—or what would be the living room if Rachel didn't use hers as a studio. It's why we generally hang out at my place when we want to chill or watch TV. Rachel doesn't even own a TV. "Really? Can I see it?"

She grunts. "It's on the easel, but don't go look yet because I want to know what happened with Cameron last night, and I'll fall asleep if you don't tell me now."

I sigh and drop onto the corner of her bed.

She picks her head up long enough to look at me quizzically. "What's with the sigh? Did you get your hat back?"

I nod. "I did."

"Annnnd?" she says, clearly growing exasperated.

"I met him at the provost dungeon. He texted me a picture of Mr. McGregor wearing my hat, which was actually pretty cute, but then we ended up getting locked inside the dungeon, and he wouldn't talk about anything, but *I* talked about everything, which I think is what he wanted the whole time, and now I'm just confused."

She looks at me blankly. "I don't know if I'm really tired, or if you mumbled a bunch of nonsense."

"Probably both."

"Okay." She sits up and crosses her legs, rubbing her eyes for a second before leveling me with the first lucid look I've seen from her this morning. "Let's break this down. First of all, who is Mr. McGregor?"

"He's the customs officer that lives inside the dungeon."

Her forehead wrinkles. "Like, all the time?"

"Yes. Oh, but he's a mannequin. Not a real person."

"I thought you said he was a customs officer."

I wave my hand in frustration. "He's a mannequin dressed up as a customs officer from 1771. The docents at the museum gave him a name. Mr. McGregor. And Cameron texted me a picture of Mr. McGregor, the mannequin, wearing my hat."

She nods. "Got it. I think that was probably more confusing for me than it would have been if I'd had a full night's sleep. Then what happened?"

"Then we nerded out on dungeon history for a few minutes, and we kept hearing all these scary noises."

"Um, of course you did. I've heard the stories about how haunted that place is."

"Oh, I believe every single one of them. Which is saying something for me. You know how long it's taken me to admit Matilda might be real."

"True," Rachel adds sagely.

"So we end up hugging after one particularly loud noise—"

"Wait." She holds up her hands and cuts me off. "By hugging do you mean you climbed him like a baby sloth?" She grins, and I frown, wishing I'd never used sloth imagery when talking to Rachel.

"Something like that," I say. "But I was really freaked out. And honestly, he didn't seem like he minded. We even held hands later. And I told him all about my window boxes."

Her mouth drops open. "You did?"

"I know! It's so crazy. But he's a very good listener. He is also terrible at talking about himself. The only thing I learned about him was that he actually *is* from Walterboro. His family still lives there, but he's about as willing to talk about them as I am to talk about the time in high school when I accidentally showed the entire cross-country team my boobs."

Rachel giggles. "That's still one of my favorite Darcy stories."

"The point is, he *is* hiding something."

"Is he though?" Rachel asks. "Or does it just seem like it because all the things you thought you knew about him aren't really true?"

"Maybe. I honestly don't know what to think."

"Maybe you don't think anything. Maybe you just get to know him. Consider this an opportunity to start over. How was the hugging? And the handholding?"

"Very sweet," I say. "He smells good. And he has good muscles. And I felt weird tingly things whenever our hands touched."

"Awww, did he walk you to homeroom next?" Rachel says. "Middle school is so fun!"

"Shut up. You asked. And middle-schoolers don't have muscles like Cameron Hunter."

She flops back onto her pillow and stretches out, her feet nudging me off the bed. "So what's your next move?" she asks through a yawn. "Are you going to see him again?"

I stand up. "I don't know. I want to, I think. If only to figure him out."

"Yeah," she says suggestively. "Figure out if he's a good kisser."

"Now who's in middle school?"

She's quiet for a beat before she finally says, "I'm sleeping now, k?"

I straighten her comforter and smooth it over her shoulders. "You need me to wake you up later?"

She yawns one more time. "I set an alarm. I'm . . . good," she says, the last word a mumbled whisper.

It blows me away the way Rachel can fall into her art—create without any awareness of time or space. I tiptoe out to her studio and admire the painting on the easel. This one looks like Sullivan's Island—long stretches of sand and shallow tide pools dotted with shiny, white sand dollars. The sand is in the foreground, the grains so distinct, the painting almost looks like a photograph. It isn't a wonder she stayed up all night. The sand alone must have taken her hours.

I wander back to my apartment, not even flinching when a loud thud sounds somewhere off to my left. "Good morning, Matilda," I say out loud. "What do you think? Should I give Cameron a chance? Get to know him a little bit?" The only response I get is silence, but if I were a ghost, I'd save my thuds for negative responses, so I'm taking the silence as a good thing.

***

I only do one tour on Sundays; in the summer months, I keep it early. It's too hot to be out in the middle of the day. But when the weather is mild, the air crisp and the humidity low, I start at noon. I've found people like the opportunity to walk off a Sunday brunch.

Today's tour is easy, the group small enough that we're able to talk and get to know each other a little bit. That's how I like it, even if it isn't the most lucrative way to run my business. After I say goodbye, I walk home the long way. I always do on Sundays. It gives me the chance to pass Vivian Abernathy's gardens without a tour group to worry about. I can mosey down the sidewalk as slowly as I want, admiring as much as I can from the limited vantage point the street provides. She's already refreshed her window boxes for spring, but it wouldn't surprise me if she updates them again. If I had a greenhouse as large as hers, it would be hard not to swap the flowers out weekly just because I could.

It occurs to me that Vivian Abernathy's greenhouse could be full of broken crates and empty milk jugs. Just because a greenhouse sits on her property doesn't mean she uses it. But the rest of her gardens are so gorgeous, she must.

I slow as I near the corner that marks the beginning of her property. From here, a tall wall edges the east side of the garden, extending up to the next corner, then wrapping around to the gate that hides the driveway. Past the gate, the house fills up the west end of the lot, extending back to the kitchen house that Cameron includes on his tour, and of course, the greenhouse.

The only reason I even know there are such gorgeous gardens on the other side of the wall is because sometimes the driveway gate is open, allowing a narrow glimpse into the winding pathways and manicured beds. It's a wonder I've never been caught standing on the sidewalk, staring awkwardly onto her property.

At least I don't have to sneak to see her window boxes. Like most houses in Charleston, the side of hers butts right up to the sidewalk, with a privacy door that leads onto the long front porch. There are two windows that face the street, and they are always dressed to kill.

I round the corner, hoping to find the driveway gate open, and pause in my tracks.

An elderly woman is several yards ahead of me, her arms buried deep in the soil of one of the window boxes. She looks more like she's dressed for an afternoon tea than gardening, her hair perfectly coiffed, her matching sweater set a perfect complement to her pink tweed pants. When she glances my way and smiles, she could be wearing a tiara and a princess ball gown for all I care.

It's her. The woman I've been dying to meet. Right there on the sidewalk. Smiling almost as if she expected me.

"I'm sorry, this is terribly rude, but do you think you could help me a minute?" she says, her tone warm and friendly.

I look over my shoulder, positive she's talking to someone else. "Me?"

"It will only take a minute," she says. "If you don't mind?"

I hurry forward. I absolutely do not mind. "Of course," I say as I approach. "What can I do?"

"See, I've got my fingers cupped around the roots of this begonia, and I don't want to jostle it." She eyes me knowingly. "It's a begonia rex. Finicky little things. They don't particularly like to be messed with, so I'm trying to be gentle."

"That sounds perfectly reasonable," I say, utterly charmed by the woman's lilting Southern accent. Every word sounds like a song.

"There's a bucket behind me, up next to the house. Do you see it?"

"Yes, ma'am," I say. I reach for the bucket and pull out a smaller flowerpot, sensing that's what she's needing. I hold it up. "Is that what you want?"

"Yes. Perfect. Can you hold it up for me?"

I cradle the pot as she deftly pulls the begonia from the window box and nestles it into its new home.

"I thought it might do well out here," she says as she takes the pot from my extended hands. "But it hasn't been thriving. I'll baby it a bit back in the greenhouse and try again another year."

I barely suppress the urge to cheer. Her greenhouse is *not* full of broken crates and empty milk jugs.

"Now, to decide what to put in its place."

"Ranunculus," I say, almost without thinking. "Violet ones."

Mrs. Abernathy's eyes go wide. Or, I assume she's Mrs. Abernathy. She has to be, doesn't she?

"Sorry," I quickly say. "That was . . . I'm sure you'll know what to put there. I don't—"

"No, no," she says. "It's a good suggestion. Unexpected. But good." She looks at me with a gaze serious enough that I drop mine to the sidewalk. I notice her shoes for the first time. A pair of clogs in a crazy floral print that reminds me of a painting Rachel once did of a hibiscus plant that curls over the back wall of Washington Square Park. "Do you know a lot about flowers?"

I lift my eyes to meet hers. "I'm still learning," I say. "But I do okay."

She pulls off her gardening glove and holds out her hand. "I'm Vivian Abernathy."

"Darcy Marino."

"What a pretty name," she says. "It's lovely to meet you, Darcy."

I've heard the rumors circulating among other tour guides that Vivian Abernathy is a cold, intimidating woman. The fact that even though so many others have asked, Cameron is the first guide to ever gain access to her kitchen house seemed to substantiate them. But the woman standing before me is far from cold and intimidating. She has a presence about her, but her smile is warm and welcoming.

"It's lovely to meet you as well. I love your garden," I say, the words tumbling out and landing in a heap at her feet. "And your window boxes. I walk by your house every Sunday just so I can admire them."

Her smile widens, reaching all the way up to her eyes, deepening the wrinkles there. "Do you have a few minutes?"

"Right now?"

"I was thinking you might want to help me pick out something to fill this spot. I don't have any ranunculus but come on back to the greenhouse with me. I've got all kinds of things growing back there. There's bound to be something that will complement what's already here."

Excitement pulses through me as I take a steadying breath. "I would love that."

She offers me the plant she just uprooted from the window box. "Here. You can carry her."

I take the begonia while she picks up the empty bucket and a gardening shovel leaning against the side of the house. I follow her through the privacy door and across the porch, trying not to gawk as we pass by the enormous planters that line the front of her house. They are filled with different colors and varieties of shade-loving impatiens and coleuses, and they are gorgeous, the colors expertly grouped in a way that looks haphazard but I'm positive is intentional. It has that feel of organized chaos that I love most in gardening--when plants look so completely at home it feels as though they were never planted. They've simply existed there forever, growing and thriving, their leaves blending and mingling with the plants surrounding them. It's a style choice—not one all gardeners like. Some like gardens to be precise. Perfectly straight lines of tulips. Neatly trimmed hedges. But I love a wild garden. A window box bursting with life and color. It thrills me that, from the looks of things, Vivian Abernathy feels the same way.

I follow her down a wide set of steps at the back of the porch and down a winding path that cuts through the garden to a narrow door at the rear of the greenhouse.

"Excuse the mess," she says as we pass through a workroom filled with bags of potting soil and fertilizer and other odds and ends. A familiar scent tickles my nose—that dirt/fertilizer combination that I love so much. It smells like possibility.

Vivian puts the bucket on the floor by the door and continues forward, moving into the main area of the greenhouse. It's warm inside, a little warmer than it is outside, and it is brim-full of plants. So many plants. Orchids. Hibiscus. Roses. Snapdragons. Hydrangeas. Lobelia. I've never seen anything like it.

Clearly reading my expression, Vivian only smiles. "Go on. Look around."

The path through the room is like an elongated circle, with plants on either side and in the middle. I walk slowly, my eyes darting from one side of the path to the other. Nothing is labeled, but I recognize almost everything. I stop at a deep purple flower I've never seen before. "What's this?" I ask, pointing.

"A guaria morada," Vivian answers, from where she's following behind me. "Pretty, isn't it? It's an orchid. And the national flower of Costa Rica."

"It's lovely."

We continue like that for several minutes, me asking questions, her sharing tiny details about how each plant came to be a part of her collection.

It occurs to me as I make my way around the back half of the greenhouse that now I'll have nothing to demand of Cameron if I end up getting the magazine feature. I can't bring myself to care. Because I'm here. Seeing it. Chatting with Vivian about flowers like we're old friends.

I stop in front of a deep green plant with tiny white blooms. The contrast of the dark leaves will look beautiful against the vibrant coleuses that are already filling the window boxes.

"This one," I say, pointing to it. "Can it handle the cooler spring temperatures?"

She nods. "Sweet alyssum. I think that's the one."

"It isn't as bold as something with a little more color, but the combination of this deep green and white will complement the lighter green of the vines tumbling over the left side of the box. And the white will look nice with the red accents of the coleus right behind it."

Vivian nods. "You've got a good eye."

A surge of pride fills me like I've never known before. I do have a good eye. I just need an opportunity to use it.

"Is this a hobby?" she asks me. "Or a job?"

"What, the flowers?" I ask as we head back to the window box out front, the sweet alyssum in hand.

"Sure. You obviously know what you're talking about."

"It's only a hobby right now." A tiny thrill shoots through me. "I want it to be a job though," I admit. "That's the goal."

"What's your job now?"

"I'm a tour guide. My degree is in history. I was supposed to teach, but I'm not sure I'm made for a classroom. I like being outside too much."

"Then you're in the right profession. Though I can't say I'd want your job in August."

"No one wants my job in August. And yet, it's when the most tourists come."

She smiles slyly. "I'll never understand why. The beaches, I suppose. But the beaches are also lovely in April before the heat starts to cook us all."

She turns the alyssum over and gently shakes the bottom of the pot with one hand, her other hand cradling the stem of the plant as it pulls free. "There we go," she says gently, and it's clear she's talking to the plant, not to me.

I hold back the leaves of the surrounding plants as she nestles the new one into the vacant spot and pulls the extra dirt forward, smoothing it around the stem. "I know another tour guide. He brings his groups through to look at the kitchen house out back. Cameron Hunter. Do you know him?"

Heat flames my cheeks and I resist the urge to cover them with my hands. I'm not sure which would be more conspicuous. An obvious blush, or me trying to *cover* an obvious blush.

Vivian chuckles. "You do know him. And well, I'm guessing. Judging by the color in your cheeks."

"I don't. Not really."

The expression she sends my way tells me just how much she doesn't believe me.

I sigh. "We're sort of friends, I think?"

"Sort of friends? What does that mean?"

"I wish I knew, Vivian. I honestly wish I knew." I pause and look up. "I'm sorry. Is it all right if I call you Vivian?"

She reaches over and pats my hand. "Of course, child. Please do."

I brush the dirt off my hands, sad that the project, small as it was, is over. "Do you . . ." I hesitate, but only for a moment. This is too good an opportunity to pass up. "Would you . . . could I help you some other time? With anything, really. I don't have many opportunities to garden. I'm renting this tiny apartment and we don't have any garden space. And . . . I miss it."

She smiles. "Can you come over this week? I've got some rose bushes I need to move before it gets much warmer."

"Yes. Absolutely, yes."

"Tuesday afternoon?"

I mentally review my booking calendar. I'm technically open for tours on Tuesday afternoons, but when I checked this morning, I still didn't have any bookings. It's likely if I leave it open, someone will book last minute. That happens a lot. Or . . . I could just delete the tour from my calendar and come plant rose bushes instead.

"Tuesday is perfect."

Vivian walks the few steps that separate us and pulls me into a hug, giving my shoulders an extra squeeze. "Darcy, I'm glad we ran into each other today."

As I walk home, it feels particularly noteworthy that even though I feel like he's keeping secrets, even though I basically know absolutely nothing about the man except for where he went to high school and that he makes my stomach swoop whenever he looks at me, Cameron is the person I want to tell about Vivian.

Not Rachel. Not Tyler. Not Mom or Dad or anybody.

Cameron.

The thought burns me as much as it thrills me. How has he worked his way so thoroughly into my psyche? How has he turned my loathing into something so heady, so intoxicating?

And what am I supposed to do about it now?

Chapter Fourteen

Cameron

I leave Darcy's apartment on Friday night uneasy. Things ended better than I thought they would when we left the dungeon. But I can't shake the fact that with Darcy, I keep managing to say the wrong thing. Or I say the right thing, and she takes it the wrong way anyway.

It's at least good news that I get a thumbs-up text from Vivian on Sunday afternoon. Darcy passed by her house exactly when I suggested she would, and the two of them met. They spent an hour in Vivian's greenhouse talking about plants. Vivian had been skeptical enough that I wasn't sure she'd go through with it.

That she did just reminds me I need to finish up the paperwork for her kitchen house's historical landmark designation. That, and a hundred other things on my to-do list.

I normally attack my work with single-minded focus. But here lately, Darcy has been messing with my focus. Keeping me from doing the things I really ought to be doing. Like giving great tours and finishing up the grant proposal I promised Jerome I'd have ready by the end of the week.

The land for the education center has been cleared so that construction can begin, but we ran into some issues with drainage—not an uncommon problem when your land is only three feet above sea level—and we need fifty grand to install a drainage system that will keep the foundation of the education center from flooding every time it rains. We anticipated it might be an issue. Half of Charleston's streets are temporarily under water whenever it rains. But we hoped our location on Johns Island, on donated land at the edge of the Oakwood Plantation, would be high enough to avoid any issues. No such luck. Jerome hired an engineer who was able to come up with a workable solution, just one with a fifty-thousand-dollar price tag. For now, we're moving forward, but the cash we're using is cash allocated for other things, which means I have to drum up more money.

So far, I've managed to raise that amount twenty times over, so I'm not worried. There's a lot of money in Charleston; not everyone who has it is interested in furthering education focused on the black experience in the Lowcountry, but there are plenty of people who are. And I'm good at finding them.

An inside tip from a friend let me know the Coastal Community Foundation has some unclaimed grant money up for grabs that should get me halfway to where we need to be. I just need to submit the proposal.

And yet, here I am, the Tuesday after Darcy and I were trapped in the dungeon, at the downtown library researching newspaper archives for mentions of the house Darcy lives in.

Know what I'm not doing? Writing a proposal.

Here's the thing. Most of the ghost tours that walk Charleston's streets are embellished for entertainment value. People don't see ghosts half as frequently as tour guides claim they do. But Charleston is a really old city full of really old stories.

I haven't had a personal experience with a ghost—unless you count Friday night in the dungeon with Darcy. (I still can't figure out how the door closed on us.)

But I've heard enough stories from people I trust that I'm not discounting the possibility.

It's also possible I just want an excuse to see Darcy again.

For a brief moment on Friday night, I wondered if we'll ever be able to communicate without bickering. But then on the drive home, the tension broke, and we laughed and . . . things with her just feel so good.

I shouldn't have judged her desire to achieve her goals no matter the means necessary. Will the feature have a more lasting impact on my business? Definitely. But there's no reason for that to be Darcy's priority. Especially when she doesn't know the first thing about what I really want my business to accomplish. And why the financial boost would matter so much for me. For my family.

I like the idea of sharing those things with Darcy about as well as I like giving tours during a muggy August rainstorm.

But Darcy's initial dislike demands honesty from me in ways nothing ever has before. A shiny exterior isn't enough for her. If I want to get to know her, I'm going to have to let her in, no matter how uncomfortable it makes me.

I think back on the feel of her hand in mine, of her arms wrapped around my waist. A pulse of electricity flows over my skin, an echo of the response she triggered when I held her, when I let my hand slide over the curve of her back. The crackle of chemistry between us tells me being real with Darcy will be worth the effort, but that doesn't extinguish the fear flickering in my gut.

My eyes catch on a news article with a headline too sensational to ignore. "Charleston's Most Haunted Houses." The article is dated November 4th, 1907, and is organized in list format, with a short summary of the supposed haunting occurring at each of the listed addresses. I quickly scan the list, my heart rate picking up when I come across Darcy's address. 53 Queen Street.

I read the attached summary twice. It gives a quick history of the family who originally built the house in 1844, then documents why the current occupants believe the house to be haunted. The story is what you might expect. A tragic, untimely death. A grieving family. Most of the stories in the article are similar. Still, if Darcy hasn't already done the research herself, she'll probably find this interesting.

I email myself a digital copy and leave the library, heading straight for Darcy's house. I still have a couple of hours before my afternoon tour starts at four. If she isn't home, I'm at least headed in the right direction because her house is within walking distance of the gift shop where my tours start.

I saw her briefly this morning before our morning tours, but she was talking to someone and aside from briefly making eye contact, we didn't interact.

I park a block or so away from her house—my car will be fine here for the rest of the afternoon—and check my reflection in the rearview mirror, making sure I'm not wearing any of the lunch I scarfed down on my way to the library. The fried green tomato BLT from Brown Dog Deli is a sandwich worth scarfing; it is also easy to drip the pepper jelly that makes it taste so good down your shirtfront. Or wear some of it in your teeth.

This would be my luck. Hanging out with Darcy as Aloysius, my jeans hiked up to my ears, isn't embarrassing enough. I also need to smile at her with pepper in my teeth.

My phone rings on the way to Darcy's front door, and I smile when I see my dad's image fill the screen. It's a shot Maggie took of him and my two little brothers when they went to Botany Bay. Jackson and Maddox are both draped across his back, one on either shoulder. Their smiles are wide, their eyes, the same shade of blue as mine, reflecting the joy they're obviously feeling. A tiny, niggling fear needles into my gut. I was fourteen the first time Dad got sick, and I was too young to lose him.

Jackson and Maddox definitely are.

I turn around and face the other direction, not wanting to pace right in front of Darcy's house while we talk. "Hey, Dad."

"Hey." His voice is gruff, like always, but he sounds well. Like he's feeling good. "Where are you? Are you downtown?"

My steps slow. "Yeah. In between tours. Are you?"

"Waiting to see the oncologist at MUSC. Are you going to be busy in an hour?"

"I've got a tour at four. Are you here for your scan?"

"Yep," he says as if it isn't a monumental event. The scan could mean more chemo. More radiation. It could mean we have reason to be optimistic, or reason to shore up our defenses and prepare for battle. "Four o'clock?" he asks. "Is that later than usual?" Dad's Southern accent is thicker than mine and his words roll into each other, their edges smooth and lilting.

"Yeah. It's a special booking. A corporate group who's using the tour as a team-building thing."

"Ah," Dad says. "Well, this won't take long. Maggie's been thrifting in Mt. Pleasant again and she found you a jacket she says you're going to love. Can you come by and get it? Or I suppose I can bring it to you on my way out of town."

Maggie's ability to find incredible deals never ceases to amaze me. She married my dad the summer before I started my freshman year at the College of Charleston and was determined to outfit me for "city life." That she still hasn't stopped, even though I've been done with school and living on my own for almost five years, is one of the things I love most about her. Not the stuff. Just that she cares. That she thinks about me and looks for ways to help me feel like I'm part of the family.

"No, I'll come to you." I glance at my watch. It'll cut into the time I spend with Darcy, but I haven't seen Dad in a couple of weeks. I can't miss the opportunity when he's so close. "I'll have time. When will you get the results of the scan?"

"In a few days, I suppose. But I'm not worried about it. I feel good. The news is going to be good."

I appreciate his optimism, but he's always optimistic. Even when he doesn't have reason to be. Most of the time, I rely on Maggie to give me updates about his health. She's a nurse—they met when she helped take care of him the first time he got sick—and is always honest with me about how things really are.

"Make sure you call me," I say.

"Of course, of course," Dad says. "Oh, hey. They're calling me back. I'll call you when I'm done, and we can meet up for a minute."

We say goodbye, and I end the call.

When I turn around to head back to Darcy's, she's standing in front of me on the sidewalk, her arms folded and her expression curious.

"Darcy," I say as I slip my phone into my pocket. I take a few steps toward her. "Hey."

"Hey. What are you doing here?" she asks.

"I, um, I have something to show you. I'm glad you're home."

"I'm not, actually. Well, not anymore. I was just heading out."

I resist the urge to ask her where she's going. It isn't my business, even though every second I spend with her makes me realize how much I want it to be. Except—I glance at my watch—she's probably going to work. Most of us start our afternoon tours at two. *My schedule is delayed today, but hers wouldn't be.* "Right. Your afternoon tour."

"Um, not today. Her gaze skitters away, and she bites her lip. "I don't have anyone booked this afternoon. Funny thing though." She finally looks up. "I'm on my way to help Vivian Abernathy replant some rose bushes."

I feign surprise, hoping just this once, Darcy buys what she sees on the surface. "Really? How did that happen?"

"I ran into her on my way home Sunday afternoon. She was outside working on her flower boxes. We started talking, and . . ." She shrugs. "I don't know why everyone thinks she's so intimidating. She's so nice."

Bless you, Vivian. "Yeah. She really is. That's amazing. So . . . you saw the greenhouse?"

Her face transforms in a way that makes me feel like if I lifted my feet off the ground, I'd soar straight into the sky. It's that smile—the one I first saw when she talked to Jerome about horticulture. Except now she's smiling at me. "It's amazing, Cameron. You wouldn't believe the plants she has in there. It's more incredible than any nursery I've ever seen. And she tends to her plants like they're people. Talking to them, telling stories about them. It's amazing."

I have no idea if a connection to Vivian Abernathy will do anything to help Darcy get her business off the ground, but I am so happy that she is this happy, that I had a small part in helping her get here, even if she'll never know it was me.

I take a step forward. "Do you have a quick second to talk before you go?"

She studies me for a long moment, indecision clear in her expression. Her scrutiny isn't exactly comfortable, but I do appreciate the opportunity to stare into her eyes. Her irises are a deep dark brown that in lower lighting, would probably look black. But in the bright afternoon light, I can pick out swirls of honey around the edge. There is a battle raging behind her eyes, and I can only hope that whatever side wins, it'll be the side that includes me.

"I've got a few minutes," she finally says. Her expression shifts to something warmer, more welcoming. Something that looks a lot like *I'm interested, but not in talking.*

I swallow. Staring at Darcy has left me

completely . . . bewildered. "Right. Um . . ." I pull my phone out of my pocket. My hand is shaking, which is ridiculous. *Ridiculous.* I am not a man prone to losing his cool. Especially when it comes to Darcy. If anything, she generally brings out my sarcasm and wit faster than anyone. But that was when I thought she loathed me. When hatred sprouted from her like the weeds in Maggie's tomato garden, the ones with prickly leaves and deep roots.

I clear my throat. "I was at the library just now, and I happened across this list. Your house is on it."

I offer her my phone.

"The most haunted houses in Charleston," she reads. She looks up. "Seriously?"

"Crazy, right?" I say, my nerves starting to ease. "It was written in 1907, so it isn't exactly up to date, though I don't think ghosts have an expiration date."

"Where's the part about my house?"

I reach across her hand, the side of my pinky brushing hers as I scroll down to the section I previously highlighted. "Right here."

"You've read it?" she asks. "Do I want to? Is it going to freak me out?"

"It shouldn't, I don't think."

She starts to read out loud, and I hope my assessment is true. Filling her head with ghost stories about a house she sleeps in every night might make her like me less than she did when she thought I locked her in a dungeon on purpose.

"A man and woman by the last name of Hildebrand built the home located at 53 Queen Street in 1844," she reads. "There are few written records regarding the Hildebrand family, but neighbors who knew the family well all tell a similar story. The family had three children. Their youngest, a girl named Mary Beth, was possessed of a particularly friendly nature and would sit in her bedroom on the third floor and wave out the front window at those passing by on the street.

Tragically, just before the girl's thirteenth birthday, she leaned out too far and tumbled to the ground below. She initially survived the fall but succumbed to her injuries four days after the incident occurred."

She looks up, her eyes catching on mine before her gaze shifts to her house. "The third story window. That one." She points. "Right there."

"I guess so. It's the only one that faces the street."

She takes off, heading toward the door of her house.

I stay where I am, not sure what she expects.

At her porch steps, she turns and looks at me over her shoulder. "Are you coming?"

Anywhere you want me to.

I jog up the sidewalk, catching up to her as she pushes through the heavy front door.

I follow her up three flights of narrow stairs to what I assume is her apartment. She leads me through the living room, stopping at a narrow door at the front of the room, the side closest to the street, and turns to face me. "Rachel lives directly across the hall. Our apartments are basically mirror image, right down to this closet. She has one exactly like it in her apartment."

"Okay," I say, unsure where this is going.

She opens the door. There's no light installed overhead, but light *does* filter in over the top of what appears to be a brick wall at the back of the space. It stretches nearly to the ceiling, with only a few inches of room between the last brick and the plaster overhead. The closet is mostly empty, save a few boxes pushed off to the side. It's wide enough to walk in, so I move to the wall, Darcy following behind me.

"What on earth?" I touch the wall, the bricks cool under my palm. "Is it bricked off on Rachel's side too?"

Darcy nods. "But it isn't the same wall. There's space between them."

"A room?"

She shrugs. "I guess so, though it can't be very big. We've measured our steps across the landing in the hallway between our apartments and compared it to the length of each closet. We're guessing there's maybe four, five feet in between the walls."

"About the width of the window we saw outside," I say, finally beginning to understand.

"Exactly. But why? Though, if someone fell from the window . . ."

I nod, easily following her train of thought. "Maybe in their distress, after Mary Beth died, it was the only way her family knew how to cope."

"Why do you think they left space at the top of the wall, though? For the light?"

I shake my head. "My guess is it wasn't intentional. They just worked until they ran out of room."

"The bricks were too big for them to add another row. That does make sense."

"But I still don't get it. Why not just close the door to the room? To build a brick wall inside your house? It seems a little extreme."

Darcy shakes her head. "Except, maybe there wasn't a room. Or a door. Maybe this was attic space. You see how narrow the third-floor stairs are compared to the second. If this was all open space, maybe they built three walls around the window, cutting it off from the rest of the space completely."

"Right. Then when the house was remodeled, divided into two apartments . . ."

"They hid the back section of the brick when they framed out the landing between the apartments," she finishes. "It makes sense."

She puts both hands on the brick wall and looks up at the glow of light filtering over the top. "Poor Mary Beth. What a sad story."

"Will you call your ghost Mary Beth now?" I say, my tone light.

A thump sounds from somewhere on the other side of the wall, and Darcy's eyes go wide. "I have to now, don't I?"

I lean my shoulder onto the brick, enjoying the forced proximity the closet provides. "How does Rachel feel about your ghost? She lives right next door, right?"

"Oh, Rachel loves it. She talks to her like she's a roommate."

She leans on the wall across from me, mirroring my pose, her expression playful. She is close enough that every cell in my body is charged, tuned in to her every move, aware of her every breath.

A piece of her hair is caught on the bricks beside her, and I reach up to loosen it, my fingers sliding down the silky strands.

She laughs softly. "Why do I suddenly feel like I'm at a middle school party playing seven minutes in heaven?"

"Seven what?"

There is just enough light filtering over the wall for me to see a blush climb up her cheeks. "The game. You've never heard of it?"

I shake my head. "I didn't go to a lot of middle school parties."

She looks away, her palms pressing to her cheeks. "I'm sure you can guess by the title. Two names are randomly drawn from a hat, and those two people are supposed to go into the closet and make out."

I chuckle. "Are you trying to tell me you want to make out with me?"

She rolls her eyes. "You would ask that, wouldn't you?"

"You're the one who brought it up."

She steps closer, one hand lifting and playing with the edge of my button-down shirt. It isn't quite a touch, but my body reacts anyway, like a bonfire doused with gasoline. I force a calming breath; she has the reins here, and I want it to stay that way.

She looks up, her eyes on my lips as she leans toward me. I bend down to meet her, our noses brushing before she takes an enormous breath and leans away, her eyes closed.

"Sorry," she whispers. "Sorry."

"Sorry for almost kissing me?" I ask tentatively.

Her eyes shoot open. "No. Sorry for *not* kissing you."

"Oh, good. Just making sure we both understand that kissing me would not require an apology."

She smiles softly, her eyes down. "My body definitely wants to kiss you, Cameron," she says. She looks up, and I see my own desire reflected in her gaze. But then she taps her temple. "But my mind isn't so convinced it's a good idea."

"Why is that?"

She studies me, hesitation playing across her face. "Tell me about the women at the Darling the other night."

Ah. I've wondered if she would ever bring that up. "That was entirely accidental. Both blind dates that Jerome's wife set up. One canceled, so Angie found me a second date. Then the first date showed up anyway. I wasn't interested in either of them."

She purses her lips. "But you were interested in me being there. You told Rachel to bring me."

"I did," I admit, unsurprised that Rachel told her. "I didn't know that Angie found me a second date, so I was hoping it might give me the opportunity to spend some time with you."

She nods, her expression serious. "You must not be very confident about winning our bet. Couldn't just wait to see how things shake out? Claim your dinner with me when you win?"

I shrug. "I'm confident. Just . . . impatient."

She presses her palm flat against my chest, and my breath catches. I lift my hand to cover hers, and she turns her palm so our fingers entwine. "How do I know you aren't just messing with me? Trying to get in my head?"

"Darcy, that's not . . . I'm not like that."

She squeezes my hand. "But you still want to win?"

There's only one way to answer that question. "Don't you?"

"Of course I do."

There is more conviction in her voice than I expect, and it occurs to me that hearing her talk about her desire to work with flowers, seeing her excited to spend time with Vivian, has changed the way I view her business. Because it's so obvious that she really needs to be doing something else. But this is the path she's chosen for herself, the path she believes will take her to her dreams.

"I just feel like we have to let this thing play out first," she says.

"The competition."

She nods.

"Except, you're already hanging out with Vivian. What do you get if you win since you've already gotten what you asked for?"

She looks at me, her expression coy, and I suddenly feel like even if Darcy does get the magazine feature, I won't be losing.

"I want to make sure if we do this, we do it for real," she says. "That it isn't about winning. About messing with each other."

"I'm not messing with you, Darcy. That's not what this is."

"I think I believe you. But I also don't know you."

"So get to know me. Ask me anything." Even as I issue the challenge, an uneasiness creeps into my gut.

This is what I want with Darcy. That doesn't mean it's easy.

"How do you know Jerome Dawson?" she says.

I relax the slightest bit. That's an easy one.

"He was my roommate in college. And now he's my best friend."

She nods. "Okay. Why don't you tell people you're from Walterboro?"

I choke out a sigh. "I don't *not* tell people."

"Yes, you do. You know you do."

"It's complicated. It's just . . . easier this way."

She shakes her head. "I don't buy it. Maybe I have made assumptions about you. But I can only know what you show me. And right now, I have no idea who you are. Which makes me think maybe you're messing with me. Maybe this is all part of your plan to win."

"How do I know you aren't messing with me?" I shoot back. I reach forward and catch her other hand, so that we're standing toe to toe, all four of our hands tangled together.

"You can't," she says matter-of-factly as her thumb brushes over the back of my hand. She leans a little closer. "Which is why we have to wait until we're through this. Stay away from each other until this magazine thing is behind us. Or until I figure out why you're keeping so many secrets."

"I'm not keeping secrets," I say.

"Who were you talking to outside my apartment just now? Before you saw me."

I tense, and she responds by tightening her grip on my hands. I don't necessarily *want* to keep my personal life private from Darcy, but old habits are hard to break. "My dad," I manage to say.

Concern wrinkles her forehead. "Is he sick?" She frowns and gives her head a small shake. "Sorry. I didn't mean to overhear. I was waiting for you to see me . . ."

I swallow. "He's . . ."

I suddenly suspect that Darcy is exactly the kind of person who, if given the opportunity, will pick up any person's burden and carry it alongside them. She has that warmth, an empathy that radiates from every inch of her. If I give her this, she'll take it, she'll make it hers. She'll want me to talk about it. To give her updates. She'll *care too much*. And I'm not ready for that.

"He's fine," I choke out.

Her shoulders immediately drop, and a faint sadness fills her eyes. She knows I'm not telling her the truth. She tugs her hands away. "Okay," she says simply as she moves past me.

I follow her out of the closet and into her living room. "Darcy, it's just . . ."

"Complicated?" she finishes for me. "Yeah. I know. Life generally is."

"What's complicated about your life?" I say, the animosity in my tone surprising even me.

She eyes me warily. "Lots of things. But that's not—I'm not asking you to treat this like a therapy session where you tell me everything that's complicated in your life. I just want you to be real. I want to feel like the man I'm getting to know is the real you."

"I was real on Friday night."

She offers me a small smile. "I liked you on Friday night." She glances toward the door. "I have to go, Cameron. Vivian is expecting me."

"Right. Sorry. I'm—I actually need to go too." Dad hasn't texted yet, but he probably will any minute.

We stop on the sidewalk out front. "So we're still doing this thing?" I ask. "Still competing?"

"Whether we want to be or not, we still are," she says. "There's no way around that. We might as well have fun while we're doing it." She grins and lifts a shoulder. "Besides, I've been anxious to see how you get me back for those text messages."

"Nothing I do will ever top those text messages," I say, relieved to be back in a place where we can banter like this. This is a place I'm comfortable.

She starts off down the sidewalk, taking a few backward steps as she yells back to me, "Aw, come on. Don't quit now. You want to take me to dinner or not?"

I watch her as she turns and walks away, her dark hair glistening in the afternoon light.

My thoughts and emotions are completely muddled together. Darcy challenges me in ways that are uncomfortable and thrilling at the same time. She demands I take off the mask, be real with her. But I've worn it so long, I'm not sure I know how.

I only know she makes me really want to try.

Chapter Fifteen

Darcy

It is surprisingly easy to find a couple of street musicians willing to follow Cameron and his tour group around the city on Thursday morning. I have to pay extra for them to play "Death of a Clown" by The Kinks on loop the entire time—pretty sure they had to learn the song in order to play it—but after what Cameron did to me? The extra investment is well worth it.

Cameron hired an actual clown to follow me around last week. Dressed in full circus finery, giant red shoes and all, the clown showed up beside me as I led my group across Broad Street and didn't say a word. Just walked behind us for the entire tour, standing a few paces away from everyone else. There's no way I won't get reviews mentioning the creepy, silent clown who stalked us all over the city.

Meanwhile, every time I see Cameron, it feels like literal fireworks are exploding overhead. The knowing smile he gives me whenever our eyes meet. The way we track each other all over the gift shop.

I probably should have let him kiss me at my apartment the other day.

But there is also something delicious about the anticipation. About the tension building between us.

"Seriously," Rachel says, dropping a box of grits on the floor beside the counter. "How much longer is this going to go on between you two? Can you please just jump him already? The tension is even killing me now."

"Talk a little louder, why don't you?" I say. "I'd love to draw attention to our conversation. Maybe I should text Cameron directly and let him know we're talking about him."

She rolls her eyes. "I'm sure he'd be so surprised since you two are undressing each other with your eyes every chance you get."

"Gross. We are not."

"Yeah. *Gross*. I'm sure that's how you really feel."

There is zero part of Cameron in any state of dress, or otherwise, that sounds gross. Even just his exposed forearms are enough to repeatedly draw my eye. I can't imagine seeing more of the man. I'd probably lose my actual head. But that doesn't mean I want to talk about it with Rachel in the middle of the crowded gift shop.

The weather is finally starting to warm up, which means the tourists are starting to show up. That's good for business, but you wouldn't know it looking at my calendar. I've been spending multiple days a week in Vivian's greenhouse; I've even canceled a couple of scheduled tours to free up more time.

If I didn't have to pay actual bills and, you know, do basic stuff like eat, I'd cancel them all and spend every day with my hands in the dirt. It didn't take Vivian long to figure out there's something I'd rather be doing than leading tours, but she isn't pushing me to admit to more—something I appreciate. I'm not sure I could tell her about my plans at the flower show without it sounding like I'm asking for her help. Not that I wouldn't love to have it. I just don't want to take advantage. Her company is more than enough.

Besides, I ran into Bethany Morgan the other morning in the gift shop, and she mentioned that the lady from the magazine specifically asked her if there were any female tour guides they could feature. She gave her my name.

Probably a very good reason for me to stop canceling tours.

I glance at my watch; I'm early today. Early means more time to see Cameron before we go our separate ways. Every day that passes, I look forward to seeing him more and more. Today, he's noticeably absent, which has me nervous for an entirely different reason. It's been a few days since I bombarded him with "Death of a Clown."

He owes me. His absence tells me he's about to pay up.

Still, I can't be annoyed. He's been sending me texts lately. Little things about himself. *Real* things. And it is going a long way to strengthen his case.

When I was in the fourth grade, I slipped in the bathroom and broke my arm. I felt lame about how it happened, so I told everyone at school I fell off my skateboard while I was practicing tricks. I still don't know how to skateboard.

I was sixteen before I discovered that beets don't come out of the ground already pickled.

That one made me laugh.

Don't hate me for this one. I don't like shrimp and grits. I lie to tourists all the time because they really should try them, and I don't want to dissuade them. But I've never liked them.

I forgive him for this gross offense against our Lowcountry roots because he at least admitted that grits themselves are perfectly fine. It's only the combination he doesn't like.

"Look what he texted me last night," I say to Rachel, pulling up the string of texts. I flip my phone around so she can read it.

"I've never been on a yacht," she reads. We make eye contact. "Man. You really were wrong about him, weren't you?"

I shrug. "He's definitely not what I thought."

"Darcy Marino?" a voice calls from the front of the shop. I turn and see a man framed in the glass doorway. He hasn't come inside. And he won't. Because he's holding a dog leash. A dog leash with a very real, very large dog on the end of it.

I look at Rachel.

"Oh, he's good," she says, her smile wide.

"Are you Darcy?" The man repeats.

I manage a nod. "But that is not my dog."

The guy shrugs. "I don't know the details, ma'am. Just that he's supposed to stay with you."

"Says who?" As if I even need to ask.

"Says the guy who paid me twenty bucks to walk him over here. I honestly don't care though. If you don't want him, I'll just let him go."

"No, no. Don't do that," I say. I have no idea who the dog belongs to, but he doesn't deserve to wander the streets alone. "Does he have a name?"

"Bailey," the guy says.

I take the leash, and the man disappears. "What the everlovin'—"

"Nice dog," someone calls out.

I look up to see Cameron standing across the street, leaning up against a light post like he doesn't have a care in the world.

"Cameron Hunter, what am I supposed to do with this?"

He grins. "I don't know. He looks like he's up for a walk."

Oh, he is so going down for this one. How am I supposed to do my entire tour with a dog?

The answer is: not very gracefully.

I manage. But only just. Twice I get the leash tangled around my legs and nearly fall flat on my face. And when we're standing on the battery, talking about Fort Sumter and its role during the Civil War,

Bailey sees a pod of dolphins swimming a little ways off shore and gets so excited, he nearly tugs me straight off the battery wall and into the water.

Had one of the dads on the tour not been there to stop us, we'd have both been swimming.

After the tour, I have no idea what to do with Bailey, so I take him home with me. There's no way I'm doing a second tour with him along, and there isn't much in my apartment he could ruin, so my plan is to leave him here.

I'm pretty sure Cameron didn't intend to actually give me Bailey. He's a gorgeous dog. A golden retriever who looks well-loved. He belongs to somebody. How long Cameron will push this prank is another question altogether. Hopefully not much longer or else Bailey will be eating sandwich meat and cheddar cheese slices for dinner.

I've only been home twenty minutes or so when Cameron shows up.

I buzz him in and wait for him to climb the stairs from my apartment doorway. His grin is wide as he crests the final stair. "How was your tour?" he asks.

I glance over my shoulder at Bailey, who is lounging on my couch like he owns the place. "Oh, fabulous," I say. "Aside from the part where Bailey nearly dragged me into the Cooper River."

I level him with a glare, and he frowns. "He didn't hurt you, did he?"

The genuine concern in his voice knocks me slightly off-kilter. I shake my head. "Not really."

He nods. "Jerome promised me he was well-behaved. That he wouldn't bite anyone or do anything stupid."

So Bailey belongs to Jerome. "He was a perfect gentleman most of the time. And there were kids on the tour who thought he was fabulous so all in all, it wasn't terrible having him along."

He steps closer, and my breath catches in my throat. "Are you telling me I need to up my game?"

I swallow. "Are you telling me you're holding back because you like me so much?"

He only smiles and shakes his head, like he doesn't know what to do with me.

I know exactly what I'd do with him, but my couch is currently occupied, so I take a step back and push my hands into my back pockets, hoping that will keep me from reaching out to stroke his sweater. It looks particularly soft. Like it might even be cashmere.

What would cashmere feel like stretched across Cameron's broad chest?

Whatever his reasons for dressing like a preppy frat boy while he's leading his tours—and I'm still not sure I understand them—I cannot complain about this sweater. It's working in magical, beautiful ways.

"I need to get Bailey home." His voice is low and throaty and sends a shiver racing up my spine. Warmth blossoms in my gut, spreading from my toes to my fingertips, and my eyes drop to Cameron's lips. He's normally clean-shaven, likely an intentional part of his pretty-boy socialite look, but right now, it looks like he hasn't shaved in a few days. The blond of his beard is tinged with red, and I barely resist the urge to rub my palm across the stubble.

I close my eyes and take a step back, my entire body charged with crackling energy. The man only has to stand there to make me feel warm all over. But with that husky voice and his bedroom eyes . . .

Get a grip, Darcy. I am in serious trouble if talking about his best friend's dog is starting to sound like foreplay.

I nod and manage to squeak out an "okay" before I step out of the way so he can retrieve Bailey. He pauses on his way out and leans forward, his lips brushing across my cheek. "Bye, Darce," he whispers, his lips close to my ear.

He leaves me standing in the door of my apartment, my heart in my throat.

Or worse. My heart following him down the stairs and out the front door.

As I fall asleep later that night, I half-wonder if I should cancel what I have planned for Cameron's afternoon tour. Afternoon, because I need to be free to make this one work.

It's a relatively benign prank—less intrusive than having a couple of buskers serenade him for a few hours. But I'm beginning to wonder if it's time to call everything off. He seemed ready a couple of weeks ago when we almost kissed in my closet. It was me who insisted we keep the competition going, convinced that if I held a little more tightly to our rivalry, it might help me keep a firmer hold on my heart. Or at least slow down the falling that was beginning to feel inevitable.

But now, I'm pretty sure the falling happened regardless.

Cameron Hunter has my heart.

***

On the back side of Vivian Abernathy's property, there is a narrow alley that cuts between her house and the one beside it. It is gated and only accessible with a key, a key Cameron possesses. It allows him to walk his tours down the narrow alley—which is magical all on its own, with its ivy-covered walls and centuries-old cobblestone—and view the kitchen house, a historic relic that is likely the highlight for most people who take his tour. The alley continues all the way across the property and comes out one block over, so the gate on Charlotte Street isn't the only way to access the kitchen house.

But it is the most convenient way.

I glance at my watch, hoping I've timed things correctly. My friend John, who works at the nursery I like to wander around whenever I have a free afternoon, sticks his head out the window of the nursery's small box delivery truck. "Am I close enough?" he yells.

"Just a tiny bit farther," I say. He'll get fined if we leave the truck parked on the sidewalk for long, and I promised him that wouldn't happen. I maybe shouldn't have promised something I can't guarantee, but it shouldn't happen. This is a relatively low-traffic area, and it's not like I haven't seen other trucks and service vehicles pulled onto the sidewalk before.

Plus, I only need him to stay here long enough to thwart Cameron's efforts to cut through the alley. With the truck positioned as it is now, Cameron will be able to *see* the gate that leads to Vivian's kitchen house, but he won't be able to open it.

"Okay, stop right there. That's perfect." I hold up my hands.

John nods and cuts the engine. He joins me on the sidewalk and pockets his keys. "Now what?"

"Now you get out of here. If we do get in trouble, I don't want you anywhere nearby. I'll text you when it's safe to come back and move it."

He eyes me warily. "You're lucky the weather's nice right now. And I better not get a ticket."

"You won't. I'll be watching the whole time. Twenty minutes, John. That's it."

He lifts a hand and waves as he walks away. "Yeah, yeah. But you owe me."

Now there's nothing to do but wait.

I crouch down in front of the truck only to decide I don't want Cameron to see me with the truck. But then, if he doesn't see me, will he know I'm the one responsible? Or will he think some idiot just parked in a way that unluckily blocked the gate?

I don't want to distract him from his tour—he really will only need to walk around the block to get where he wants to go—but I do want credit for what I think is a pretty ingenious prank.

I hear Cameron before I see him, his deep voice echoing off the houses that crowd the narrow lane that will lead him around the corner and into view. I dart across the street and hide behind a car, hopefully far enough out of Cameron's line of sight that he won't see me.

His words trail off as he approaches the truck, and he sighs.

Like, a bone-deep sigh. One that feels heavier than anything I've ever heard from Cameron before. My heart pounding, I peek over the hood of the car.

He turns—does he legitimately have eyes in the back of his head?—and we make eye contact. His jaw tenses, then he starts walking toward me.

"Give me just a second," he says to his group.

So we're doing this now, I guess.

Except no, I don't want to have any kind of confrontation with the man storming toward me. I have enough sense to recognize that Cameron was likely having a bad day before I blocked the alley with a box truck. But I'm not sure, based on his expression, that Cameron has enough sense to recognize as much.

I dart away from the car and hurry down a narrow driveway that cuts between two homes.

"Darcy," Cameron calls after me.

I stop and turn around, immediately struck by the fury that is clouding his features.

For the first time, Cameron's mask of impeccable calm and composure has slipped. His cheeks are mottled, his jaw firmly set, and his eyes are sparking with a rage I've never seen. Behind Cameron's tailored clothes and perfect hair, there is a real man, with real emotions. He doesn't want anyone to see that man. But I see him now. And he's . . . hurting.

It frustrates me that I don't know enough about Cameron's life to guess what's going on. We *have* been getting to know each other, but he still hasn't told me much about his family, about his life outside of work.

"Move the truck," he says calmly, a little of his control slipping back into place.

"I . . . don't know what you're talking about," I lie.

"Like hell you don't. Move the truck."

A tiny flicker of heat ignites low in my belly, a wave of attraction washing over me. Angry Cameron is a little bit sexy.

Except, no. That isn't what he needs right now. He's dealing with something bigger than my little prank.

I step closer and press a hand to his chest just over his heart. "I'm sorry," I say softly. "I can move the truck. Only . . . Cameron, tell me what's wrong."

A myriad of emotions flash across his face in rapid succession. Fear. Anger. Pain. There is a storm behind his eyes, and for the first time, I see all of it. He's *letting* me see all of it.

He lifts his hand and slides it over mine, squeezing my fingers. "How do you see so much?" he asks, his voice low. He tugs me closer, and the air around us shifts, his eyes sparking with desire.

Any response I might have given stalls in my throat.

That's more than a spark.

That's a roaring forest fire of red. hot. desire.

Okay, so maybe this is what he needs right now.

His arms are around me before I even realize what's happening. He lifts me, and my legs wrap around his waist as he presses me to the brick wall at my back.

I don't know if I start kissing him first, or if he starts kissing me, but I know I can't get enough of him. I have lost all sense of reason. All awareness. I know only the taste of him, the warmth of his mouth as it presses against mine, the strength of his arms as he holds me up, the brush of his stubble as he turns his head, parting his lips in invitation.

I respond willingly, matching his desire with my own, then asking for more. There is a rightness to the feel of him against me, our bodies pressed close. We have been building to this inevitable conclusion for a long time.

Maybe I always knew it. Always wanted it. Even if I wasn't ready to admit it.

A throat clears behind us, and we break the kiss, our breathing fast and heavy. A look passes between us when we make eye contact. Something like wonder. Even reverence.

That was not just a kiss.

We turn at the same time to find a woman standing at the end of the alley, a child under each arm and her palms pressed against their eyes.

"This isn't exactly the education I thought my children would be getting when we signed up for a walking tour," she says pointedly.

I bite my lip, my face immediately flooding with embarrassment. But I can't regret what happened.

Cameron slowly lowers me to the ground. "I, um . . ." He clears his throat. "I'm so sorry. I just . . . need a minute."

"Oh, I'm sure you do," she says pointedly. "Come on, children. Mr. Hunter will be back in a moment to see if he can earn back a few of the stars I just knocked off his Google review."

She disappears and I finally let myself laugh. "I'm sorry," I say through my giggles. I press my face against his chest.

"I'm not," he says, his hand sliding over my hair and gently clasping the back of my neck. He holds me there, pressed against his chest like it's the most natural thing. Like I belong in his arms. He kisses my temple. "We're going to talk about this."

I nod. "I know."

"I'll call you?" he asks, a new trepidation in his voice. It is utterly adorable and my heart squeezes at the sound.

I smile. "Okay."

He leaves me standing in the shadows of the moss-covered wall—a wall I will never pass by again without thinking of this moment. He stops at the end of the alley and looks back. He smiles and shakes his head, his expression saying he doesn't know what happened either, but he enjoyed it as much as I did.

It's the most genuine smile I've ever seen on Cameron, and I realize with utter certainty that I will do anything to see it again.

Chapter Sixteen

Cameron

To say it is difficult to focus on the rest of my tour is an understatement. That kiss. The way she looked at me, the way she knew, even without me explaining, that there was something else going on.

Blocking the alley was clever, but that shouldn't surprise me. Darcy is always clever. The "Death of a Clown" thing was genius.

Any other day, I would have laughed to find the alley blocked, but I started this tour hanging onto my composure with my fingernails.

Dad's scans were not great. Not horrible. Just not the good news we were hoping for. It means another round of treatment, which is news we've heard before.

That doesn't make it any easier.

Dad was optimistic when he told me, insisting that his tumors—in his leg, this time—are responding well to the treatment and one more round is likely all it will take. Maggie confirmed when I followed up with her, so I haven't worried too much about him.

But then Dad fell getting out of his truck this afternoon, right before my second tour started. Maggie called to tell me they were on their way to the hospital.

I wanted to leave right then, drive over to meet them, but I had twenty people waiting for me to entertain them for two hours, and Maggie promised there was no reason for me to rush.

I kept it together. Barely. Until I found a box truck blocking the alley that leads to Vivian Abernathy's kitchen house.

I reacted like an idiot, fueled by the exhaustion that always overwhelms me whenever I think about how fragile Dad really is. But then Darcy changed everything.

I don't know how she sees me like she does.

Dad is stable, and Maggie thinks they'll release him soon. They want to be sure his fall was caused by exhaustion and isn't linked to some underlying condition. I'm still worried about him, but not so worried that I can't relive my kiss with Darcy over and over again. Her hands around my neck, her breath coming in jagged rasps as my lips moved across the line of her jaw. The way her body molded so perfectly to mine.

I pull out my phone to text her, but I hesitate. She knows something else is going on. There's no way she won't ask about it.

But Dad's okay. The fall wasn't anything serious. There's no reason to even tell her, really.

Also no reason to text Jerome, though he'd feel otherwise if he knew Dad was in the hospital.

Except, I want to text Darcy.

And there's the difficulty.

I'm torn between wanting her here for my own sake, and wanting to keep her at a distance for *her* sake. She doesn't need my burdens. My drama.

I spend way too long crafting a text, typing and deleting so many different versions, what I finally end up sending almost seems laughable for how simple it is.

Cameron: Can I see you tomorrow?

Darcy: Absolutely. Is everything okay?

I both hate and love that she asks so quickly, that the question comes so easily.

Cameron: Yeah. Rough day. I'm working tomorrow, but only in the morning. Picnic lunch?

I tap my phone into my palm while I wait for her to respond.

Maggie finds me this way, sitting on a long bench in the hallway outside of Dad's hospital room. His doctor is with him now.

I sigh and try to release some of the tension in my shoulders as Maggie drops onto the bench beside me. "What are you frowning over?" she says as she covers a yawn. "You look as tired as I feel."

"Nah, I'm good. Just . . ." I'm suddenly tired of the pretense, and I let it fall away. ". . . texting a woman," I finish.

She smiles. "That explains it. I take it you like this woman?"

An ache pulses up from my gut—a longing I'm not sure I've ever felt for anyone. I run a hand across my face. "She's special, Maggie. Honest and real, and open with her emotions."

She smiles and nudges my shoulder. 'Then I'm not sure I understand why you're frowning."

"Because I know I'm *not* very good at those things. I can't help feeling like once she really gets to know me, I'm going to disappoint her somehow."

"Isn't she already getting to know you? You're texting, aren't you?"

"Yeah, but . . . the real me, you know?"

She scoffs. "As opposed to the *you* you're pretending to be? You've always been more than your fancy clothes and your charming words." She nudges me again. "You've never given yourself enough credit, Cameron. Just be yourself. If she likes you, she does. If she doesn't, she doesn't. It's that simple."

I wish it felt that simple. But it's more than that. It isn't my *life* I'm worried Darcy won't like. It's me. "Maggie, I've never had a serious girlfriend."

She rolls her eyes. "You don't have to remind me. Your father worries over that very fact all the time."

"It's not that I don't want one," I say. "I just . . . I don't think I know how to let people get close."

Her expression softens. "But this girl . . . you want her to get close?"

I nod. "It's early. But yeah. I really think I do."

"And you're worried you're going to screw it up," she says, a statement more than a question. "My word, child. You really are like your father."

I huff out a laugh. "I can't decide if you think that's supposed to make me feel better."

She shrugs. "Maybe. He figured it out with me, though Lord knows it took a lot of talking, and even some therapy." She pats my knee. "You'll figure it out. Trust your instincts. And don't let what happened with your mama make you think you aren't worth a woman sticking around. You're a catch, Cam." A yawn swallows the tail end of her words, and I suddenly wish there was more I could do for her.

"Hey, do you guys want to stay at my place tonight? It's a long drive back to Walterboro."

She waves away my concern. "Nah, we'll be all right. You know how your daddy is about sleeping in his own bed. Plus, he'll want to see the boys. Make sure they know he's okay."

"How are they?"

She smiles. "With a sitter and as happy as a couple of clams at high tide. I let them order a pizza for dinner."

"I'm sure they loved that." With their budget stretched as tightly as it is, even an ordered pizza is a treat. "When do you see the doctor again?"

"Tomorrow. But he's coming out to the satellite office in Walterboro, so we won't have to drive back over here." She stands. "Come on. I'm sure they've got Jake ready to go by now. Walk with us to the car?"

My watch pings with a text notification while I'm helping Dad—annoyingly, according to him—into the passenger seat of his truck. "You better let him help you," Maggie says from the driver's seat. "Or you'll fall again, and then where will we be?" She looks at me. "Thanks for your help, Cam."

"Call me tomorrow?" I say. She nods, and I grip Dad's shoulder. "I'm glad you're all right, Dad."

He shrugs, and his smile stretches wide, almost countering the deep circles under his eyes. *Almost.* "You know me," he says with his customary optimism. "I'll always be all right."

Maggie rolls her eyes and smiles at him affectionately. "You'll be saying that when you're a hundred years old and on your deathbed."

I watch them pull away, then grab my phone to read the text I hope is from Darcy.

Darcy: A picnic sounds lovely. Unfortunately, I'm tour-less tomorrow. Will you finish in your usual spot? How about I pick you up?

Tuesdays are often slow, but Darcy has no one scheduled? I really could start funneling people from my waiting list over to her, though she'd probably hate me for it. And her lighter schedule could be intentional. Vivian says they're spending an awful lot of time together.

Cameron: Sounds perfect.

***

I am nervous when I see her leaning against her car the next morning, her ankles crossed in front of her, her eyes on her phone. She looks gorgeous, in jeans and yet another pair of sneakers I've never seen before.

She doesn't see me approach, doesn't even look up when I'm standing right in front of her. I nudge the side of her shoe with my toe, and she looks up, startled.

She smiles wide, her expression warm and welcoming, and some of the nerves coursing through me ease away. "Sorry," she says as she pulls out her AirPods. "I didn't hear you."

"How many pairs of these do you have?" I ask, looking back at her sneakers.

"Oh, that is a dangerous question. But the answer is never enough. I've been collecting them since I was in high school. How was your tour?"

"Uneventful. But sometimes those are the best kind."

"No clowns?"

I chuckle. "And no musicians."

"Or dogs. Or box trucks."

"Or text messages," I add. "It's a wonder Google reviews haven't tanked for both of us."

"Oh, I got a good one after the clown thing. It said something like, 'I never could figure out if the clown was a part of the tour or not. It made the whole experience memorable, but also, why? Is there some connection to Charleston history I missed?'"

"I still can't believe he didn't talk the entire time. That was all him. I only told him to be a little annoying."

"He was definitely annoying. In the creepiest way possible."

We climb into her car, and I direct her to where my Honda is parked a few blocks away so I can grab the cooler and picnic basket out of the trunk, then we swing by The Brown Dog Deli to pick up the sandwiches I ordered in advance. I didn't use to be good at things like this, but I've been friends with Jerome long enough that some of the best parts of him have rubbed off on me. His care and attention to dates is one of those things.

Still, I'm anxious in a way I never have been before. I may be very good at first or second dates, at impressing women when everything is easy and fun and casual. But this is Darcy. Everything is different with Darcy.

She follows my instructions and drives us out to Oakwood Plantation on Johns Island. I send her down an access road that skirts around the main property and spits us out right beside the construction site for the Gullah Education Center.

She climbs out of the car and stands, her hands perched on her hips, and surveys the site. The site is empty, work temporarily halted until the drainage system has been fully installed, which won't happen until next week. She turns to look at me. "Where are we?"

I retrieve the picnic basket, sandwiches, and cooler from her trunk. "The future home of the Gullah Education Center," I say.

Her face brightens. "Right. This is what Jerome is doing, isn't it?"

I nod. "It started as research for his PhD and turned into this."

"I remember him touching on it during the lecture I attended," she says. "His ancestry goes all the way back, right?"

"To the enslaved people who worked this very plantation." I motion to the grounds around us. "Which is why the land donation was particularly significant. His grandmother is also a commissioner for the Gullah Geechee Heritage Commission. His roots in the Gullah community are deep."

"I love that. That he's doing this. That it's working."

We walk a little ways from the car to a flat spot under the swooping branches of a live oak. One of the conditions of the land donation was that construction neither damage nor require the removal of any of the live oaks on the property. It took some extra creativity from the architects to come up with a building design that skirts clear of the trees, but it was a small price to pay for free land.

I pull a blanket out of the picnic basket and shake it out before handing two corners to Darcy. She takes the corners, but instead of backing up so we can spread the blanket on the ground, she surprises me by stepping forward and giving me a quick kiss.

"There. Done," she says, her cheeks blazing pink.

I raise my eyebrows, and she presses her palms to her cheeks. "I'm blushing, right?"

I grin. "A little."

We spread out the blanket, and she drops onto it with a huff. "I've just been stressing about us kissing again. Will it be awkward? Weird? Will you even want to kiss me again? I wanted to get it over with, break the tension and all that, but I think I made things worse."

I lower myself to the blanket beside her, struggling to hide my smile, and open the picnic basket.

Darcy reaches for it. "I'm starving. Are you starving?"

"Hey," I say, slipping my hand over hers.

She stills, turning her hand and entwining our fingers. Finally, she raises her gaze to meet mine.

I lift my free hand to her face, my fingers sliding into the hair just behind her ear. I lean forward and press my lips to hers. She is soft and yielding and warm, and I resist the urge to shove the picnic basket out of the way and pull her closer so I can lean back onto the blanket and feel the weight of her against me.

But this is still so new. There is reason to go slow, to let her lead. I break the kiss but keep her close. "You'll never make things worse by kissing me," I say softly.

"Well, that's a relief," she says, a grin spreading across her face. Her stomach rumbles and her eyes go wide, a hand flying to her midsection.

"But clearly feeding me should be your top priority," she says.

I chuckle, then open the basket and pull out our sandwiches.

"While we're eating, maybe you can tell me why we skipped the half of the plantation with gardens and river views to hang out next to a construction site full of mud and concrete."

Her words aren't judgmental, just observational. And a little playful. Like she knows I must have a reason and is hinting that she's ready for it.

I hand her a to-go box from Brown Dog Deli. "A fried green tomato BLT. Is that all right?"

"I've never had one, but it sounds perfect."

I toss her a bag of chips and set a container of macarons from Cristophe's, a French bakery downtown, on the blanket between us. "How have you lived in Charleston all your life and never had a fried green tomato BLT?"

"It's that good, huh?"

I nod, motioning for her to go ahead and try it.

She takes a bite, then closes her eyes with a moan that makes me want to toss her sandwich to the side and kiss her again. "I think I love you, Cameron," she says before taking another large bite.

I grin. "That's all it takes, huh?"

"I am a very simple woman."

"Shoes and sandwiches?" I hand her a water bottle out of the cooler.

"And flowers," she says after taking a long swig.

"I shouldn't have forgotten that one."

Her eyes dance as she says, "And kisses from you, I think." Heat smolders in her gaze, the energy between us sharp and crackling.

"So . . . the education center," she prompts.

"Right. Yes." Focusing is not going to be easy with her looking at me like that. "You said you wanted to see the real me. This is part of it."

"Because of Jerome?"

"Partly. This is his project. I wouldn't be involved if not for him. But I care about real history. History that hasn't been sanitized or whitewashed for more comfortable consumption. It's what I'm trying to do with my tours, too. But what Jerome's doing out here—it's huge. I got a master's degree in nonprofit management, hoping it would create an opportunity for me to work with one of the historical foundations in town. I'm not there yet, but I've been using what I know to help Jerome with his fundraising. Writing grant proposals, pitching, schmoozing."

"That's why you were so dressed up that morning," she says.

I nod. "When you're asking Charleston's finest to donate more money than I've made . . . *ever*, you dress to impress."

"I bet they eat you up."

I raise an eyebrow, not sure what she means.

"Oh, come on. You had me convinced. They're probably happy to donate money to one of their own. Isn't that the way it works?"

"But I'm not one of them." My freshman year of college made that clear enough, but that's not a story I want to share with Darcy. Some stories are best left in the past. I push the painful memories aside. I can't dwell on them or the embarrassment might send me into an anxiety spiral, which, considering present company, I'd rather avoid.

"You let them think you are though," Darcy says. "Just like you do with the tourists. Like you did with me."

She isn't saying anything I haven't heard before, but her willingness to name it for what it is surprises me.

"Code-switching," she continues. "That's what you're doing, right? You talk to people in whatever language they need to feel most comfortable." She sits up on her knees and reaches for the cookies, opening the container and offering me one. "It's a brilliant skill, honestly. And it makes sense. It's why everyone likes you so much."

"Everyone, huh?"

"Look, I'm coming around," she says sheepishly, "but you didn't do yourself any favors."

"Why did you hate me so much?" I ask, finally voicing a question I've wondered about more times than I can count.

"Because you came across as exactly the kind of guy I don't like," she says. "Entitled. Spoiled. And yet you were so good at your job. You make it look easy, and it's never been easy for me." She takes a bite of another cookie, wiping a crumb from her lip in a move that thoroughly distracts me from her words.

"Cameron," she says, and my eyes dart back to hers.

"Hmm? What?"

She grins. "Why did you hate *me*?" she says, and I realize she had to repeat her question.

I shake my head. "I never hated you, Tinkerbell."

She rolls her eyes. "Yes, you did. You were awful to me."

"Only when you were awful to me first."

"That's not . . ." Her words trail off. "Okay, maybe that is true."

"It was the opposite for me. I moved the meeting place for my tours because of you," I admit. "So I could see you every day."

"So you could call me Tinkerbell every day."

I lean back on my elbows, looking up through the branches overhead to the blue sky beyond. "Now, that I *did* do to annoy you."

She shoves my chest playfully and I catch her hand, holding it against me and tugging her close as I lean all the way onto the blanket. She settles in next to me, her head resting against my shoulder. "We wasted so many months hating each other."

"Except I didn't—"

"I know, I know," she says. "You didn't hate me. The point is, we spent so many months being awful to each other when we could have been doing this." She leans up on her elbow and leans forward until her nose brushes against mine. "I'm going to kiss you now, okay?"

Her kiss is feather-light, her lips warm, and she tastes like salted caramel and vanilla and the future I want for myself. I wrap an arm around her waist, pulling her gently until the weight of her falls against me, pliant, molding to me like our limbs were made to be in constant contact.

Her hand slips beneath the hem of my shirt and she presses her palm flat against my abdomen.

I stifle a moan at the touch, but then . . . she *giggles* against my lips.

"What?" I say, suddenly self-conscious. I lean up, propping myself up on my elbows.

"Seriously? Did you just do that on purpose?" She runs her hands over the ridges of my stomach, which is flexed only because of how I'm sitting. "How do you even have time for this? You *walk* for a living. Walking doesn't build muscles like these."

I grin, a hint of embarrassment warming my face. "I live in Park Circle. There's a great gym over there. But genetics also help. My dad still looks ripped, and he's in his forties and in the middle of—" I was about to say cancer treatments, but I don't want to spoil the mood by talking about cancer. "He doesn't work out much anymore," I say instead.

Darcy's expression is curious, but somehow still guarded. I wish I could read her as well as she reads me. She takes a deep breath as if settling on some sort of decision, and leans back onto my shoulder, shifting so we're lying flat again. She leaves her hand on my stomach, tracing small circles over my skin in a way that has me closing my eyes, afraid to breathe too deeply else she'll stop.

"Your dad's only in his forties?" she asks after a minute or two of silence.

I feel safe with Darcy. Comfortable. But the words she's asking me to say aren't comfortable. Because they're mine, and I don't want anyone else judging them. I know she won't, that she's only asking because she wants to know me. But it takes me a long time to say them anyway.

"He was seventeen," I finally say. "My mama was sixteen." The words roll off my tongue like they always do when I think about home—a little less Charleston-refined, a little more small town.

There is so much more I could say. That my parents both dropped out of school, got married, and Dad got a job unloading trucks at UPS. That Mama wasn't around much unless she needed cash for booze, or a bed to crash in to sleep off a hangover, that is, until Dad got sick, and she finally left for good. That I was mostly raised by my dad and his mom, who kept me while he worked, God rest her soul.

But the words are lodged in my throat, and I leave them there. Festering. Knowing I ought to say them. To own them for what they are, for how they shaped me, good and bad. But I am too practiced, too good at hiding them away under a sheen of carefully crafted polish. It's hard to call them up.

Darcy wraps her arm full around my middle and squeezes, and I feel her acceptance of the one small truth I managed to say. "How do your tours fit into all of this? Into your goals?" she asks.

It's still a question that requires vulnerability, and it makes me itchy; I'd rather get up and run around the field than sit here. But I have to give her something. "It's why I want the magazine feature," I say simply. "I want to grow. Expand the business. Hire other tour guides that I can train. Build something that makes a consistent effort to keep the bar high and share history that hasn't been whitewashed and glossed over."

"I love that," she says simply. She looks up at me, her chin resting on my chest. "Your reasons for wanting the feature are better than mine." I stop just shy of telling her I'd also love to help out Maggie and my dad. Pay down some of their medical debt. Provide more for the boys.

I shake my head. "We all have our reasons. Yours are no less important."

She rolls her eyes. "But they are way more selfish."

My phone rings, an interruption I hate and love at the same time. It's becoming a common pattern whenever I'm with Darcy. I want it. Want her. But I know what she'll demand of me, and that's terrifying.

I glance at my watch to see it's Maggie calling and immediately sit up. "Sorry. I gotta take this."

Darcy nods and shifts away. I stand and walk a few paces toward the massive trunk of the oak beside us. "Maggie? Is everything okay?"

"Your daddy's fine. It's not him I'm calling about," she says, and I take a deep breath, relief coursing through me. "I do need your help though," she continues. "If you're not busy."

"Sure. Anything."

"I'm at the oncologist with your dad and we've been waiting forever to find out when the next round of chemo will start. I'm not going to make it back home in time to get Maddox off the bus, and I already called my neighbor, and she isn't picking up. I know it's a drive, but can you go meet him at the bus stop? They won't let him get off if there isn't an adult there. They'll just take him back to the school, and the last time that happened, he cried for three days."

I glance at my watch, already calculating how long it'll take me to get back to my car and all the way out to Colleton County. "What time does he get off the bus?"

"Just past two-thirty. You'll have to leave now if you're going to make it."

I *could* leave now, but my car is at least fifteen minutes away. "Maggie, I won't make it. I'm out with a friend, and I don't have my car—"

Darcy appears in front of me and her hand curves over my forearm. "We can take mine. Wherever it is, I can come. I don't have anything else to do today."

The implication of accepting her offer sits like lead in my gut. Taking Darcy home?

Well. That's one way to unpack all my secrets.

But this is Maddox. I can't not go. "I'll be there," I say to Maggie. I mouth a thank you to Darcy. "I'll get him and stay until you guys are home. Don't worry about it."

"Thank you, Cam." She hesitates a moment. "Is that her?" she asks. "The woman I just heard talking. Is she the one you were texting?"

Darcy is hurriedly gathering up the remnants of our picnic, haphazardly shoving things into the basket. "Yeah. That's her. Her name is Darcy."

I can hear the smile in Maggie's voice. "Well, I'm excited we'll get to meet her."

Excitement isn't exactly the word I'd use for what I'm feeling. But I'll go with it. The alternative—unpacking what's really going on—might take an entire team of therapists and a few shots of bourbon, and that feels too hard for a regular Tuesday afternoon.

But ready or not, I'm taking a woman home to meet my family.

The last time that happened was three weeks shy of never.

Chapter Seventeen

Darcy

I have processed a lot of information in the past fifteen minutes. Cameron has brothers. Tiny ones. Like, tiny enough to be his own kids tiny. He also has a stepmom, Maggie, and a dad who I think is sick in some way. Though, for how vague Cameron is being, he could also just be a drunk.

I have way more questions than I do answers. Where is his mom? Does he have a good relationship with his dad? Or is it a bad relationship and that's why he doesn't talk about where he's from? Does he get along with his stepmom? Are his little brothers as cute as he is?

The thought of two little mini-Camerons has my body reacting in ways I cannot adequately describe. Let's just say I'm pretty sure if my ovaries could talk, they'd be screaming, *Yes, please! We want one!*

Cameron is driving my car; I tossed him the keys before we left the plantation mostly because I didn't want him to feel pressured to talk, to keep me—the driver—entertained. This way, he can focus on the road, and I can play games on my phone in comfortable silence as opposed to an awkward one.

Whatever his reasons, this clearly isn't easy for him.

This. Me. Being here. Going to see his home. To meet his family.

The man has high walls, walls I sense he built on purpose, and I'm blowing right through them.

That's not to say I'm not happy to be doing it. I want to know the real Cameron, and I have a feeling this is as real as it gets.

But I want him to be okay more than I want to satisfy my curiosity.

We pull up to a tiny house at the end of a narrow dirt road. A couple of steps lead up to a concrete slab porch, where a pair of rocking chairs sit to the left of the front door. The house has chipped white paint and shutters that look like they started out black but have faded to a dusty gray. A tiny bicycle leans against the porch, and a t-ball stand is in the middle of the yard, a discarded whiffle ball and a plastic bat on the grass beside it. Dormant rose bushes line the walkway that leads up to the house. I can only imagine how beautiful they look in the summertime when they're all in full bloom. The house looks a little worn down, but it also looks *warm* and welcoming. Like a family lives here. A happy one.

Cameron climbs out of the car without making eye contact, and I quickly follow. "The bus will stop up where the gravel starts," he says, motioning up the road we just drove down.

We walk in silence, though it is no more uncomfortable than when we were driving over.

I've only been to Walterboro a few times, back in high school mostly, when we came to Colleton County for sporting events. It's beautiful, full of enormous trees and wide green lawns. And peaceful in a way Charleston could never be. I reach over and take Cameron's hand, threading our fingers together, and he smiles down at me in a way that makes my heart grow two sizes.

It's the oddest sensation. My feelings for Cameron are new, but my heart isn't treating them like they are. It's more like love snuck in and elbowed hate out of the way but decided to take full advantage of the root system left behind. *These feelings are all worked in nice and deep, might as well take advantage!*

Seeing Cameron like this, in his hometown, his emotions so close to the surface, it's hard to imagine how I ever hated him. There is so much I misunderstood about him. So much I missed.

The bus pulls up seconds after we reach the end of the road. Cameron crouches down as a little boy with blond hair the same color as his and a blue backpack strapped onto his tiny frame climbs down the oversized bus steps. As soon as he sees Cameron, his face breaks out in an enormous grin.

Oh, my heart. He really is a miniature version of his big brother.

"Cameron!" Maddox calls. He pauses on the bottom step and looks back at his bus driver. "It's my big brother Cameron!"

Cameron waves to the bus driver, then scoops Maddox up in an enormous hug. He stands tall, Maddox's legs dangling, and wiggles back and forth a little, a dramatic gesture that makes Maddox burst into giggles.

"What are you doing here?" he asks through his giggles.

Cameron finally lowers him to the ground. "Your mama is stuck at a doctor's appointment with Dad. I thought about seeing if your bus driver would bring you all the way to Charleston, but you have better snacks at your house, so here I am."

Maddox laughs again. "Mr. Joe would never drive all the way to Charleston. He has to get home to feed his dog, Rambo."

"Rambo?" Cameron says. "That's a cool name for a dog."

"He says it's from some old movie that was made before I was born."

Cameron smiles. "That old, huh?" He looks over and catches my eye, and Maddox turns too, noticing me for the first time.

"This is my friend, Darcy," Cameron says. "She's going to hang out with us this afternoon."

Maddox scrunches up his nose and studies me, as if he doesn't know how to feel about that. "You know any good games?" he finally asks.

"I . . . bet I can come up with something," I say, though honestly, I'm a little out of my depth. I haven't spent a ton of time with kids. "What about you? Do you know any cool games?"

He nods. "Tons. But I'm warning you, I am really hard to beat."

"Oh, I don't doubt it," I say, my tone serious.

"You sound awful cocky, Maddox," Cameron says. "You sure you've got the chops to back up all that swagger?"

"I'm not cocky," Maddox says, sounding more sixteen than six. "I'm just confident."

Turns out, Maddox has every reason to be confident. The kid schools me in checkers *and* Mario Kart, even though it's the same old-school version I played when I was growing up.

But something more significant is happening to my heart. On the drive over, I suspected watching Cameron with Maddox would be satisfying, and it has not disappointed. Cameron is completely at ease with his brother. Kind, gentle, and so invested. When he talks to him, there is nothing patronizing about his mannerisms, nothing dismissive. He listens like every word Maddox says is important and worthy of his time.

But beyond that, Cameron wears no mask when he's talking to his brother. He's just . . . himself. It's the first time I've ever seen him this way, and I feel like I'm stealing glimpses, soaking up what I can of this more open version. His walls are down, and he's relaxed and completely at ease.

Except, not completely at ease when he looks at me.

He's still worried about me being here.

When Maddox settles in to watch some TV, Cameron and I move

out to the front porch. I drop into one of the rocking chairs, and he sits on the top step, facing me, his back leaning against the post behind him.

"I like it here," I say.

He smiles. "Me too."

"You're here a lot?"

"Not as often as I should be, probably. I come every other weekend pretty regularly, and I try to make it to t-ball games and whatever school stuff Maddox has."

"He looks a lot like you. I bet people think he's yours."

"All the time. They think my dad is the grandpa. Wait until you see Jackson, though. He looks even more like me."

"Where's Jackson now?"

"At a daycare center near the hospital where Maggie works. Dad isn't working right now, so sometimes Jackson can stay with him." He hesitates and runs a hand across his face. "Just depending on how he's feeling."

So there is something going on with his dad. "He's sick?"

Cameron slowly nods, his gaze fixed and distant, but he doesn't offer any further explanation.

He's retreating, building his wall up a little higher.

I slip out of the chair and drop onto the porch. I sit cross-legged, facing him, and I hold out my hands, palms up.

He eyes me curiously, then slips his hands into mine.

"You don't have to talk about it," I say. "You can if you want to. Whenever you want to. But if it feels like a lot, that's okay too. But I want you to know I'm not judging. Not you." I look around. "Not any of this."

He squeezes my fingers. "I know. It's not—" He's quiet for a long moment. "It's not that I don't want you to know. Jerome asked me once if I'm so private because I'm ashamed. I'm not. Far from it. I'm not ashamed of my family. But I know there are people who will judge me regardless. Who would think less of me because I don't come from much. I know that's on them. And I don't want to be associated with people who make such shallow judgments. But sometimes it's the shallow people that determine whether you get ahead. You gotta play the game, you know?"

I don't, really. Sure, there are people like Cameron is describing. And Charleston is full of enough old money that it might even have a higher percentage of those people than normal. But in my experience, you can always find the good. The people who see bigger, who honor all kinds of stories. For being someone who cares so much about authentic history, about telling stories with integrity, it seems odd to me that Cameron is so cagey about his own.

It makes me wonder who hurt him. Who showed him that walls are what he needs to keep himself safe?

A car pulls into the driveway, and we both stand, my nerves skittering to life at the sight of Cameron's family pouring out of the SUV. A woman who must be Maggie climbs out of the driver's seat and immediately moves to the back where she helps a toddler out of his car seat. Jackson. Cameron was right. He does look even more like him than Maddox does.

A man I assume is Cameron's father is the last to get out. He moves around the car capably, but with slow movements that speak of exhaustion. He looks fit—Cameron said that about him—but there are shadows under his eyes and a gauntness to his cheeks, though had I not known he was ill, I might not have noticed. He tousles Jackson's hair as the trio moves up the walk. When Jackson notices Cameron, he echoes his brother's excitement and lunges forward, running and leaping into his arms.

Maggie approaches me. "You must be Darcy."

I smile and nod.

"Can I give you a hug?" Maggie asks, already opening her arms.

I quickly reciprocate. "I love hugs."

She squeezes me tightly. "You must be something special," she whispers. "He's never brought someone home."

I look over my shoulder and see Cameron holding Jackson, he and his dad in conversation. "Oh, I don't know. I'm not sure he had much of a choice."

"Oh, honey, trust me. If he didn't want you here, he would have crawled up the interstate naked to find an alternative. You know how he is."

More like, I'm learning how Cameron is. I have so many questions I want to ask. Maggie is easy and warm in a way only Southern women can be, and I have a feeling she'd tell me anything I want to know.

"Jake, say hello to Darcy," Maggie says.

I smile at her gentle bossiness. She and my mama would get along.

Cameron's dad turns and looks in my direction; I am immediately struck by his eyes. They are the same piercing blue as Cameron's, but there is an openness to them that's different, like I can see right into his heart. As I shake his hand, I get the sense that he is a man incredibly comfortable in his own skin.

"It's nice to meet you, Darcy. Thanks for keeping Maddox company this afternoon." He looks at Cameron. "And for putting up with this oaf."

"Oh, hush," Maggie says. "If he's an oaf, what does that make you?"

"An oaf's daddy, I reckon," he says with a grin.

Maggie rolls her eyes. "Y'all come on inside." She ushers Jackson through the door and into the living room, where he heads straight for the couch and plops down next to his brother. "Can y'all stay for supper?" Maggie asks, looking from Cameron to me.

He glances at me, a question in his eyes, and I nod. I'll stay all weekend if he wants to. I'm loving this glimpse of him, this window into the man behind the mask.

Cameron's dad, Jake, wraps his arms around Maggie from behind. "What are we eating? How about breakfast for dinner? I'll cook."

"You'll do no such thing. Sit down and entertain our guest. You need to rest." An expression that reminds me of Cameron flits across his face, and he shakes his head. "Maggie," he says softly. "Let me. I'm fine. And you've been on your feet longer than I have today."

She sighs and shakes her head. "Fine. But I'm still making the biscuits."

"Yes, ma'am," Jake says with a grin. "Cam, you want to go check for eggs? Maddox will probably want to help."

"Me too! I go!" Jackson says, jumping from the couch. Cameron crouches down and picks his brothers up at the same time, and in a move that almost looks choreographed, flips them both upside down so their arms are dangling. "All right. Let's go see the chickens."

The boys giggle in unison and wave at their parents as they disappear out the back door. Cameron sends me a look over his shoulder before he disappears out the door, and my heart climbs all the way up to my throat.

Maggie chuckles beside me. "Oh, you've got it bad."

My cheeks flame, and I lift my palms to cover them. I shouldn't be surprised. Even before I realized I liked the man instead of hated him, Cameron sparked me to life just like this.

I move to the counter beside Maggie and watch as she shakes self-rising flour into a wide, wooden bowl. She hands me a stick of butter and a knife. "Want to cube that up for me?"

I work beside her, happy to have something to keep my hands busy.

"How did you and Cameron meet?" she asks.

"Oh. Um, I'm a tour guide too. We start our tours at the same place." I wonder if she's heard of me. If she knows about my rivalry with Cameron, but if his track record is any indication, I'm guessing he's not much for sharing.

"Well, that's exciting," Maggie says. "Do you like it? The tour business?"

"Right now, it pays the bills," I say simply, growing more comfortable with owning my own truth. Vivian's constant praise and encouragement are helping with that. "But what I'd really love to do is work with flowers. Design the window boxes you see all over downtown."

"The flowers in that city. So gorgeous."

I nod. "There's this flower show this summer that I'm doing. I'm hoping it will help me get my start."

She smiles wide. "I love that for you. I mean, touring is nice, I'm sure. But if you have the chance to do what you love? You best grab it."

"I'm trying. Cameron is a much better tour guide than I am."

"Oh, I'm sure that's not true." She scoops up the butter and starts working it into the flour with her fingers.

"No, it is. And I'm okay with that. He has a passion for history that I don't, and he's just good with people. Charming. Everyone loves him."

"It's funny, isn't it? He can talk all day every day about history and everything else, but the minute you ask him something personal, he shuts up like a possum that's found a sweet potato and doesn't want to share."

I laugh. "Sometimes I wish I were more like that. I tend to lean more toward oversharing, which brings its own set of complications."

"Maybe you'll be good for each other," she says. "Balance each other out." There is hope in Maggie's tone, and I'm struck by how openly she loves her family. "Are things going well?"

"Things are still so new. But . . ." I shrug. "I'm hopeful."

She nods her understanding and leans a little closer. "Well, I'll tell you this much. The Hunter men—they take a long time to let people in. Cameron's even worse than his daddy, and that's saying something. But once they do?" She levels me with a serious stare. "Honey, no man will love you better."

I take a deep breath, unexpectedly relieved to know it isn't just me who Cameron keeps at arm's length. That he isn't doing so just because I'm, well, *me*. "Has he always been that way?"

She nods. "As long as I've known him. I think his mama did a number on him when she left." She motions to Jake, who is at the stovetop behind us frying bacon. "On both of them." She tilts her head toward the buttermilk sitting beside the bowl. "Want to pour that in for me?"

I open the jug, my heart aching at the thought of someone leaving Cameron on purpose, especially his mama. "Do I need to measure?"

"Nah. Just pour. I'll tell you when to stop."

I smile. "You make biscuits like my grandma."

"And my grandma. And probably her grandma too. It's the best way to do it."

I pour until she stops me and watch as the dough forms beneath her kneading fingers. "I didn't know his mom left."

She looks up like she's surprised, but then she smiles. "I suppose he wouldn't have told you yet. Not if things are still new. She left when he was fourteen. The first time Jake got sick."

"What is—?" I stop, unsure how to phrase the question.

Maggie gives me a knowing look. "He hasn't told you that, either? Lord, child, what has he told you?"

I laugh. "I learned about his brothers on the way to your house today. So not much."

"I bet he knows a lot about you though."

"So much. But I'm a talker and an open book. And he's a really good listener."

"True enough. He and his daddy have that in common." She drops the dough onto the counter, sprinkling it with flour before rolling it out. "Osteosarcoma," she says. "That's what Jake has. Bone cancer. But he beat it the first time, and he'll beat it this time too." Her expression softens. "That's where we met. I was the nurse who administered his first round of chemotherapy. One look at those eyes, and I was done for." She chuckles and shakes her head. "The finagling I did to make sure I was always on shift when he came in. I was ridiculous."

"I thought I was just lucky," Jake says over his shoulder, and Maggie grins.

"I never said a word," Maggie says. "I truly thought I would only ever admire him from afar. But then a year later, when his treatments were over—"

"And my divorce was final," Jake adds.

"He called the front desk and asked for my number." She shrugs. "The rest is history."

Cameron and the boys bustle back into the kitchen, Maddox carrying a basket holding seven beautiful brown eggs, and the conversation shifts to easier things. T-ball and Legos and whether biscuits are better with strawberry jam or butter and honey, the warming weather and how excited the boys are for the community pool to open up in a few more weeks.

The longer the conversation goes on, the more Cameron relaxes and settles into himself. He is so different than the man I watched across the gift shop. The man I taunted and teased and judged.

As we eat our simple meal of grits, eggs, bacon, and fresh biscuits, as I watch him do the dishes with his stepmom and play one last game of checkers with Maddox, as we say our goodbyes and step into the chilly March air, I realize how close I am to falling right into love. It's a terrifying realization. I'm at the beginning of something *big*. Something like . . . forever.

I won't tell him. He's already skittish enough. But I'm all in. Maggie said if I hold on long enough for him to truly let me in, no one will love me better. All right, then. Challenge accepted.

"Do you want to drive?" Cameron asks, pausing beside my SUV. He holds out my keys.

"Sure. But first . . ." I push up on my toes and press my lips to his, my hands resting on his shoulders. This is the third time I have kissed him today, but judging by his response, he doesn't mind. His hands settle on my waist, and he pulls me close, taking a step back until we're leaning against the car. The pressure of his kiss increases as he explores my mouth with his, and I give in willingly, savoring the taste of him, the rush of the heat coursing through my limbs. I am struck again by the rightness of this—*us*. He has to feel it too. Has to recognize this is more than just chemistry.

I do *hear* the sound of a door opening behind us, but it doesn't quite register in my brain until a tiny voice says, "Daddy, why are they kissing like that?"

Cameron stills, his lips still pressed to mine, and a chuckle rumbles through his chest. He steals one more kiss, his teeth grazing across my bottom lip, before he pulls back, though he keeps his arms around me.

"I guess they really like each other," his dad says. "Maddox, go on inside. I'll be right in."

I lean into Cameron's chest. I have no desire to have a conversation with his dad based on what's running through my head right now, so I stay put, my face down and buried in Cameron's shirt.

"You, uh, left your phone inside," his dad says, his voice closer now.

"Oh. Thanks," Cameron says like his dad didn't just catch us making out. "I didn't realize." How is he not acting awkwardly? I want the driveway to swallow me whole, and he sounds like he's chatting about the weather.

He shifts, one arm falling away as he takes his phone and puts it in his pocket.

"No problem. I'll be sure to have Maddox call you if he has any questions about the biology lesson y'all just gave him."

"Very funny," Cameron says.

His dad laughs softly. "Goodnight, y'all. I'm not saying don't enjoy yourselves. Just maybe not in my driveway."

"What is it with kids catching us making out?" I whisper as his dad retreats. "We have got to get better at choosing our locations."

He kisses my temple with a tenderness that almost has more of an impact than our earlier kiss and finally releases me. "At least I didn't kiss you in the dungeon."

"True." I open the driver's side door and pause. "Did you want to?"

He buckles his seatbelt and gives me a pointed look, his eyes reflecting the openness I saw in his father's eyes. I'm seeing the real Cameron, and the sight nearly takes my breath away. "I wanted to kiss you the first day I met you," he says. "And I've wanted to kiss you every day since."

I lean over and kiss him one more time—how could I not?—before starting the car. "Thank you for letting me come with you," I say as I pull out of the drive.

"I'm glad you were here."

"Your family is amazing, Cam." A thought suddenly pops into my head. "Is that why you always winced whenever I called you Cam? Before? When we still hated each other. Because it's what your family calls you?"

"I liked it when you called me Cam. I just didn't want you to realize it."

I roll my eyes, struck again by how much time I wasted thinking so many rotten things about him. "Maggie told me about your dad's cancer." I eye him cautiously. "And about your mom."

He meets my gaze for the briefest moment. Even in the dim light of the car, I can see a tiny part of him shutter closed. He nods slowly. "Okay." The word in and of itself isn't dismissive, but I'm getting better at reading his body language. If I push, I suspect he'll give in. But I swallow my questions anyway. A lot happened today. I can respect the distance he needs now. What's more, a part of me wants him to talk to me when *he's* ready, and not just because I demand it of him.

We talk about nothing and everything on the way home. Flowers. Food. Books. Favorite restaurants. Favorite bands. Favorite tour guide stories. (His? The time his entire group was in on a staged flash mob wedding proposal. Mine, when two Broadway actresses from the cast of Hamilton the Musical took my tour and serenaded the group with "Dear Theodosia" outside of Theodosia Burr Alston's home on Church Street.)

It's after ten when I finally turn onto the downtown street where Cameron left his Honda. I ease to a stop directly behind his car and shift into park. If it were up to me, we'd sit here another hour talking and laughing like we have been.

And kissing. Surely there aren't any kids around to spot us now.

Cameron leans his head back against the seat and smiles. "I had a really good time today," he says.

Best day ever in my whole entire life. "Yeah. Me too."

"I'd like to see you again."

A million times yes. "Okay."

"Tomorrow?"

It's getting harder to suppress my own enthusiasm when he's being so open. So honest. "Impatient, are we?"

"Yes," he says simply. "Can I see you the next day too? And also the one after that?"

I drop my face into my hands. "Cameron, what is happening?"

He grins. "Let's find out together, yeah?" He leans over and kisses me on the cheek. "I'll call you."

So I guess we're doing this thing.

Me.

Him.

Us.

It's been a long time since I've had an us.

I smile the rest of the way home and try to ignore the niggling sensation in my gut that says this might be too good to be true.

Chapter Eighteen

Darcy

Days turn into weeks and the weather slowly warms up. Flowers all over Charleston wake up, blooming and splashing the city with color. It's my favorite time of year and has always been my favorite time to lead tours, though you wouldn't know it by how much I'm neglecting my business.

Even with Cameron funneling his waiting list over to me, I'm still barely scraping by. Not that I care all that much. I'm spending multiple afternoons a week in Vivian's greenhouse, sketching out the designs for my booth at the flower show, brainstorming unique combinations that will be eye-catching without looking like I'm trying too hard.

The dream that has lain dormant in the back of my brain for years is finally coming to life, and I couldn't be happier. I haven't come right out and asked her, but Vivian has hinted multiple times that whatever help with flowers I need, she'll be happy to provide, loaning me every flower in her greenhouse if that's what it takes. I hate to ask it of her, and I keep hoping I'll figure something else out so I don't have to ask. At the same time, I believe her when she says talking flowers with me brings her joy.

I haven't thought about the magazine feature for days. Cameron is the obvious choice. He's focused on his business, focused on ways he can improve the historical narrative of the city, focused on supporting Jerome and his efforts. I'm not thinking about it because I'm positive they're going to pick him. And they should.

"How is that man of yours?" Vivian asks. We're walking side by side across a narrow foot bridge that crosses the Ashley River on the south end of Magnolia Plantation. The old plantation house is restored and open for tours, but in the spring, the gardens alone are worth the short trip outside the city. Vivian likes to come up every March to see the azaleas in bloom. I jumped at the chance when she invited me to come along.

"He's good," I say, unable to stop my smile. Things *are* good. I see Cameron almost every day. He is attentive and sweet, and the chemistry still crackles between us, which is enough to keep things exciting all on its own. But I still can't help feeling like Cameron's keeping himself apart from me—like there is some imaginary line between us that only he can see.

If I push, ask him more personal questions, ask him to open up, he responds. Still, it's almost as though he has figured out how to give enough of himself to appease people, but not enough to let people get really close.

"I sense there's a 'but' to that response," Vivian says. We reach the end of the bridge, and a long stretch of azalea-covered riverbank comes into view. She reaches out and grips my hand. "Oh, Darcy. Look. I came a few days late last year and some of the blooms had fallen, but this . . . this is perfect."

I follow her gaze and let out a small gasp. It *is* perfect. Azaleas in shades of purple, pink and white cover the entire bank, the blooms so profuse you can't even see the green of the leaves behind them.

"My brother's best friend got married here a couple of years ago," I say. "A little later in spring. It was still beautiful, but it doesn't compare to this."

"People don't realize how early spring starts down here," Vivian says. "With azaleas, the most impressive blooms are always the earliest. Come on. Let's keep walking. There's more to see, and I want to know what's really going on in your love life."

I have hashed and rehashed the finer points of my newly formed relationship with both Rachel and my mom over the past week or so, but I have felt such a kinship with Vivian over the past month, it feels wrong not to answer her question honestly.

I pull her arm, which is looped over mine, a little tighter, giving her the chance to lean on me if she needs it. Vivian is spry, but she's still in her eighties, and we've walked nearly half a mile already.

"Things really are good," I finally say. "Cameron is amazing. He's also very private. And I think I maybe feel like he isn't really letting me in. Like, if something were to happen, something hard for him, I don't think he'd call me. Not because he'd call someone else. I just . . . I'm not sure he'd call anybody."

"And you'd like to be the person he would call."

"Isn't that what we all want?"

"Sure," she says simply. "But people are all different. We need each other in different ways. Maybe his way of needing you looks different than your way of needing him."

"I suppose that's true."

"Or he could just need more time. My Frank was the kind of man who took his walls down slowly. Always so stoic. But he talked when it mattered. I had to be a little more patient than I wanted to be, at least at first."

The thought gives me pause. Am I being impatient? Expecting

too much from Cameron too soon?

"Just ask yourself this question," Vivian says. "Do you want Cameron to open up to you for your sake? Or for his?"

I stop in my tracks. Vivian is coming very close to unlocking something in my brain. I feel it tickling, nudging me toward a truth I need to realize, but I'm not quite there yet. "I'm not sure I understand. Is it okay if it's both?"

"It will always be a little bit of both. Just be sure you aren't making Cameron's opening up to you, or his lack of doing so, about your own need for validation."

Whoa. There it is. And it hits me like a punch to the gut. "So, Cameron opening up to me shouldn't be about making me feel like I'm a good person—a good girlfriend."

She smiles slyly. "Good girl. You can want him to open up, to trust you, to know he can rely on you. But if you keep your focus in check, you might have a little more patience, a little more grace while he gets there."

I sigh. "So you're telling me I shouldn't give up."

She purses her lips, as if considering something. Finally, she nods and leans forward. "Can I let you in on a little secret?"

I nod.

"You told me once that you thought meeting me was the greatest stroke of good luck you've ever received."

I nod and reach out to squeeze her hand. "I do feel that way."

She shakes her head. "Honey, it wasn't luck."

"I don't understand."

"Cameron told me about you. He said, 'Vivian, she'll be your new best friend if you meet her. She knows everything there is to know about flowers, and she's the nicest person in the entire city.'"

"He said that?"

She nods. "Mm-hmm. Then he told me exactly when you pass by my house on Sunday afternoons. It only took a little bit of brainstorming to come up with a reason for me to be outside so we could meet."

I don't even know what to say. "But why would you—? Vivian, I was a stranger. And you went to all that effort."

"You weren't a stranger to Cameron. And it was obvious to me how much he cared about you. And look where it got us. You have brought so much joy to my afternoons, Darcy. I don't know anyone that can talk to me about flowers like you can."

All this time, all the help Vivian has offered, the way she has spurred me forward in my plans to change careers—I owe all of that to Cameron. I suddenly wish he was here so I could hug him. Thank him.

"Now don't be going and telling him I spilled the beans," Vivian says. "I told him I'd never tell, but judging by the look on your face, it's a good thing I did."

I smile. "I won't tell him. Honestly, I can't believe he convinced you to hang out in front of your house until I happened to pass by."

"Well, when you say it like that, I can't either. But what can I say? That man is so charming, he could probably convince me to walk across Broad Street topless."

I laugh. "You would never do such a thing."

She shoots me a saucy grin. "How do you know I haven't already?"

My jaw falls open. Vivian Abernathy is nothing like I expected. And I mean that in the best way possible.

"The point is, that man is a catch, honey," Vivian adds. "You shouldn't give up."

"Vivian, you give really good advice."

She chuckles. "Oh, I've got a degree or two. I haven't been called Dr. Abernathy in years." She drops my arms and adjusts her sweater like she's posing for a professional photo. "How did I do? Not too rusty, am I?"

I put my hands on my hips. "You're a doctor?"

"Of psychology. Went back to school after my children were raised, then had a private practice out of my home for twenty-five years before I retired."

"Vivian! You've been holding out on me. Why didn't you say anything?"

"Oh, pish. That part of my life is ancient history. I'd much rather talk about flowers." She takes my arm again, and we resume our walk.

"Well, you've done it now that you have told me. I'm going to start bringing you all my relationship questions."

"Bring them all, dear. As long as you promise to listen to me. I hate it when people ignore good advice. And I only give good advice."

I smile. "I'm sure you do."

We stop under the arched branches of a live oak and settle onto a bench near the base of the tree. "I've invited him to go home with me in a couple of weeks," I say as I pull a couple of water bottles out of my bag. I twist the top off one and offer it to Vivian. "For my brother's wedding."

"That feels big." She takes the water and takes a ladylike sip. I stifle a giggle. Only a woman like Vivian Abernathy can make drinking from a plastic water bottle look poised and polished.

I shrug. "I mean, maybe? I would have tried to find a date to take no matter what. But I guess this is bigger because I like him so much."

She holds out her hand for the water bottle lid. "Do you think you might love him?"

I consider her question—the same question I've been asking myself for days. "It's too soon for that. But I think I want to love him. I'm scared, though. What if him *not* letting me in really just means he's not feeling it?" Even as I say the words, they don't ring true. I may still have questions about our relationship, but Cameron isn't a player. He wouldn't be spending time with me, wouldn't have agreed to come to Tyler's wedding, if he wasn't feeling something.

"The way your eyes are darting around, I'm guessing you just answered your own question." She reaches over and pats my knee. "Let things play out, dear. I have a good feeling about you two."

Chapter Nineteen

Cameron

Jerome leans against the doorframe of my bedroom and watches me pack for Tyler's wedding. The college is out for spring break, and he took Evie swimming at the rec center near my house. Now, Evie sits in the center of my bed, an iPad in her lap, and giggles her way through an app that's helping her learn her numbers. "One, fwee, seben . . ." she says, clapping her chubby hands.

"One, two, three," Jerome says, and Evie nods.

"One, two, seben . . ."

He grins and shakes his head. "Angie's worried she's never going to get it," he says.

"She will. Maddox and Jackson were the same way. Jackson still can't get past seven without messing up, and he's, what, a full year older than Evie?"

"Yes, but Angie's mother insists *Angie* was doing basic addition by the time she turned three."

I chuckle. "That would not surprise me about Angie, but seriously, Evie's fine. She's perfect."

He sighs and drops onto the edge of my bed and Evie crawls over, climbing onto his back. "Wuve you, Daddy," she says.

He leans forward so Evie tumbles over his shoulder and into his arms. She squeals and giggles as she falls, then settles into his lap, her thumb in her mouth.

"Angie talked to Maggie the other day," Jerome says, eyeing me warily.

I look up. "What? Why?" Angie and Maggie know each other—would even call each other friends. Jerome has been around too long for that not to have happened. But they aren't "have casual phone conversations" kind of friends.

"She's worried about you," Jerome says simply. "She says your dad isn't doing well, and she isn't sure you're . . . processing."

I shrug dismissively. "I'm processing just fine."

"Why haven't you told us, Cam? Me, Angie. Does Darcy know?"

My heart twinges when he mentions Darcy. "What do you want me to tell you? He's got cancer. Is anyone ever doing well when they have cancer?"

"It's not that simple and you know it."

I stuff a final pair of socks into my bag. "I'm fine, all right. Dad's going to be fine."

His expression tightens, but he doesn't argue with me.

"Daddy, wisten," Evie says from beside us. "Eight, eweven, fibe . . ."

He smiles. "That's great, Evie." He eyes my suitcase as I zip it closed. "You ready for this?"

"I think so. The only person in Darcy's family I haven't met yet is Tyler, and she says he's great, so I'm not too worried."

"Things are getting pretty serious between you two, yeah?" he asks, his expression guarded.

An uneasiness spreads through my gut. Things are getting serious. I see Darcy almost every day. But if past relationships—if you can even call them that—are any indication, we're fast approaching the time when I tend to retreat, pulling back emotionally enough that women get too frustrated to hang with me.

Jerome knows this, which is exactly why he's asking.

But the judgment in his tone makes it seem like I do it intentionally. Like I'm playing women. But that's never been the case. I've just never had a relationship feel right.

Or maybe the psychology major I dated a little over a year ago—Alexis—was right and I really do have a deep-seated fear of rejection that keeps me from making myself emotionally available.

Dates with her were *awesome*.

"Things are good," I say to Jerome, as casually as I can. "Great, even."

He narrows his eyes. "You're lying."

I haul the suitcase off the bed and drop it at my feet. "I'm not. Things really are good. We're going away together for a weekend. I'm meeting her family. How is that not good?"

He shakes his head. "You're being all cagey. Not meeting my eyes. You've been here before, man. She's getting close. Taking down your walls. Just own it. This is usually when you freak out."

I pull the suitcase out of the bedroom and into the living room. "You don't know what you're talking about."

He follows. "Don't I?"

I spin around. "You're wrong. I've never been here before. I've never been with anyone like Darcy. Things are different this time."

"Which is exactly why I'm looking out for you." He hoists Evie higher in his arms. "I don't want you to screw this up."

My shoulders fall. I don't want to screw things up either, but I can't say I haven't been scared of that very thing happening. I've sensed Darcy pulling away the last few times we've been together. It terrifies me because I don't want to lose her, but I also don't know how to be what she needs.

Except, that isn't exactly it. What I don't know is how to let *her* be what I need. And she's too empathetic a person to be okay with that—with me not needing her like she wants to be needed. "I'm trying, all right?" I finally say. "I don't want to screw things up either."

He walks over and Evie reaches for me, wiggling until Jerome shifts her into my arms. She snuggles into my shoulder, one arm looping around my neck.

Sharp yearning blooms in my gut. I want this. And I'm pretty sure I want it with Darcy.

I just have to figure out how to let her all the way in.

***

Darcy has fallen asleep by the time we pull down the long drive that curves its way through Stonebrook Farm. A traffic accident that stopped traffic an hour outside of Charleston for almost two hours meant we missed the rehearsal dinner, but Tyler assured Darcy everyone was still together at the farmhouse and wouldn't leave until we arrived.

Sure enough, the massive farmhouse is all lit up and cars are parked everywhere.

There are multiple guest rooms in the farmhouse where the wedding party is all staying. Darcy will be staying in the bridal suite tonight, with Olivia and the rest of her bridesmaids, slumber party style, for a bachelorette party girls' night in, leaving me to fend for myself in one of the other guest rooms. Darcy insists Tyler, Isaac, and the rest of the guys won't let me spend the evening by myself, though I'm not sure I'd mind it if they did.

I reach over and nudge Darcy awake. "Hey," I say softly. "We're here."

She looks around for a second or two, confusion marring her features until her eyes meet mine and she smiles. "Hi," she says softly.

"Hey, sleepyhead."

She stretches. "How long did I sleep?"

"Just an hour or so."

She reaches over and slips her hand over my arm, her fingers loosely curling around my bicep. "Sorry. You were probably so bored."

"Nah. I don't mind the quiet." It's normally the truth. I generally like long, quiet drives. Right now, it's only mostly the truth.

Even if I denied it when Jerome brought it up, Dad isn't doing great—he started his latest round of chemo and he's completely wiped out—so the silence was mostly filled with my own worry.

I nearly backed out of coming to the wedding, thinking I'd be of more use at home, but Maggie insisted they were fine, said she would call me if things got worse. She's right—there isn't much I can do besides keep the boys occupied, and that's covered with her mom back in town again.

Darcy studies me closely, her gaze narrowed like she's trying to puzzle me out, like she senses there's more going on in my head than I'm telling her. I force a wider smile and unbuckle my seatbelt. "It looks like everyone else is here," I say cheerfully. "You ready to go in?"

She sighs a little too heavily. "Yeah. Let's do it."

A chorus of cheers and hellos erupts as we enter the farmhouse. Darcy's mom reaches us first, and she hugs us both. "Hello, Cameron," she says as she squeezes my shoulders. "I hear y'all hit some traffic."

"Yeah, it was rough. I'm glad you guys made it out before it hit," I say.

"Me too, though we only just missed it based on when Darcy called." She steps back, and I shake Darcy's dad's hand, then swallow as Tyler approaches. There's no mistaking his dark eyes. Darcy's eyes.

He's intimidatingly tall, and though his expression is warm and open, meeting him is ten times more stressful than it was meeting Darcy's parents. Tyler has been her person for a lot of years.

"Nice to finally meet you, man," he says, gripping my hand tightly enough that I don't mistake his meaning. *I see you. You better be good to her.*

"Yeah, likewise. Congratulations on the wedding."

His entire expression shifts as he looks over his shoulder at a woman with deep red hair. She looks up and smiles, then moves to stand beside Tyler. "Thanks. This is Olivia."

She reaches out and gives me a hug. "Darcy has told us so much about you. Thanks for being here." She and Tyler exchange a look so full of unfettered love that my chest tightens. I rub the spot and look at Darcy who has been consumed by a pod of enthusiastic women. They've formed a tight circle around her, and she appears to be telling some kind of story, talking with her hands, her expression animated; she is literally glowing under their attention.

The introductions continue until I've met everyone in the room. Tyler's best friend Isaac, and his wife, Rosie. Isaac's sister Dani, and her husband, Alex. Isaac and Dani's parents are also around, as well as Olivia's entire family, including her very famous movie-star brother, Flint Hawthorne. Even with the advanced warning Darcy gave me, I'm still proud of myself when I maintain at least a measure of nonchalance when I meet him.

Soon, I'm settled into a chair next to the oversized fireplace, a drink in my hand. It's full warm down in Charleston, the weather already inching toward summer temperatures, but up here in the mountains, it's still cool at night, so the fireplace is roaring, filling the room with comfortable warmth.

I try not to feel intimidated by the collection of men filling the chairs around me, but it's nearly impossible not to. The breadth of experience and talent in the room is unusual. Flint and Isaac are one thing, with their very successful careers in the public eye, but the rest of these men are just as accomplished, excelling in their respective fields. I suddenly feel like the guy with the kind of job you're only supposed to have while you're waiting for your real job to start.

Still, this is a game I know how to play.

When Olivia's brother Lennox sits down beside me and starts up a conversation about fine dining restaurants in Charleston—he's a chef—I start to relax. I haven't eaten at half the restaurants we discuss, but I've been making food recommendations to tourists long enough, I have half the city's menus memorized. Lennox nods along as I talk about the best shrimp and grits on the peninsula. "It's got to be Poogan's Porch," I say. "Possibly SNOB—Slightly North of Broad, depending on how you feel about gravy."

"Excellent. You're making me want to take a trip to the city. You've always lived there?"

I hesitate, but only for a moment. "It's been home for a long time."

It's the kind of half-truth I'm used to telling—one that leads people to conclusions that may or may not be true. It's always been easy to talk like this, to keep people at arm's length, but this time, it doesn't settle well. It's Darcy's influence probably, and I feel a sudden desire to do better for her. "I grew up in a small town about an hour outside the city," I add. "But I went to school in Charleston, and I've lived there ever since."

Lennox nods. "Right on. There's something to small towns, isn't there? I'm getting ready to move back here from Charlotte. There's a part of me that's hesitant to leave the city, but . . . I don't know, man. I'm looking forward to a slower pace for once."

"Yeah. Definitely. I make it back to see my family a few times a month. I can't find quiet in Charleston like I can at home."

The conversation is completely benign and inconsequential. All I did was admit to being from Walterboro. But it feels like a victory all the same.

Half an hour later, a text from Darcy pulls my attention away from a conversation I've mostly just been listening to between Tyler, Flint, and Isaac. They're geeking out about movie plots, debating whether an element woven into the latest Marvel movie was meant to be foreshadowing for a future storyline.

"I can end this once and for all," Flint says as he pulls out his phone. "I'm texting the director. I've got his number right here."

"Well, that's convenient," Isaac says.

"It's the worst." Brody, another of Olivia's brothers, tosses a pillow at Flint. "We can't just talk and speculate about movies like normal people. He's always got to play his celebrity card and get us the *real* answers."

Flint deflects the pillow with a grin, his thumbs still flying over his phone. "You didn't seem to mind my celebrity card when Scarlett Johansson called you to wish you a happy birthday."

"Best day of my life," Brody deadpans. "Hands down."

I half listen as the conversation continues, my eyes on Darcy's text.

Darcy: Are you busy? Can you sneak upstairs a sec?

Tyler is the only person who seems to notice me leaving. He raises his eyebrows when we make eye contact, but he doesn't say anything to stop me, so I lift my chin in a gesture I hope says *I'm cool* and head to the stairs.

When I reach the top, Darcy darts out of a shadowed alcove and pulls me back in with her. There is a window behind us, filling one of the giant dormers that line the front of the house. A low bookshelf stretches across the space under the window, with a padded bench on top. Beside the shelf, there is a round rug, an overstuffed chair, and a reading lamp.

"It's perfect, right?" Darcy says. "If I lived here, this would be my favorite place."

"This feels like a very Darcy place." I wrap my arms around her back and hold her against me. "How are you?"

"It's good to see everyone," she says. "How are you? Are they being nice to you?" Her hands slip up my chest and clasp around my neck.

"Everyone is great." I nuzzle my nose into her hair. "I mean, I'd rather stay up here with you, but . . ."

"Hmm, my thoughts exactly." She tilts her head up for a kiss that I willingly give. Every kiss with Darcy still fills me with wonder. Like I'm the luckiest man alive for being the one she chose. I pull her a little closer and she lets out a soft moan, her fingers moving up to tangle in my hair. The desire coursing through me fights against a new feeling that suddenly threatens to take over. Something like *fear*. It's hard not to feel like I might lose her, like this will all just . . . slip away from me.

I don't want to lose her. Don't want to mess this up.

"Hey," Darcy says softly, breaking the kiss. "Are you okay? You tensed up."

There is so much that I want to say.

I'm in love with you.

I don't want to lose you.

I don't want you to realize I don't deserve you.

"You know you can talk to me, right?" she says. "Whatever it is."

A surge of frustration courses through me; I am not frustrated with her—never with her. I hate that this is so hard for me. That opening my mouth and saying the things that I feel is so difficult. She deserves more than that. More than my silence. More than my inability to let her in.

I feel the wall going up even now. If I don't let her in, if I never say the things, well, then losing her won't hurt near as much.

I grip her shoulders and kiss her again, harder this time, pushing it full of all the words I don't know how to say. "I don't deserve you,

Darcy," I finally whisper. "I'm not . . . I'm not as good at this as I need to be."

She moves her hands to my cheeks. "Just talk to me," she says. "You're so good at talking, Cameron. Why can't you talk to me?"

Her question feels heavy, like it's something she's been thinking a while but hasn't had the courage to say.

I close my eyes and lean my head against the wall behind me, the push and pull of my emotions wearing me out. How did we even get here? Except, we've been on our way here for days. Even Jerome saw the warning signs.

Darcy wants more than I know how to give. She deserves more than I know how to give. She's hanging on, but for how much longer? The frequency of her probing looks, the ones that say *please tell me what you're thinking* is increasing.

In theory, I know exactly how to fix things. In execution? I don't know if I can.

"I should get back to Olivia," Darcy finally says. Her hands slip down to my chest and rest there, palms flat. I press my hands over hers and hold them there. *Don't give up on me. I'm trying. I'll keep trying.*

"I'll see you in the morning?" she says. The moonlight skirting in through the wide dormer window dances across her cheekbones. *God, she's beautiful.*

"Have fun, okay?" I say.

She nods and smiles, but it doesn't hide the pain lurking behind her eyes. She kisses me on the cheek before darting away, leaving me alone in the darkness.

I contemplate heading straight for my room but worry it would seem rude to cut out early, so I slowly make my way down the stairs.

Tyler is at the foot of the stairs, leaning casually against the wall, his hands pushed into his pockets. He raises his eyebrows when I hit the bottom step. "Have fun?" he says simply.

I clear my throat, suddenly feeling like I'm back in middle school when the principal caught me kissing Sophie Gellar in the stairwell. "We, um, we were just talking."

He holds up his hands. "Hold up. That came out wrong. I'm not that brother." He runs a hand across the back of his neck. "Do you want to take a quick walk?"

I nod, well aware there is no possible answer to give here but yes. "Sure."

I follow him down the long hallway that leads to the farmhouse's front door, grabbing my jacket from the coat rack on our way out. At the bottom of the porch steps, Tyler makes a right and I fall into step beside him.

"Want to meet Penelope?" he asks.

"The goat?"

He nods, his eyes trained forward.

"Um, sure." We continue walking in silence, and I start to wonder if this is some sort of intimidation strategy. The farther we get away from the main farmhouse, the more uneasy I start to feel. Based on the outbuildings that surround us, and the smell, we're on the actual *farm* half of Stonebrook. There are probably all kinds of tools and things out this way. Shovels, hammers, scythes. Wait, farmers don't use scythes anymore, do they? But a shovel would knock me out well enough.

It's an irrational thought, but with Tyler staying quiet, my brain seems plenty willing to fill in the gaps with nonsense.

Lots of land out here where someone could hide a body, my brain thinks.

Oh, great, brain. That's helpful. Let's stay on this path. Turn Darcy's brother into a murderer. That definitely won't end badly.

Tyler opens the sliding barn door of the largest building we've passed on the property and flips on a light, illuminating the corridor that runs through the center of the barn, extending from one end to the other. The air smells like hay and something else—goat, probably—but it isn't an overly offensive smell.

We pass a stall that houses a mama and three goats that look like they can't be more than a few days old.

"Born yesterday," Tyler says. He reaches out and scratches the mama goat's ears, then moves on to another stall a few paces down. A snow-white goat with a red bandana around her neck jumps up, her front hooves on the door, and bleats a hello to Tyler. I immediately recognize her from Tyler's videos, though this version of her is bigger than she is in most of what I've watched. "This is Penelope," he says.

I reach out and scratch the end of her nose, and she tries to eat my sleeve.

"Here," Tyler says, pulling a carrot out of his pocket.

I eye him as I take it. "You randomly keep carrots on you?"

"I was hoping we could take a walk. And this is normally where I go when I need to clear my head."

I nod, holding out the carrot for Penelope, who happily snatches it out of my hand. "Makes sense."

"So, Darcy," Tyler says, leaning against the stall wall.

I raise my eyebrows, not sure how he wants me to respond.

"I think she's in love with you, man."

These are not the words I expect. Darcy and I haven't said the words to each other yet, though I've been thinking them for a few weeks now. What I can't figure out is why Tyler's words sound like some kind of warning. "I, um . . . I don't know what to say."

"Listen. It wouldn't surprise me if she's fallen for you faster than you've fallen for her. She's always been like that with her feelings. All in. When she's passionate about something, or someone, she just goes for it."

"Yeah, that sounds about right," I say softly.

"You don't have to tell me how you feel about her," Tyler says.

"You don't owe that to me, and I'm not trying to make you uncomfortable. But I care about my sister. And she doesn't think *you're* all in."

I look up. "She said that?"

"Tonight, actually. To Olivia." He pulls out his phone and glances at the screen. "About forty-five minutes ago."

I stare at Penelope, watching as she jumps up and nibbles at Tyler's sleeve. I don't know what to say. I love Darcy. I know that much. What I don't know is whether I'm capable of being what she deserves.

"All I'm asking is that you don't string her along, all right? If you aren't all in? Cut her loose, man. Don't do her like that."

I shake my head and swallow the emotion building in my throat. "I wouldn't do that."

He studies me closely, his expression saying he isn't sure he believes me, but then he nods. "I'm glad to hear it." He claps me on the back. "I've got to get back inside. You're welcome to stay out here as long as you like. Penelope's a good listener. Just get the light and close the door when you leave?"

I nod. "Yeah. Sure."

I stare at Penelope as Tyler retreats. She nuzzles my hand where it curls around the top of the stall wall, the whiskers on her lips tickling my knuckles.

"Cameron?"

I look up to see Tyler standing at the end of the corridor by the barn door.

"Darcy's a good listener too," he says. And then he disappears into the darkness.

Chapter Twenty

Cameron

I don't see Darcy when I wake up the next morning.

She's already with the florist, arranging the flowers that adorn the massive pavilion where the wedding will take place. The flowers are her design, or at least inspired by her ideas. I can only imagine how happy it's making her to see her vision come to life.

I spend the morning hiking with the rest of the guys—though Tyler won't let us venture off of Stonebrook's property. "The last thing I want to do is have my wedding ruined by one of you fools falling off the mountain and breaking your legs," he says, instead pointing us in the direction of a three-mile loop that circles the perimeter of the farm. The hike doesn't disappoint—the views are unbelievable, the cool spring air invigorating, and the flowers blooming everywhere remind me of Darcy.

I don't see her until just before the wedding. She's standing with the other bridesmaids at the back of the pavilion. I've already taken my seat next to a couple of Dani's friends from New York. If I remember the introductions from last night correctly, the man on my left is the designer responsible for the bridesmaid's dresses.

I could almost kiss him for his brilliance. I've never seen anything as beautiful as Darcy in her dress. The rest of the wedding party could be wearing burlap for all the attention I pay them. She is all I see. *All I want.*

I just have to find a way to tell her.

The desire to do so presses on me with increasing urgency throughout the entire ceremony. It only grows when the reception begins, and we get to dance. We still haven't had the chance to really talk, with all the wedding party stuff she's been involved in, but I hold her close to me now and whisper in her ear. "Your flowers look beautiful."

She looks up, her face beaming. She glances around the crowded dance floor and bites her lip. Then, as if having made a decision, she tugs me off the floor and away from the crowd. "They do, don't they?" she finally says. We stop just outside the circle of light spilling out of the pavilion. It's quieter here, quiet enough for us to really talk. She leans up on her toes and kisses me quickly. "I've missed you," she says. "And I've been wanting to do that all day."

My phone buzzes in my pocket, but I ignore it. This moment is too important.

"The florist had so many positive things to say," Darcy says.

"Of course she did."

"I mean, I knew they were pretty on paper, but this is even better than I imagined." She looks toward the reception tent dotted with the massive floral arrangements she breathed into being. She could probably name every single flower in each one and explain her reasons for picking it. I suddenly want her to even if I won't understand a thing she's saying, just so I can listen to her talking about something she loves. My phone buzzes a second time, and I tense, a pulse of worry shooting through me. Maggie said she would call if things got worse.

Darcy looks toward my pocket. "Do you need to get that?"

I shake my head, wanting to stay in this moment with her a little longer. I've been working up the courage to talk to her all day. If it doesn't happen now—

"Darcy, I—"

My phone rings a third time, and the words die in my throat.

"Darcy!" a voice calls from inside the reception tent. "Can you come for a picture?"

She looks at me and bites her lip, a question in her eyes. "Go on. I'll catch up in a second," I say, already reaching for my phone.

"Who is it?" she says, her expression suddenly clouded with worry. "Cameron, is it about your dad?"

The ringing ends before I can answer it, but all three missed calls were from Maggie. I shut off the screen and drop the phone back into my pocket. "It's probably nothing," I say. I curl my hands into fists to keep them from trembling.

"Darcy!" the voice calls again, and she closes her eyes, her brow furrowed.

"It's all right. Go. I'll return this phone call and then come and find you."

She huffs out a sigh. "Fine. But if anything is wrong, Cameron, come and get me. We can leave right now if we need to."

I nod. "Okay."

She disappears back into the crowded reception tent, and I turn in the opposite direction, moving several paces away before returning Maggie's call.

She answers on the first ring. "Hey. I'm so sorry to call." Her voice is tired and laced with obvious worry.

"It's fine. What's going on?"

"I don't know, Cam." Her voice trembles. "He just got so sick, and his color got really bad. I called an ambulance. I sent him on so I could calm the boys down, and now I'm driving to the hospital myself. I didn't want to ask you to come home, but I knew you'd want to be here."

"No, I do. I'm glad you called. I'll leave right now."

"Okay. The ambulance is taking him to Colleton Medical, but I expect we'll probably end up over in Charleston so his cancer doctors can be involved."

"I'll call you from the road and find out where you are," I say. "Would you rather I go home to be with the boys?"

"No, my mom's there, and they're probably sleeping by now anyway. I'm sorry you're having to drive so late."

"No, it's okay. I couldn't sleep now anyway."

"Please tell Darcy I'm so sorry. Will you bring her with you?"

I turn and look toward the reception tent. Darcy is standing with Tyler on one side, his arm draped over her shoulder, and Olivia on the other. If I tell her what's happened, she'll want to come with me. I know she will. But navigating all this . . . I've always done things like this on my own.

I waffle back and forth, the earlier certainty I felt about letting Darcy in evaporating into the cool mountain air. Why would she want this? Why would she want to go through this with me?

"She has family who can drive her back to Charleston," I say. "I don't want to make her leave early just to sit in a hospital with me."

"Cameron, don't do that," Maggie says. "She'll want to be with you."

I turn my back on the reception lights and start walking up the hill toward the farmhouse. "I'll be there soon, all right? I'll call when I'm close. But you call me as soon as you know what's going on."

On the way to the farmhouse, I run into Darcy's mother. "Cameron, is everything all right?" she asks. "You look like you've seen a ghost."

"Actually, I need to go. There's an emergency with my family, and I need to get on the road immediately."

"Oh, gracious. I'm so sorry to hear it. Is there anything I can do?"

"If you could make sure Darcy makes it back to Charleston, I would really appreciate it. I don't want to make her leave early; it's more important that she be here."

She nods. "Of course, but are you sure? I think she'd want—"

"I'm sure," I say, cutting her off.

She frowns, and a surge of regret pulses through me. "I'm sorry. I'm not myself right now. I just . . . I really need to head out."

Her face softens. "It's all right. I'll take care of Darcy. But you better keep us posted, all right? Whatever it is, Darcy is going to want to know what's going on. We all will."

It is an offering—one I don't deserve with the way I just treated her.

She reaches out and squeezes my hand. "Go on, then. Drive safe."

I nod and continue on to the farmhouse without another word. It only takes a couple of minutes to grab my bags and toss them into my car. I don't even pause long enough to change out of my suit. Once I'm in the car, I *do* pause long enough to send Darcy a quick text.

Cameron: I'm so sorry, Darcy. Something came up with my dad, and I had to leave.

I debate about saying something more. She deserves more, I know that much is true. But am I the man who can give it to her?

I tap out one more line. It's the most I can offer in my current state. I can only hope it will be enough to keep her from giving up on me completely.

I'm trying, but I'm not as good at this as I want to be. I'll call you as soon as I can.

Chapter Twenty-One

Darcy

No matter how many times I read Cameron's text, or how many times Mom repeats what he told her on his way out, I can't make sense of things. Why would he just leave? Did he honestly think I'd be able to enjoy the reception with him gone? Does he not understand that if something is wrong with his dad, the only place I want to be is with him?

I can't say I didn't see it coming. I've sensed from the beginning that Cameron has been struggling to truly let me in, to let himself need me. You would think with all that warning, this wouldn't hurt so much.

But I'm gutted. Heartbroken. And worst of all, *so, so worried about him*.

I should be there. Wherever he is.

At first, I contemplated going after him. Borrowing Mom's car and tearing down the highway to catch him. But my pride wouldn't let me. He left me at my brother's wedding reception with nothing but a text to explain. *He left me.*

It feels like he pulled my heart right out of my chest and drove it away, only to toss it out on the highway somewhere.

Mom reaches over and squeezes my knee. We're sitting together on the window seat at the top of the stairs, my head resting on her shoulder. "You going to be okay?" she asks softly.

I sniff. "I don't know, Mom. This really hurts."

She nods. "I'm sure it does, baby. But he did say he'd call. And his daddy might be dying. That's enough to make a man act rashly. If he's worth it, you need to hold on and love him through it."

I sit up a little taller. "I know that. I do. And I don't want anything to happen to his dad. But am I just supposed to sit around and wait? Only connect with him on his terms? What about what I need?"

Cameron's text pops into my head. *I'm not as good at this as I want to be.* I pull up the text and show it to Mom. "What do you think this means?"

She reads it silently then hands the phone back. "I'm no expert, baby, but I think he sounds like a man with a few emotional battle scars. He says he's trying. Is that enough?"

I shake my head. "Tonight, it wasn't. He should have found me. He should have given me the chance to go with him. It should have been my choice, not his."

"That's fair," she says simply. "But no relationship is going to be without its stumbling blocks. I think it's probably up to you to decide how long and hard you stumble." She wraps an arm around my shoulders. "Just remember, loving has always been easy for you. You wear your heart on your sleeve and you give it quickly and generously. Not everyone is the same."

"Yeah, yeah, a golden retriever puppy. I know."

Tyler appears in the hallway before us, a bag slung over his shoulder. "Hey."

We both look up. "I thought you already left," I say, wiping my eyes. I watched them leave—we all did. Apparently, they only left for the farmhouse.

"We did, but we took a slight detour to . . ." He clears his throat. "Um, to change clothes." His lip twitches, and I fight the urge to roll my eyes.

"Is that what kids are calling it these days?" Mom says with a smirk.

Tyler stifles a chuckle and pushes his hands into his pockets. "We're heading out right now. Isaac and Rosie are driving us to the airport." He gives me a pointed look. "You okay?"

I shrug. "Not really. But it's nothing for you to worry about now. I will be."

He hardly looks convinced, but what choice does he have? "All right. I'll call you when I get home?"

I nod, and a sudden impulse surges through me. "Actually, can I ask you something really quick?"

He pauses, his hand resting on the stair banister, and gives me his full attention.

"You remember the flower show I told you about?"

He nods. "What about it?"

I take a deep breath. "I think I'm ready to truly make a go of it. I've been talking about it for too many years. I need to just do it. Which means I need a little money for start-up costs. It won't be a ton. Just enough for business cards, maybe a website—Rosie already agreed to help me with that part—and some marketing materials for the show." I bite my lip. "Do you think you could help me out?"

"Absolutely," Tyler says without a moment's hesitation. "I'd love to help."

A pulse of pride pushes through my chest, and I smile the first genuine smile I've managed since Cameron disappeared. "Yeah?"

He hurries over and wraps me in a hug. "I'm proud of you, Darcy. You're going to be amazing at this." He offers Mom and me a quick goodbye, then disappears down the stairs. Seconds later, the thump of the front door swinging shut echoes through the now-quiet house.

Mom nudges me with her shoulder. "You could have asked me for the money, Darcy," she says quietly, a touch of hurt in her voice.

"Mom, I know." I turn to fully face her and take both her hands in mine. "I know that. But you paid for my education. It didn't feel fair to ask you for anything else, not when I'm trying to stop using the degree you paid for. Plus, Tyler has it. And he's always offering to help."

Her expression softens. "What changed? What gave you the courage to do it?"

I shrug. "Cameron, I think. Both because he's always been so encouraging whenever I talk about it, and because seeing him do his job? He's so passionate about it. He's better at it than me for a lot of reasons, but mostly because he loves it so much. And I want to love what I do that much too."

She lifts her hand and cups my cheek. "I can't wait to see what you accomplish."

"Thanks, Mama."

"Welp, I'm going to bed. You gonna ride home with me and Phil in the morning?"

"If you'll have me. Daddy's leaving too early for me to want to ride with him."

She nods and we say our goodnights, Mom issuing one final motherly reminder to not stay up too late.

I shouldn't have kept *her* up so late, but I appreciated the company. With Cameron gone, Tyler and Olivia off on their honeymoon, and most everyone else in the wedding party coupled off and snuggled away in their rooms, unless I want to go downstairs

LOVE IN BLOOM

and hang out with Olivia's brothers, I'm on my own. Even with the lure of a celebrity like Flint Hawthorne—he was sitting by the fireplace downstairs when I came in—I don't want to be anywhere Cameron isn't.

My heart stretches as a pang of loneliness fills me brim full. I pull out my phone to read Cameron's last text one more time, but I'm distracted when a new message from Rachel pops up.

Rachel: Tyler just called me ON HIS WEDDING NIGHT which must mean he's really worried about you. You okay?

I sigh and key out a response.

Darcy: Are you busy?

My phone immediately rings with her call. I settle into the window seat and give her the rundown of what happened. She doesn't have much to add but sympathy. She's always been firmly in Cameron's corner, but I can hear her confidence waning.

"I don't want to tell you to give up, D," she finally says. "You know I love you and Cameron together. And your mom is right. With whatever is going on with his dad, he probably deserves a little grace. It isn't like he up and left to go off on a guys' trip or something."

"No, I know. You're right about that." She is right. She and Mom, both. Whatever happened, Cameron has the right to process his grief in his own way. If that means being alone with his family, I can't fault him that. I want to be patient, to give him room. But I also crave connection. And I don't know how to stop wondering if the simplest answer isn't the truth.

The connection is missing because he doesn't care about me, doesn't love me enough to fight for it.

Chapter Twenty-Two

Darcy

By the time I make it back to Charleston Sunday afternoon, I still haven't heard from Cameron. I want to stay mad at him, angry that he left without saying goodbye, without telling me what's going on with his dad.

But the longer I go without hearing from him, the more my anger morphs into worry. I don't have any tours scheduled, so I don't have anything to do but pace around my apartment and stress.

Rachel barges into my apartment without knocking just before six. "Where's your phone?" she says, not even stopping to say hello.

I freeze in my tracks. "What?"

"Your phone. Where is it?" She's wearing her painting smock and has a smear of yellow paint on her cheek.

"Why do you need my phone?"

"Because your pacing is driving me insane. You're worse than Matilda, Darcy. You have to call him. Call him, or I will."

I roll my eyes and fold my arms across my chest. "Her name is Mary Beth," I say with a pout.

"Oh, good grief. Where is it? I'm not lying about this."

My eyes dart to the coffee table in front of the couch where my phone is hiding under my sketchbook. I look away, hoping Rachel didn't notice the direction of my gaze. I don't doubt for a single second that she'll call Cameron, and there's no telling what she'll say to him.

Rachel lunges for the coffee table at the same time I do. She grabs my phone first, using her height advantage to hold it over my head.

"Give me that!" I say as I jump to reach it. "You can't . . . *oof* . . . call . . . *oof* . . . him." I climb onto the couch and lean onto Rachel's back, wrapping one arm around her shoulders while the other reaches for my phone.

She steps away from the couch, taking me with her. "Are you going to call him?" she says, her voice a near grunt from the strain of literally having me draped across her shoulders.

I finally wrap my fingers around the phone and pull it from her grasp, knocking us both off balance. We crash into the chair, which catches Rachel, but I topple all the way to the floor in between the chair and the table.

I am flat on my back on the hardwood, and I'm probably going to have a bruise on my butt in the morning, but I have my phone, so I'm calling it a victory. The rest of my life might be a complete disaster, but at least I have this. My best friend is *not* currently yelling through the phone at my absentee boyfriend.

A surge of laughter bubbles up and my shoulders start to shake. Or . . . wait.

I think I'm actually crying.

I press my hands to my cheeks. *Yes. Yes, those are definitely tears.*

Rachel nudges my foot. "Are you laughing or crying?"

I sniff. "I'm laughing," I say through a hiccupped sob.

"Oh, honey," she says, falling to the floor beside me. She has to shift the chair out of the way to do it, but she manages and pulls me into a sitting position so she can wrap her arms around me. "You're going to get through this." She rubs her hand up and down my back.

I sniff again and wipe my nose on my sleeve. It's either my sleeve or hers; we're close, but not that close.

"I don't know if I will, Rach," I say weakly.

"What if you just text him?" she says simply. "You're worried about him. Give him the chance to give you an update."

I nod and turn on my phone so I can pull up his last message, but I'm totally distracted by an email notification that's sitting on my home screen.

"Oh my word." I look at Rachel. "I've got an email from *Southern Traditions and Travel.*"

Her eyes go wide. "What does it say?"

I look back to my phone, opening the message and quickly scanning its contents. "I got it," I finally say. "The feature. They want to interview me next week."

"Wow," she says. "That's big. But... do you even want it anymore?"

I sink back against the front of the sofa. "I don't know. I mean, I'm flattered. A part of me wants to do it just because it's an honor to have been chosen."

"But it doesn't make sense for your business, does it? You'd cancel *all* your tours if you could do it and still get by. Don't tell me you wouldn't."

"No, you're right. I would." I close out my phone and set it on the floor in front of me. "I have to tell them no."

"Yeah, you do." Her voice filled with conviction and optimism. "Because you're a woman who knows what you want, and you're going after it."

"I am."

"You're going to have the business that you want, you've already got the very best friend on the whole entire planet." She nudges my phone toward me. "And now you're going to text your man so the best friend you love so much doesn't murder you in your sleep."

I pick up my phone. "Right. I can do this."

My fingers hover over the keyboard, but I have no idea what to type. I'm concerned about his dad, but if my message is only concerned, will that make it seem like I'm not mad at him for leaving? My worry is bigger than my anger, but I also don't want to let him off the hook.

"I don't know how to do this."

Rachel holds out her hand. "Here."

I pull the phone closer to me, and she rolls her eyes. "I won't send it until you read it." I let her snatch the phone out of my hands and watch as she keys in a message.

Any news? Would love an update on your dad. We have a lot to talk about.

"That's good," I say. "Go ahead and send it."

"There. Done." She turns off the phone and tosses it on the couch behind us. "Have you reached out to Jerome to see if he knows anything?"

"I don't have his number. Though I could probably find him at the college tomorrow."

"That's what I would do if you haven't heard from Cameron by then. Then you can decide a next step."

I nod. It feels good to have a plan.

"Now . . . you need to focus on something else," Rachel says.

"Not possible," I grumble. "Unless it's food. I could probably focus on food."

"Food it is." Rachel stands and pulls me to my feet beside her. "How about some very delicious very deep-fried Dave's Seafood?"

"Oh, absolutely yes. I want extra hushpuppies."

***

Jerome saves me a trip to the college.

He calls first thing Monday morning; he tracked down my number on my website after correctly assuming I'd want an update on Cameron's dad. He's in the ICU with pneumonia, a result of his weakened immune system, but the doctors are confident that, with oxygen and antibiotics, he'll pull through.

I am relieved that Jake is still with us, that they think he's going to heal, but knowing that Cameron told Jerome about his dad's condition when he hasn't told me... it's like I'm back in North Carolina, the pain of him leaving me behind slicing right through me all over again.

"I'm very good at nagging, Darcy," Jerome says, trying to make me feel better. "I practically forced the information out of him."

"But I was there, Jerome. We were together when he got the call. He should have just told me."

"He should have. You're right about that."

I pull a pair of sneakers out of my closet. I need to leave soon if I'm going to make it to the gift shop in time for my morning tour. "I just don't understand why he's pushing me away. I mean, I feel guilty for making anything about me when his dad is so sick, but I want to help. To be there for him."

"Or what?" Jerome asks.

"What do you mean?"

"I mean that if this is a dealbreaker for you—the distance, the lack of communication—Cameron might need to understand that. He needs to know what's really on the line."

"And that's me?"

"Only you can decide," he says. "Listen. It wouldn't matter if my father, mother, brother, sister, and fifteen cousins were all in the hospital. If I left Angie somewhere without adequate explanation, I'd be sleeping on the dog bed with Bailey for the rest of my life, *if* she decided to let me live in the first place. You have to take care of your own heart too, Darcy. It isn't only about what he needs."

It's comforting to hear someone validate my own disappointment instead of encouraging me to be patient, to give Cameron grace because of his dad's illness. If a relationship is really going to work, it can't just be one person that's doing all the compromising.

Still, I can't deny how I feel.

"I love him, Jerome."

The tone of his voice softens. "Then hold him accountable. Make him step up and take care of you the way you deserve."

Jerome's words stay with me all through my morning tour and into the afternoon. He's right, but I also know if my dad were in the hospital, I wouldn't know which end is up. Cameron shouldn't have left me. He should be talking to me. But now is probably not the time to march into the hospital and demand a define-the-relationship talk.

I waffle back and forth over what to do. Give him the space he clearly wants? Go support him like I would want to be supported? Show up with food and clean clothes and camp out until he realizes he really does need me?

I settle on something in the middle.

It's an excellent plan.

A practical plan.

One I feel perfectly capable of executing. Right up until Wednesday evening—I'm proud of myself for giving him two whole days of space before making a move—when the elevator doors slide open on the seventh floor of the hospital and Cameron is standing directly in front of me.

My heart jumps into my throat and my fight or flight reflexes kick in, this time screaming for *flight*. I can't do this. Can't see him. Can't talk to him. Can't keep myself from wrapping my arms around him and loving him.

But I'm already here.

I'm holding sandwiches.

I can't back out now.

"Darcy," he says. "You're here."

He looks terrible. Dark circles rim his eyes, his clothes are rumpled, and his face is shadowed with scruffy, unkempt facial hair. He looks like he hasn't slept in days. He probably *hasn't*.

I step off the elevator and hold out the bags I'm holding. "I brought food," I say simply. "From Brown Dog Deli. And a few stuffed animals for Jackson and Maddox. I know they probably aren't here, but maybe the next time they are, you could pass them along."

He nods and takes the bags, peeking into the one from the deli.

"I got you a fried green tomato BLT."

He offers me a small smile. "I was going down to the cafeteria, but this sounds so much better."

"Good. There's enough for Maggie, too. I wasn't sure what she likes, so I picked out a few of my favorites."

"I'm sure she'll appreciate it, whatever it is." He holds my gaze, the warmth in his eyes triggering an ache deep in my belly. For a tiny moment, I let myself revel in how good it is to see him. It's only been four days, but my worry stretched that time into an eternity.

"Thank you for this," he says. "Really."

I shake my head. "I was happy to do it." I push my hands into my back pockets and rock back onto my heels. "How's he doing?"

"Better today," Cameron says. "They think they'll be able to move him out of the ICU and into a step-down unit by tomorrow."

"That's good news."

"Yeah. Yeah, it is."

I bite my lip. "And Maggie's okay?"

He nods. "She's the toughest of all of us."

We stand there in awkward silence for almost a full minute, the air between us heavy with all the words we aren't saying.

I should go. Leave him to eat his sandwich in peace. But I haven't said everything I came to say.

"So, um, I heard from *Southern Traditions and Travel*," I finally manage, and his eyes dart up to mine. "You got the magazine feature, Cameron."

He narrows his eyes. "I don't understand."

I scrunch up my nose. "Technically, I got it first," I say. "Which is unbelievable considering I've canceled as many tours as I've given this month. They were hoping to feature a woman—that's the only reason they picked me—but I convinced them to feature you instead." I hold my hands up. "I explained you were in the middle of a family thing—I didn't say more than I absolutely had to, I promise—and they agreed to delay your interview a couple of weeks. You should get an email with all the info soon if you haven't already, but I wanted you to know how things went down in case they mentioned me."

He pushes his hands into his pockets. "Darcy, you didn't have to give up the feature for me," he says, even as gratitude shines in his eyes.

I shrug. "I know. And I didn't, really. I gave it up because I don't need it. Tyler has agreed to help me cover start-up costs, and Vivian is letting me use flowers out of her greenhouse for the flower show. I'm doing this thing—this different thing—so the magazine feature doesn't really make sense for me anymore. Besides, you deserve it more than I do."

He takes a step toward me, then glances over his shoulder toward the glass-enclosed waiting room behind us. "Do you want to stay with me for a little bit?" he asks, a flicker of hope lighting his expression. "Maybe share a sandwich?"

Pain rips through my gut. I want to say yes. To take him in my arms and pretend like none of this ever happened. But I can't do it.

"I can't stay," I say softly.

He seems to sense that what I really mean is *I won't stay.*

"Darcy, I'm sor—"

"Stop," I say, cutting him off. "Don't apologize. Not here. Not after I came to you, showed up with food and drinks and . . ." I tug at the ends of my hair. "It's too easy. And I'm still mad enough about you leaving without talking to me, about you completely ghosting me for the past four days, that I *can't* make this easy for you."

"Darcy, I wasn't trying to hurt you."

"I know that. But you did hurt me. And I still can't figure out why. I would have been here with you, Cameron. Supporting you. Taking care of you." I hesitate. "*Loving* you." I shake my head and take a step backward. "I'm ready to be all in," I say. "That's what I want. *You* are what I want. But I can't do this unless you are too."

I spam-push the down button on the wall between the elevators.

I have to get out of here.

I can't be more than three seconds away from tears falling, and I do not want that to happen with Cameron watching.

"Darcy," Cameron says, pain etched in his voice.

I shake my head, steeling my courage, remembering Jerome's counsel to hold Cameron accountable. "Just get through this thing with your family," I say. "They need you the most right now."

"Then what?" Cameron says.

I shrug. "Then figure out what you want."

Chapter Twenty-Three

Cameron

I have an email from the magazine by the following morning. After Darcy's explanation of my circumstances and her glowing review, they're excited to include me in their magazine feature and hope I'll accept.

One particular line gives me extra pause. *Darcy spoke highly of your commitment to truth and historical integrity and your ability to entertain without sacrificing facts.*

I'm not surprised that she was so generous. That's just the way Darcy is.

And she wants to be with me.

Well. Maybe. Every hour that passes, I grow more and more convinced that she's probably already changed her mind. I hurt her. Shut her out. And why?

The answer pulses deep in my mind. I can sense it hovering, close enough that if I reach a little deeper, I'll see it. Embrace it. Process it.

I have been at this crossroads before. And I have run from the answer like it's a pack of starving lions and I'm a gazelle. But Darcy makes everything different. She makes me want the answers I've been running from. If the lions are answers, I'm a gazelle hobbling on three bloody legs . . . . wait.

My metaphor clearly needs work, but the point is, I don't want to hide anymore. I don't want to escape.

I slowly climb the stairs to my dad's hospital room. He's officially out of the ICU and is slowly regaining his strength. After a few more weeks of recovery, his doctors will tweak his chemotherapy and he'll resume his treatment. But for now, it's nice that he can focus on getting better.

Dad has had cancer a long time, if you count months collectively, both times he's been sick. But I have never been so scared of losing him. We've never come so close.

Maggie is coming out of his hospital room as I approach. She smiles when she sees me. "Hey! Look at you. You're all cleaned up."

I run a hand across my freshly shaven cheeks. Up until this morning, I hadn't shaved since before Tyler and Olivia's wedding. It became weirdly symbolic for me. Not shaving as long as Dad was in the ICU. Symbolic . . . and *itchy*. I also haven't run a single tour, eaten a single meal made outside of a restaurant or the hospital cafeteria, or washed a single article of clothing, but who's keeping score, really?

And I haven't called Darcy.

She probably should have given up on me. Instead, she came to the hospital laden with gifts and food.

I don't deserve her. But I also don't think I can live without her.

Now I just have to figure out what to do about it.

"How's he doing today?" I ask Maggie, tilting my head toward Dad's door.

"His spirits are up," she says. "He hates the bed, hates being bound to it. But I promised I'd bring Maddox up to play checkers with him tonight, so he's looking forward to that."

I smile. "Are you going to get the boys now?"

She nods. "Mama's got to get home. She's already stayed longer than she originally thought she would. Plus, they miss Jake. They've never gone this long without seeing him. Now that Jake's stable, he'll have to suffer longer stretches without me."

"I can help too," I say. "I can stay here while you're with the boys or keep the boys with me when you're here. I can even go stay with them at home. Whatever you need."

"I know you will, Cam. And I'll probably have to let you. But hopefully not for long. I expect Jake will be strong enough to go home with me in another few days."

"Well, until then, my place is your place. And I can take as much time off as you need to be with the boys."

Her expression shifts, and I sense she's about to ask me about Darcy. Maggie tries to hide it, but sometimes I catch her staring at me with this sad look on her face. The way I've mucked things up, I probably deserve her pity. But I don't want it. This is a mess of my own making. Having people feel sorry for me just makes me feel worse.

"I'll stay with Dad until you get back, all right?"

Her lips press together like she wants to say something else, but she finally shakes her head and heads down the hall toward the elevator.

Dad is sitting up, his back propped against some pillows and his phone in his hand. He's thinner than he should be, and he's still pale, but his eyes are bright, and his smile is genuine. He looks like he feels good, which goes a long way to ease my worries.

"Hey," I say as I settle into the chair beside his bed. "It's good to see you sitting up."

"It's good to *be* sitting up."

"How are you feeling?"

"Like a hippo is sitting on my lungs. But the hippo's losing weight every day, so I'm not complaining." He leans back into his pillows and rests his hands on his stomach, offering me a searching gaze. "How are you, son?"

I breathe out a long sigh. Odds are pretty good that Maggie already told him Darcy hasn't been around. But where do I even start?

"Maggie told me about you leaving the wedding." He coughs a few times and I jump up to help him take a drink of water. "Darcy didn't want to come with you?" he asks.

I guess we're starting here. I shake my head but keep my eyes down. I'd rather avoid Dad's ability to stare into my actual soul. He's been turning me inside out with that gaze since I was barely talking.

"Are you shaking your head to say no, she didn't want to come with you?" He pauses. "Or no, you didn't even give her the chance?"

"You're asking like you already know the answer," I say, finally lifting my eyes to his.

"I do. Maggie told me everything," he says with an easy grin. "I'm just trying to figure out how *you* feel about it."

I pause for a long moment, my elbows propped on my knees, my eyes staring at the floor between my feet. "I screwed up, Dad," I finally say. "And I don't know how to fix it."

***

Two days later, I stand in a narrow alley around the corner from the historic foundation gift shop and adjust my fanny pack. Dad's advice about fixing things with Darcy was simple. "Get over yourself and let her in, Cameron. You're only shooting yourself in the foot here."

Of course, he followed that up with a bunch of stuff about his experience in therapy and how it helped him realize all kinds of things about himself. How Mom's choices impacted his ability to trust people, his fear of rejection, his tendency to keep to himself and avoid risk.

He could have been talking about me for how much it all resonated. Those answers I felt hovering just below the surface, Dad tossed them at me in rapid succession. Turns out, Alexis, the psychologist I dated a few months back, might have known a thing or two.

I will not be calling her to let her know.

But I do plan on calling Dad's therapist to see about scheduling my own appointment.

That's one of the things I'll tell Darcy today. Assuming she'll talk to me.

No, assuming she'll talk to *Aloysius*.

"Wow. I missed seeing this get-up the last time." Rachel approaches, waving a hand up and down to encompass my entire ensemble. "You look even more ridiculous than I imagined."

I smile and slide on my glasses. "What do you mean by *get-up*?" I say in my nasally Aloysius voice. "This is how I dress all the time."

She shakes her head and laughs.

"Thanks for doing this, Rachel," I say, shifting back to my regular voice. I pull a set of keys out of my pocket and hand them over. "Vivian won't be home until noon, but the smaller key will get you into the alley behind her house, and the larger one will get you into the greenhouse. The delivery truck should be at the back gate by eleven-thirty."

"Got it. And I'll know where to put all the plants?"

"Yeah. Vivian and I cleared out a section for her yesterday. You can't miss it."

She nods. "I hope this works."

A pang of fear shoots through me. I've been so focused on working through the logistics of my plan, I haven't given much thought to the possibility of Darcy rejecting me.

Calling her family and friends was the easy part. Rachel gave me

Tyler's number—he was nice enough to answer my call even though he's on his honeymoon—and he had numbers for everyone else that means anything to Darcy.

Darcy's family and friends love her a lot. Every single person I called was willing to chip in a few bucks (or a lot of bucks; she has some very successful friends) to stock a corner of Vivian's greenhouse with plants that can belong to Darcy alone.

Vivian already agreed to loan Darcy anything she needs for the flower show, but I know Darcy well enough to know how much she'll appreciate starting a collection and having a place to keep it. Vivian was most excited about that part—about Darcy having a key to the greenhouse and a reason to be there as often as she wants.

I get the sense that Vivian has really enjoyed Darcy's companionship over the past couple of months.

Finding the plants and arranging delivery on such short notice was a little trickier. But with Vivian's help, and a last-minute drive up to Summerville to pick up one particularly unique species of orchid Darcy loves, everything has fallen into place.

It has been an exercise in vulnerability to orchestrate everything. Because justifying everyone's involvement required me to explain why I'm so desperate to do something nice for her in the first place.

Nothing like admitting I screwed up to every single person who loves Darcy as much as I do.

But that's exactly why I had to do it. Because I *do* love her.

And I don't want to lose her.

I look up at Rachel. "It *will* work, right?" It occurs to me as I ask the question that even if it doesn't, I don't have any regrets. Even if *I* can't make Darcy happy, a space of her own in Vivian's greenhouse *can*. And she deserves that. She deserves the chance to do what she loves. With or without me in her life.

Warmth fills Rachel's eyes. "Do you love her?" she asks.

I nod, a deep certainty filling me from the inside out.

"Yeah. I really do."

"You tell her that with the same moony look you have in your eyes right now, and everything will work out just fine."

Chapter Twenty-Four

Darcy

It has only been four days since I saw Cameron at the hospital on Wednesday night, eight days since he left me at Tyler's wedding reception.

And that is a long time to go without seeing the person you have just discovered you love.

I am positive that Cameron will eventually call. Even if he's calling to say he doesn't want a relationship the same way I do, he's too much of a gentleman to end things by ghosting me. I'm trying to be patient because his dad is still in the hospital, but to say my nerves are shot is the understatement of the century.

I nearly canceled my tour scheduled for this morning.

Moping around my apartment and listening to sad love songs sounded much more appealing, but food also sounds appealing, and my bank account balance just dropped into double digits, so here I am.

I lean against the local authors' shelf while my tour group pokes around the gift shop, and I flip through the pages of my favorite Pat Conroy novel, feeling nostalgic over the role the books played in bringing Cameron and me together in the first place.

"Darcy Marino?" a too-loud voice calls from the front of the gift shop. "I'm looking for a Darcy Marino."

My heart falls into my shoes.

I replace the Conroy novel with trembling hands and move around the corner.

Cameron is standing by the checkout counter, his eyes roving around the room. When they land on me, he smiles. "Are you Darcy Marino?" He strides toward me, but it's not Cameron. It's Aloysius Butts, and I never thought I'd be so happy to see him again.

He's wearing khakis this time, pulled just as high as he wore his jeans, and a pair of suspenders over a button-down shirt. The shirt is buttoned all the way to the top.

He stops directly in front of me. "Aloysius Butts here," he says, still talking loud enough for everyone in the room to hear him. A couple of kids standing with their parents start to giggle. "I'm looking for my tour guide."

I press my lips together, trying not to laugh. "I don't recall seeing you on my bookings list this morning," I say. "Are you sure you've got the right tour guide?"

His eyes turn serious. "Positive," he says, his tone soft, a hint of the real Cameron breaking through. "Maybe you can squeeze me in with your group?"

I feel like squeezing him, all right. In the biggest and longest hug ever. I extend my hand. "I think I have room for one more. It's nice to have you with us, Mr. Butts."

His eyes sparkle as he slips my fingers into his. "The pleasure is all mine."

I can hardly keep my wits about me as I start the tour. I don't want to talk about history for two hours. I don't want to talk about anything. I mostly just want to pull Cameron into every alley we pass, press him up against the wall, and kiss him senseless.

I know it can't be that easy. That he has some explaining—some apologizing—to do. But he's here, and he's smiling, and I'm just so happy to see him looking happy.

Aloysius is so well-behaved for the first half of the tour, I start to wonder why Cameron is even dressed up. He tells a few funny stories and asks a few ridiculous questions, but he's clearly playing for laughs instead of trying to annoy me. He doesn't even walk near me for most of the tour, instead choosing to hang in the back and chat with the two kids who giggled over his last name back in the gift shop.

I do my best to stay focused on history, to give my guests the experience they paid for, but I'm more distracted than I was when I had a creepy clown following me around.

Cameron is *here*. With me. *AS ALOYSIUS*.

It has to mean something, but what?

It isn't until we're inside the Dock Street Theater at the close of the tour that he maneuvers himself to the front of the group.

"Darcy?" he says with particularly dramatic flair. "I was hoping I might tell a brief story before we all say goodbye." He sweeps his arm out to include the entire group.

I bite my lip. "Oh. Um, okay. That should be fine."

He rubs his hands together and faces the group. "You see, I'm a bit of an amateur historian myself, and I love a good story. This one is about my great, great grandfather Harry."

Oh, he did *not* just say Harry. As in *Harry Butts?* No one else in the group seems to make the connection, and Cameron doesn't even flinch, but I have to press my hand to my mouth to keep from laughing.

"Harry was a fine man," Cameron continues, "but he wasn't particularly good at talking about his feelings. Whenever he grew frustrated or worried or scared, he turned inward, keeping his own company, and shutting out the people who cared about him. Likewise, he wasn't very good at telling his wife how he felt about her. This made his life very difficult. And it bothered his wife a great deal." Cameron looks around the group, his gaze serious until it locks on me, then his expression shifts, and he smiles. "Harry knew he ought to do better. He loved his wife more than anything—"

Oh, my heart.

"—and he wanted her to know how special she was, how much he wanted her with him always." He steps toward me, his attention so focused, everyone in the group starts to look between us, their eyes darting from him to me, then back to him again.

He takes off his fake glasses and slides them into the pocket on the front of his shirt. "One day, Harry decided that if he was going to save his marriage, for his wife was very near ready to leave him, he needed to put the old adage, *practice makes perfect* to the test."

The closer he gets to me, the more normal he sounds.

"He decided he would tell his wife he loves her at breakfast every day for the next thirty days," he says, finally stopping directly in front of me. "And then, each day, he would share something personal that he's never told anyone else." He's all Cameron now, his Aloysius voice completely gone.

"This is a dumb story," one of the kids in the group whispers.

"It is not," the mom quickly whisper-yells. "Did it work?" she asks, her voice normal volume.

Cameron is so close. Close enough that it's taking all my willpower and the kids watching from a few feet away to keep me from shifting into baby sloth mode and climbing on.

"The jury's still out on whether it worked," he says, giving me a knowing look. "Hi," he says softly.

"Hi."

"Sorry to crash your tour."

"No you're not," I say, my smile easy. "Harry Butts? Really?"

He chuckles. "I wasn't sure anyone noticed." He links a finger around my pinky, a question in his eyes. "Darcy, I'm so sorry," he says. "I shouldn't have left you. I just . . . panicked. But I'm going to do better." He tugs on my pinky and turns my hand so our fingers entwine, our palms together. "I'm all in," he says, a new vulnerability filling his eyes. "If you still want this. Still want *me*."

I push onto my toes and kiss him—fitting there are kids watching us *now*, too—cradling his face in my hands. His arms wrap around my back, holding me against him as the rest of the tour group claps and whistles and cheers.

He stays close to me as my group files out of the theater, offering hugs and congratulations and especially generous tips. Only one little girl frowns as she approaches with her parents. She's maybe ten or eleven and has a serious expression on her face as she motions for me to come closer.

I crouch down in front of her, and she leans forward. "I'm just saying, he's cute and all, but if you marry him, your name will be Darcy *Butts*."

I press my lips together, hardly containing my laughter. "It's a good thing I love him so much, huh?"

***

We walk down Church Street slowly, hands clasped. The weather is pleasant, the sun warm on my shoulders, and the air smells like a sea breeze and flowers.

I'm having a hard time believing I'm here. With Cameron. Holding his hand, the reality of our present turning into a very real future stretching out before me.

At the next corner, Cameron tugs me onto a quiet side street. "Do you have anything else to do today? Or can you spend a little bit of time with me?" he says. There is trepidation in his voice that wasn't there before, and I give his fingers a quick squeeze.

"I'm all yours," I say. "I only had the one tour scheduled."

He nods and drops my hand, using both of his to run his fingers through his hair.

He almost seems . . . nervous, maybe?

He takes a slow, deep breath.

Okay, *definitely* nervous.

I reach out and touch his shoulder. "Hey, you okay?"

He stops and leans against the fading red brick of the building beside us. "My mom left when I was fourteen," he says quickly.

My eyes go wide.

"Sorry, I know that was abrupt. It's just a thing I have to say."

I lean against the wall beside him and hold out my hand. He slips his fingers into mine.

"Maggie told you that, right? That she left?"

"Just briefly. She didn't tell me any details."

He breathes out a sigh. "She left when I was fourteen, right after Dad was diagnosed with cancer the first time. I never saw her again. She died of an overdose the summer before I left for college."

My heart stretches and pulls toward Cameron, and I scoot a little closer. "That's really sad."

"Yeah. Except, I can't say it wasn't the best thing for the rest of us. I know that makes me sound like a horrible person. But she was awful to my dad. When I look at the life he has now, with Maggie and the boys, I imagine Mom showing up, messing with him, wanting things from him. Because she would have. And I could never wish that on him."

"I don't think that makes you a horrible person. Real life isn't always pretty. It doesn't always make sense."

"I've spent a lot of years trying to explain away her behavior. To make excuses for some of the choices she made. But the reality is, she hurt a lot of people before she died. She was only a kid when she had me. Had she had the chance to grow up in her own way, instead of the way life demanded . . ." He shrugs. "I don't know. Maybe things would have turned out differently for her."

I place a hand on his shoulder but don't say anything. If there's more he needs to say, I'll wait as long as it takes.

"She wasn't around much when I was little. When Dad was at work, I stayed with my grandma. Mom would show up every now and again, mostly when she needed money. But she was never really a mom to me. And yet, even with all that, she was still my mom. I don't know how to *not* love her."

He nudges me with his shoulder but keeps his eyes on the sidewalk in front of us. "I'm not trying to make excuses for pushing you away. And I'm not trying to turn you into my therapist. I'm going to get one of those, the same one who helped my dad out, and I think it'll do me some good. But I want to be real with you. I want to be comfortable letting you carry my hard things." He lifts one shoulder. "And this is my hardest thing."

"I will carry all your hard things," I say.

"And I'll carry yours. Everything. I really am all in. And I'll spend however long it takes to convince you of that." He turns to me, his expression earnest. "That's the first personal thing. I really do intend to give you something new every day for thirty days."

"Just like Harry Butts?"

He smiles. "Just like Harry Butts. Can you forgive me, Darcy? I can't promise that my first instinct when things get hard isn't going to be to clam up and retreat. And I'm not always going to be good at talking about my feelings. But I can promise I'll work on it."

"Cameron, you're doing great talking about your feelings. You're better at this than you think."

He shakes out a nervous laugh. "You would feel differently if you realized how much of my body is sweating right now."

I laugh. "I'm sure it isn't that bad."

"Please don't test your theory. You will be disgusted and then this whole thing will end before it ever truly gets started."

I raise my eyebrows. "Haven't you heard? Sweaty is the new sexy."

He pushes off the wall, already looking lighter. "Come on. There's something I want to show you."

We make small talk as we walk. About his interview with the magazine that's happening next week. About his dad. About Rachel's new attempt to paint Mary Beth—something I'm still not sure I fully understand. I'm so engrossed in our conversation, in the thrill of having Cameron close again, I don't even realize where we're going until we're standing at the back alley that leads onto Vivian's property. The gate is propped open, which seems odd, but I don't ask any questions as Cameron leads me toward the greenhouse.

"So, quick tour guide question for you," he says as we wind past the kitchen house and approach the greenhouse door.

"Okay."

"Have you ever thought about doing a garden-themed walking tour? A parade of the best window boxes, maybe? The best gardens in the city? I bet you'd get a lot of interest."

I stop in my tracks. Energy zaps down my arms and makes my fingertips tingle. "That's kind of a brilliant suggestion."

He only grins.

"I can't believe I've never thought of doing one before. I mean, I doubt I could book more than one a week, but still."

"I was thinking if you didn't feel like keeping up with your tour website when you switch to flowers fulltime, I can add it to my website and book it for you. Then you can run the tour, and I'll pay you for it."

I look at him slyly. "Cameron. Are you asking my tours to move in with your tours?"

He tugs me to a stop and wraps his arms around me. "Something like that." He kisses me quickly—a little too quickly, if you ask me—and then opens the greenhouse door.

The air inside is humid and heavy, but to me, it feels like home. I narrow my eyes as he leads me forward, not stopping until we're standing at the very end of the greenhouse, in the corner where Vivian used to keep her miniature roses. The space—an area no bigger than forty or fifty square feet—is mostly cleaned out now. Right in the center of the long wooden counter, a collection of plants sits together in several rows. They're organized by color, the hues shifting from lightest to darkest, and I suddenly think of Rachel. Everything in her apartment is arranged by color. Her books. Her throw pillows. Even the wall color in her bedroom is a gradation—midnight blue at the top melting into a sky blue along the floorboards.

I turn to Cameron. "What is this? And was Rachel here?"

He smiles. "It's yours. And yes, she met the delivery guy here this morning."

I look back to the plants. Begonias, petunias, zinnias, nasturtiums, geraniums, heliotrope. And so many others. Some I don't even recognize. "I don't understand."

"I cleared the space out with Vivian yesterday." He reaches forward and grabs a set of keys off the table and drops them into my hand. "Now you can come whenever you want. And fill the space up with your own plants."

I shake my head, still not fully processing. I step forward and finger the leaves of an orchid, studying it a little closer. It's in bloom, its lavender and yellow petals vibrant and lush. "Is this a Siam Song?"

Cameron nods. "Vivian said you've been looking for one."

My breath catches in my throat. "I don't even know what to say." I look again at the spread of flowers in front of me, my gut suddenly tightening. "Cameron, how did you pay for all of these flowers? You shouldn't have—"

He holds up a hand to stop me. "I didn't. Not all of them. But you have a lot of people in your life who love you. None of them needed any convincing. Consider them housewarming gifts," he says, and I swallow my urge to complain about taking other people's charity. He's right. I do have a lot of people that love me. "Whenever you're here seeking inspiration, you can think of your friends and family and let us inspire you too."

I move to the greenhouse counter and press my hands flat against the warm wood. Once my business is up and running and I have actual clients I'm working for, I won't be filling window boxes from my own greenhouse. I'll be using my ideas, my designs, but I'll have access to bigger budgets and expansive nurseries. But to have this—a space of my own where I can create and play—it's more than I could have ever hoped for.

"If you don't want it," Cameron says, "I can talk to Viv—"

I lunge across the room and silence his words with a kiss. He catches me, his hands on my waist, and holds me close. There is a tenderness to this kiss that makes it feel different than all the others we've shared.

This one feels like a promise.

My hands move from his face down to his shoulders—*oh, those shoulders*—and slip around his biceps.

A promise . . . that quickly turns *heated*.

We stumble to the counter, my back bumping into the wood, and Cameron hoists me up so I'm sitting on top, bringing my face closer to his. I turn my head, deepening the kiss and eliciting a small moan from somewhere in the back of Cameron's throat. The back of his shirt is damp, reminding me of his earlier nerves, but it only makes me want to pull him closer.

I once believed Cameron too polished, too perfect, to even be real. He was sexy as the Yacht Club Weekly version of himself, but this—this living, breathing, flawed man in front of me—is so much sexier.

My hands slide to his chest, snagging on the fake glasses stuck in his pocket, and I break the kiss. I pull the glasses out and put them on. "These really do complete the costume," I say.

"It's ridiculous that you actually make them look good," he says, and I grin.

"Thank you for all of this," I whisper.

"Do you really like it?"

"It's perfect. It's too much, but it's perfect."

He leans forward and kisses me one more time.

"I know you think you aren't good at communicating, but you are good at this part," I say.

"What, the kissing?"

I chuckle. "Yes. Definitely that. But that's not what I mean. Words are a love language I appreciate. But I also see your actions, Cameron. Vivian told me what you did, how you nudged her into meeting me. You didn't have to do that, but you did anyway." I take a shaky breath. "And then all of this . . . I guess what I'm saying is it's okay if sometimes we *show* someone how we feel even if we aren't good at saying it."

"Agreed," he says. "Actions can speak louder than words. But Darcy, I can also say it."

"Right. I'm sure you can," I say. "But if you decide to show me how you feel with flowers sometimes, ones that come with roots and dirt, I won't be opposed."

He laughs. "Okay, I see where this is going. Flowers, not words. Understood."

I love that he's teasing me, and I do love that he's done so much to show me how he feels. But I suddenly crave the validation that hearing the words will bring. "Or . . . maybe we stick with flowers *and* words?" I slide my hands around his middle, pulling him more fully into the space between my knees. There's too much room between us, too much air cooling my skin. I want him flush against me. I want to fall asleep in his arms and wake up to the sight of him in the morning.

I want to make him laugh. I want to hold his hard things and support him through tough times and kiss away his worries and carry his babies—

Oh. Whoa. That thought came out of nowhere.

But I mean, let's be honest. I do.

Cameron lifts a hand to my cheek. "Hey."

I look into his clear blue eyes. "Hmm?"

"I love you, Tinkerbell," he says with a wicked gleam in his eye.

My mouth drops open, and I scoff. "You did not just ruin this moment by calling me *Tinkerbell.*"

"I did," he says, stretching out his words and nodding as though I made a serious observation. "What're you going to do about it?"

"I'll start by kissing that smug look right off your face," I say. "But not until I tell you that I love you too."

Later that night, stretched out on Cameron's sofa, his arm around me and my head resting on his chest, he nuzzles his nose into my hair. "We can do this, right?" he whispers. "It's going to work?"

I look up, propping my chin on his chest so I can look into his eyes. "It might not always be easy," I say. "We have to turn to each other when stuff gets hard. I'll hold you up when you need it, and you'll do the same for me."

He threads his fingers through mine. "Thank you for not giving up on me," he says softly.

I snuggle into his chest, barely stifling a yawn. "I never will. But only if you promise to never call that clown guy again."

His chest rumbles with laughter. "I'm going to hire him to follow you down the aisle when we get married." The minute the words are out of his mouth, he freezes, his eyes going wide, his face stricken with panic. "Wait. That wasn't a proposal. I'm not—not that I wouldn't—eventually, you know, when—"

I grin and press a quick kiss to his lips, silencing his excuses, before nestling back into his arms. "You're going to dig yourself into a hole if you don't stop," I say playfully. "Let's leave it at I love you for now, yeah?"

"I love you doesn't feel like enough."

I squeeze his waist. "It's enough."

"For now," Cameron adds. "But you can't stop me from making plans."

My eyes drift closed, Cameron's words the promise I didn't know I need until I hear them.

I fall asleep certain that here, encircled in his arms, my heart has finally found its home.

Epilogue

Cameron

One year later

"I understand what you're telling me," I say, pacing on the sidewalk in front of the soon-to-open storefront of *Hunt for Truth Tours*. "Unfortunately, your roommate's grandmother's cat passing away is not a good enough reason for you to miss work. You have a ghost tour scheduled tonight, with twenty people expecting to be entertained and educated."

"What did he say?" A female voice—not the voice of the employee, Devon, I've been speaking to—sounds through the phone. "Did he buy it?"

"Seriously? Shut up!" He clears his throat. "Sorry, boss. That was—I didn't want to cancel. She was pressuring me. But don't worry about the tour. I'll be there."

I hang up the phone with a sigh.

"Devon again?" Darcy asks, stepping up beside me.

I nod. "Managing people is hard."

"Probably the hardest part," she says. She messes with the flowers in the giant planter that sits to the right of the storefront door—one of her creations—and pinches a few dead flowers off at the head. She wraps her arms around my waist. "You're a good boss though. You're doing an amazing job."

I lean down and kiss her, not even caring that every person we love is currently inside the shop, nothing but a glass wall between us, celebrating the opening of *Hunt for Truth*.

The space isn't much. A big welcome area that includes a few benches and chairs where groups can gather and wait for the start of their tour, and a few display boards highlighting historical locations in Charleston dedicated to true and transparent history. Soon, Jerome's education center will be featured front and center.

Behind the gathering area, there's a lounge for employees, as well as two offices, one for me, and one for Darcy to use as a home base for her business.

Right now, the space is decked out with soft lighting, Darcy's flowers, Rachel's art, and enough food to feed half of Charleston. Vivian decided she wanted to throw the party, and she didn't hold back. "I've got money to burn, Cameron," she said when I tried to insist it wasn't necessary. "Let me burn it."

"You coming back in?" Darcy asks.

I nod and let her lead me back to our friends and family.

A thought pops into my head, sending a tingle of nerves down my spine.

Everyone we love is here. My dad—in remission for six months and finally looking like himself again—Maggie and the kids, Jerome and Angie and Evie. Darcy's family is here too. Tyler and Olivia made the trip down from North Carolina, despite being less than two months away from the birth of their baby girl. And Rachel is here with her boyfriend, Jamal. Close friends round out the rest of the crowd. Isaac and Rosie, Dani and Alex, and Vivian, of course. None of this could have ever happened without Vivian. Even my therapist is here, and she probably deserves just as much credit.

Which is why I need to ask Darcy to marry me right now.

Here. Tonight.

It's an impulsive moment, even if it isn't an impulsive idea. I've had a ring almost as long as we've been together.

But I don't have the ring with me. It's back in the drawer of my nightstand, tucked away in a place I know Darcy won't find it.

My original plan was to dress up as Aloysius and crash her weekly garden tour with a surprise Aloysius-themed proposal.

But I suddenly can't stand the thought of waiting another minute.

Darcy tugs on my hand—I'm still standing in the doorway—and gives me a funny look. "You okay?"

I smile, but I give my head a little shake. "I'm not okay," I say.

The people closest to us must have heard me because they grow still as Darcy moves directly in front of me. The silence quickly spreads until everyone in the room is watching us, tension filling the air. She reaches out and takes my hands. "What's wrong?"

I let out a little chuckle. "I didn't plan for this," I say. "I don't have the ring on me, but we're here, and all our family and friends are here, and I just . . ."

Darcy's eyes go wide the minute I mention the ring, but she still hasn't said anything.

After a long moment of just standing there, staring at Darcy with what is probably a stupid look on my face, Jerome is suddenly beside me, one hand on my shoulder. He pushes me gently and shoots me a look, motioning toward the ground.

Right. Right. I don't have a ring, but I can at least do this part right.

I drop onto one knee.

Darcy shakes her head. She's smiling, but her expression is full of disbelief, like she can't believe I'm springing this on her here, without a ring, with all these people watching.

I look at her and shrug. "It just feels like the right moment," I say.

She starts to laugh, but then she pauses. "Wait, did you say you don't have the ring *on* you?"

"I bought it months ago," I say with a sheepish nod. "I made Rachel show you a picture to make sure it's something you'll like."

She gasps and looks at Rachel. "That's why you were showing me pictures of rings?"

"Honestly, I can't believe you didn't figure it out," Rachel says.

"I didn't," Darcy says. "I swear I didn't. You told me it was for a painting!"

"Like I said," Rachel deadpans. "I can't believe you didn't figure it out."

"He's on his knees, y'all," Tyler says from somewhere to my right. "Maybe let the poor guy get on with it?"

"Or at least give him some kneepads," Vivian says.

A chuckle sounds around the room as Darcy focuses her attention back on me.

"Marry me, Tinkerbell? I don't want to do life without you."

She pulls me to my feet and throws herself at me, but as soon as my arms are around her, she stiffens, her hands gripping my shoulders. "You have got to be kidding me."

I turn sharply, following her gaze.

There's a clown on the sidewalk. But not just any clown. *The* clown. The same clown I hired to follow her around during her tour.

She looks at me, shock filling her expression.

I immediately hold my hands up. "I swear I didn't," I say through a laugh of disbelief. "I didn't even know this was going to happen tonight."

The clown lifts his hand in a friendly wave, then continues down the sidewalk until he disappears from view.

"That did *not* just happen," Darcy says. She shoots me another glare, her hands propped on her hips.

"You have to believe me."

"If that clown is at our wedding, it's over," she says through her laughter. "All of it." She looks around the room at our friends. "Y'all heard me say it, and I mean it."

I step forward and wrap my arms around her waist. "Does that mean you're saying yes?"

She nestles in, returning my hug, and looks up at me. "Did I leave that part out earlier?"

"I think the first thing you said after I asked was, *'You have got to be kidding me.'*"

"I mean, can you blame me? It was the same clown!"

"If only Sir Isaac Haynes's ghost could join the party."

"Let's just assume he's here," she says. "That'll make the story even better when we tell our kids."

"I can't decide if I'm more happy to hear you talking about our future children, or more annoyed to hear you talk about tweaking history to make a better story."

"But in this case, there's no way for us to confirm or deny Sir Isaac's presence," she reasons. "Which means we aren't *making up* history, we're stretching the limits of possibility." She grins. "A tiny bit. Barely at all."

I kiss her nose. "I'll let this one slide then."

Tyler comes up behind us and pulls us into a group hug. "You're getting married!" he says, shaking us back and forth.

I look around the room, at my family, at my *found* family, at so many people that have been rooting for us, helping us get our businesses and our relationship off the ground.

Every single person in the room had something to do with

getting us to where we are now, and I couldn't be happier they're all here to share in the moment.

Darcy smiles from her place beside Tyler, her eyes full of warmth and joy and love.

Falling in love with Darcy Marino shouldn't have been this easy, and yet here we are.

And there's no place I'd rather be.

Acknowledgments

Charleston really is an incredible city. It isn't my native home, but I've been here almost five years and I've loved the opportunity to explore and learn so much of what makes historic Charleston unique. The food, the people, the cobblestone streets, the ancient houses. I have fallen in love and had so much fun weaving the city and all its charm into this book. I hope you get a small taste of Charleston and maybe feel inspired to visit the city yourself! All the restaurants and locations mentioned in the book are real and fabulous; if they got a mention, they are worth visiting!

 This book wouldn't exist without the generous author friends who listened and hashed and rehashed the complexities of writing an enemies-to-lovers romance. Kirsten, thank you for being so smart about stories. Emily, as always, thank you for talking about fake people whenever I need it. Melanie, Brittany, thank you reading and loving my words and making them better. Becca, your editing eye and story insight is brilliant and so, so valuable. Thank you for working your magic even though I gave you such a ridiculous deadline.

To my incredible family, thank you for being such an amazing support network. Josh, thank you for feeding me, for listening, for making me sleep, for taking care of me when I'm horrible at taking care of myself. You are the only inspiration I need to write love stories.

The Gullah people, those descended from the West and Central Africans enslaved along the coastal regions of South Carolina and other South Atlantic states are an integral part of Charleston's history. If you'd like to learn more about the Gullah Geechee Cultural Heritage Corridor Commission, you can visit their website at gullahgeecheecorridor.org.

About the Author

Jenny Proctor grew up in the mountains of North Carolina, a place she still believes is one of the loveliest on earth. She lives a few hours south of the mountains now, in the Lowcountry of South Carolina. Mild winters and of course, the beach, are lovely compromises for having had to leave the mountains.

Ages ago, she studied English at Brigham Young University. She works full time as an author and as an editor, specializing in romance, through Midnight Owl Editors.

Jenny and her husband, Josh, have six children, and almost as many pets. They love to hike and camp as a family and take long walks through the neighborhood. But Jenny also loves curling up with a good book, watching movies, and eating food that, when she's lucky, she didn't have to cook herself. You can learn more about Jenny and her books at www.jennyproctor.com.

Made in the USA
Middletown, DE
21 December 2023